DEMIGODS
AND
MONSTERS

Your Favorite Authors on
Rick Riordan's Percy Jackson
and the Olympians Series

Edited and Original Introduction by Rick Riordan
with Leah Wilson

An Imprint of BenBella Books, Inc.
Dallas, TX

BenBella Books, Inc.
10300 N. Central Expy, Suite 530
Dallas, TX 75231
www.smartpopbooks.com
www.benbellabooks.com
Send feedback to feedback@benbellabooks.com

Printed in the United States of America
10 9 8 7 6 5 4 3 2 1

Library of Congress Cataloging-in-Publication data is available for this title.
ISBN 978-1937856-36-6

Proofreading by Erica Lovett, Yara Abuata, Rachelle Sparks, and Amy Zarkos
Cover art by Ralph Voltz
Cover design by Laura Watkins and Sarah Dombrowsky
Text design by PerfecType, Nashville, TN
Composition by PerfectType and Neuwirth & Associates, Inc.
Printed by Berryville Graphics

Distributed by Perseus Distribution
perseusdistribution.com

To place orders through Perseus Distribution:
Tel: 800-343-4499
Fax: 800-351-5073
E-mail: orderentry@perseusbooks.com

Significant discounts for bulk sales are available. Please contact Glenn Yeffeth at glenn@benbellabooks.com or (214) 750-3628.

CONTENTS

INTRODUCTION

Rick Riordan

PERSONS attempting to find a motive in this narrative will be prosecuted; persons attempting to find a moral in it will be banished; persons attempting to find a plot in it will be shot—BY ORDER OF THE AUTHOR.
> —MARK TWAIN, front matter to *Huckleberry Finn*

X-Raying the Author's Head

Many years ago, before Percy Jackson appeared in my life, I was known primarily as a writer of grown-up mystery novels. One night I was doing an event with two other authors, and one of them was explaining why he liked my book *The Devil Went Down to Austin*.

"The structure is amazing," he told the audience. "It's a book about scuba diving, and as the characters go deeper into the dark murky water, the plot also gets darker and murkier. The symbolism is really clever."

The audience looked suitably impressed. I looked confused.

I use symbolism? Who would've guessed?

After the event, when I confessed to the other author that I hadn't done the murky structure thing intentionally, that perhaps it was just the result of my faulty outlining, his jaw dropped. He'd studied my writing. He'd made brilliant insights. And I'd just been telling a story? Impossible!

That doesn't mean his insights weren't valuable, or that the symbolism wasn't there. But this does raise an important point about the difference between writing a story and analyzing it.

Any book, for children or adults, can be read on many levels. We can simply enjoy it. Or we can look for hidden meanings and nuances. We can even write essays about the book, exploring it from different angles.

The writer's job is to write the book. The careful reader's job is to find meaning in the book. Both jobs are important. The meanings you find can enlighten, fascinate, and surprise. They can even surprise the author. The author, at least *this* author, uses symbols and themes subconsciously. I don't think about it, any more than a native speaker of English consciously thinks about subject-verb agreement as he speaks.

The front matter to *Huckleberry Finn* has always been one of my favorite Mark Twain quotes. Twain was adamant that readers simply read his book, not scrutinize it for morals or messages, much less a plot structure. Of course, this has not stopped generations of English majors from writing their graduate theses on the novel.

When I was first approached about editing this anthology, I wasn't sure what to think. Why would so many talented writers want to write about my children's books? And yet, when I read their essays, I was amazed. Each had a different angle on Percy Jackson—all of them fascinating and thought-provoking. Many of them made me think, "Is *that* what I was doing in the series?" It was like having someone take an x-ray of my head. Suddenly, I saw all this stuff going on inside that I was never aware of.

Maybe that's why Mark Twain tried to warn off critics who wanted to interpret his work. It's not that the interpretations are wrong. It's that they tend to be a little too close to home!

The Accidental Demigod

I never intended to write the Percy Jackson series.

When my oldest son was in second grade, he began having problems in school. He couldn't focus. He didn't want to sit down and read. Writing was a painful challenge.

Being a novelist and a middle school teacher, I had a hard time accepting that my son hated school. Then came the fateful parent conference when the teachers suggested my son get a full psycho-educational evaluation. A few weeks later we got the results: ADHD and dyslexia.

These were not new concepts to me. I had taught many students with learning differences. I had made modifications. I'd filled out evaluation forms.

But when the child in question is your own son, it's different.

How could I help him make sense of what was going on with him? How could I frame the problem in a positive way?

In the end, I fell back on what I knew best—storytelling.

My son's saving grace in second grade was Greek mythology. This was the only part of the curriculum he enjoyed. Every night, he would ask me to tell him bedtime stories from the myths, and when I ran out of them, he asked me to make up a new one.

And so it sprang from my mind unbidden—like Athena from Zeus' forehead—the myth of how ADHD and dyslexia came to be. I created Percy Jackson, a Greek demigod in the tradition of Hercules and Theseus and Perseus, except Percy is a modern kid. He has ADHD and dyslexia, and he learns that taken together, those two conditions indicate without a doubt that he has Olympian blood.

In *The Lightning Thief*, ADHD means you have finely tuned senses. You see too much, not too little. These reflexes don't serve you well in a boring classroom, but they would keep you alive on the battlefield. Dyslexia indicates that your brain is hard-wired for Ancient Greek, so of course reading English is a struggle.

My son had no trouble buying this theory at all.

In the story, Percy Jackson discovers that being different can be a source of strength—and a mark of greatness. Being academically hopeless does not mean you are a hopeless person. Percy was my way of honoring all the children I've taught who have ADHD and dyslexia, but more importantly he was a myth for my son to make sense of who he is.

When I was done telling the story, my son told me to write it down. I was dubious. I didn't think anyone would like it, and I didn't exactly have a lot of spare time. I was already teaching full-time and writing a mystery novel a year. But I made the time and wrote *The Lightning Thief*.

My son loved the final version. Apprehensively, I gave the manuscript to some of my students. They loved it too. I sent it off to the publishers under a pseudonym so I wouldn't be embarrassed by the flood of rejection notes. Within weeks, the book went to auction and was snapped up by the Disney Book Group.

At the end of that school year I became a full-time children's writer. The Percy Jackson series was soon published around the world.

If you'd told me five years ago that someone would want to create an anthology of essays based on a bedtime story I made up for my son, I would've called you crazy.

The Power of Myth

So why does the series resonate with young readers? Why do people still want to read Greek myths? These are stories from a long time ago about a very different society. What possible relevance could they have in the twenty-first century?

Certainly, you can get through life knowing no mythology, but it would be a pretty poor existence. Mythology is the symbolism of civilization. It contains our most deeply embedded archetypes. Once you know mythology, you see it everywhere—from the names of our days of the week to our art and architecture. You would be hard-pressed to find any work of English literature that does not draw to some extent on classical mythology, whether it's the hero's quest or allusions to the Olympians.

So knowing mythology makes one a more informed member of society, but its importance goes beyond that. Mythology is a way of understanding the human condition. Myths have always been man's attempt to explain phenomena—and not just why the sun travels across the sky. Myths also explain love, fear, hate, revenge, and the whole range of human feelings.

When I speak to school groups, I often ask children what Greek god they would like for a parent. My favorite answer was from a schoolgirl in Texas who said, "Batman!" Actually, the girl's suggestion of Batman as a Greek god is not too far off, because it's the same idea at work: creating a superhuman version of humanity so that we can explore our problems, strengths, and weaknesses writ large. If the novel puts life under the microscope, mythology blows it up to billboard size.

Myths aren't something that happened in the past, either. We didn't leave them behind with the Bronze Age. We are still creating myths all the time. My books, among other things, explore the myth of America as the beacon of civilization, the myth of New York, and the myth of the American teenager.

When we understand classical mythology, we understand something of our own nature, and how we attempt to explain things we don't comprehend. And as long as we're human, there will be things we don't comprehend.

On a more basic level, Greek mythology is simply fun! The stories have adventure, magic, romance, monsters, brave heroes, horrible villains, fantastic quests. What's not to love?

Mythology especially appeals to middle grade readers because they can relate to the idea of demigods. Like Hercules, Jason, and Theseus, Percy Jackson is half-man, half-god. He is constantly struggling to understand his identity, because he straddles two worlds but belongs in neither. Middle schoolers understand being in between. They are between adulthood and childhood. They feel stuck in the middle all the time, trapped in an awkward state. Everything is changing for them—physically, socially, emotionally. The demigod is a perfect metaphor for their situation, which is why the hero's quest resonates with them.

When I do school events, I usually play a trivia game on Greek mythology with the kids. It doesn't matter what school I visit or how little mythology the students have done in the classroom. The students always know the answers, and the adults are always amazed. I can almost guarantee some teacher will come up afterward, wide-eyed, and say, "I didn't know our students knew so much mythology!"

It's not a surprise to me. Young readers *own* mythology. They see themselves as the hero. They gain hope in their own struggles by following the quests. And yes, sometimes they even see their teachers as the monsters!

About This Anthology

Within these pages, you will find out what really makes Dionysus tick. You'll learn how to assign a letter grade to your parents. You'll explore the coolest monsters and most horrible villains of the Percy Jackson series. You'll decide whether becoming a Hunter of Artemis is a good deal or a disastrous mistake. You'll even learn how to unfreeze your eyeballs and recognize your own prophecy. Which essay comes closest to the truth? It's not for me to say.

About a year ago at a signing for *The Lightning Thief*, a boy raised his hand in the audience and asked, "What is the theme of your book?"

I stared at him blankly. "I don't know."

"Darn it!" he said. "I need that for my report!"

The lesson here: If you want to know the theme of a book, the last person to ask is the author. This anthology, however, offers fresh perspectives and amazing insights. If you're looking for something to lift the Mist from your eyes and make you say, "Aha! There *are* monsters!", then you've come to the right place.

Monster Recognition for Beginners

Lessons from Percy Jackson on Monsters and Heroes

Rosemary Clement-Moore

Every young hero will encounter monsters. That's a given. But will you see them before they see you? Rosemary Clement-Moore offers this handy survival guide for demigods, chock-full of tips to help you a) recognize the warning signs that a monster is near, b) avoid it if possible, and c) know what to do when you have to fight. Study up, demigods. You never know when your math teacher will start to grow claws.

W hat would you do if you woke up one morning and found a satyr on your front porch, and he explained that he was going to take you to a special camp for people like you: half-god, half-human?

You might be tempted to laugh, thinking it's a practical joke. Or maybe you'd think it was great. But if you've read the Percy Jackson books, you would also be seriously worried. Being a demigod may sound glamorous, but in Percy's world, the child of a god can look forward to a life full of hardships and danger. Heroes, whether they are on a quest or just trying to live through the school year, must always stay on their toes and on the lookout for monsters.

Imagine you're living in Percy's world: Does that donut store on the corner make a shiver run down your spine? Does the popularity of a certain coffee chain have anything to do with the mermaid on its logo? And what about the homeless man under the bridge near your apartment: Does no one think it strange that he wears a muffler and trench coat all year-round?

Or maybe you live in the country, and suddenly a lot of cattle are mysteriously disappearing. Is it a coyote problem, or a wandering monster snacking on your uncle Walt's best milk cows? What really started those California wildfires: a careless camper or a fire-breathing chimera?

To Percy and his classmates, asking these kinds of questions could mean the difference between life and death. Not to mention the success of a quest. Ignoring their instincts could lead to death . . . or worse, humiliating defeat.

If you suddenly discover you are a demigod like the ones in Percy Jackson's world, don't be lured into spending all your time on rock climbing and archery practice. These things are important, but if you really want to survive a monster attack, you need to learn how to recognize them. That way you can make a plan for fighting, or fleeing, whichever seems more prudent. Percy Jackson has had to learn these lessons the hard way. While some of his classmates might consider the constant threats to life and limb opportunities for personal growth, the wise hero should take a page from the children of Athena and fight smarter, not harder.

Fortunately, we have Percy's triumphs—and mistakes—to learn from. So just in case you do open your door to a satyr one morning, here's some of what I've learned from reading the Percy Jackson books: three easy steps on how to survive in a world full of monsters who want to kill you.

Lesson One: Monsters and You

The first thing to realize in dealing with mythical creatures is the basic nature of the relationship between hero and monster: There is a very good chance that even a random encounter between them will result in death for one or both. Simply stated, heroes kill monsters, and monsters resent that fact.

Let us take some examples from the ancient world: Bellerophon, Theseus, Hercules, and Perseus.[1] All of them heroes, all of them slayers of monsters—Chimera, Minotaur, Hydra, and Gorgon. And the monsters never forget it. Youth is no protection, either; monsters have no ethics, so they don't have an ethical problem with getting rid of their natural enemies while they are still young and vulnerable.

Now, a demigod has certain advantages over monsters. Depending on the type of creature he's facing, the demigod may be faster or more mobile. His ability to use a weapon may counter the natural advantage of, say, a bulletproof hide, like the Nemean Lion's, or seven heads that always grow back, like the Hydra's. The human half makes the hero smarter than the average monster, provided the hero actually uses his brain. The god half doubtlessly adds advantages as well, though of course this would largely depend on the god in question.

The monsters' biggest advantage—besides the obvious things like claws, teeth, poison, and superior size and strength—is that they never really die. The centaur Chiron tells us monsters are

---

[1] The original one, not Percy Jackson of *The Lightning Thief*, etc. The ancient Perseus was the son of Zeus, not Poseidon, so it's curious that his mother picked that name.

"archetypes." An archetype is the original, basic idea of something. This means that when similar characters pop up in different books and movies, all of them are based on the original archetype. For instance, the *character* of "Fluffy," the three-headed dog who guards the sorcerer's stone in the first Harry Potter book, comes from the *idea* of Cerberus, the three-headed dog who guards the entrance to the Underworld.[2]

So monsters, like ideas, can never be killed, and they have very long memories. If you're a hero and you encounter a magical creature, it may have been turned to dust many times over the years by heroes just like you. It would be wise to assume that it is holding a grudge and would be happy to help you along to your doom.

Percy Jackson has this harsh reality thrust upon him in no uncertain terms, and it's an experience we can learn from: Nothing says "your days are numbered" like a Minotaur on your doorstep.

It should be noted that children of the less powerful gods aren't going to attract as much monstrous attention as those with more powerful parents. You might think it would be "cool" if your Olympian parent was one of the major gods, but that kind of status comes with a big price tag.

Percy is the perfect example of this. Having Poseidon as his father may give him some awesome powers, but it also makes him a very high-profile target. So even if you had skills remarkable for a demigod, this in no way would guarantee you an easy time of it.[3]

The world of gods and monsters is a harsh one. A hero can't rely on his immortal parent for help. There are rules against direct interference, and it seems as though the higher in the echelon a god is, the

---

[2] Chiron wouldn't use this example, of course, because in his world there are no such things as wizards. That would be just silly.

[3] Just the opposite, since according to the agreement between the Big Three, you should not even exist, and lots of creatures would be trying to arrange it so you didn't.

more limited he or she is in stepping in to help. After Annabeth Chase runs away from her father's house, her mother, Athena, helps her by making sure she meets up with an older, more powerful half-blood. Thalia, daughter of Zeus,[4] leads her friends almost to the safety of the camp, but when she is about to be killed by a horde of monsters, all that Zeus can do is turn her into a tree on top of Half-Blood Hill.

Ultimately it is up to young heroes to watch out for themselves. A parent or patron may be some help, but it's the nature of the hero to have to face the monsters on his or her own.

Lesson Two: Types of Monsters

Monsters could be categorized in many different ways: by habitat, allegiance, intelligence, lethality, and so on. For the purpose of this lesson, I'll separate them into two main types: those who will kill you on purpose—whether it's personal, or because you've blundered into their lair—and those who will kill you by accident.

For the most part, monsters are very territorial; they tend to stake out a hunting ground and protect it viciously. When Percy's brother Tyson is attacked by a sphinx in the city, it may have been just because he ventured into its territory. Notice that the fact that Tyson himself is a monster gives him no protection.

Here we see the type of monster who may have nothing against you personally but will not hesitate to kill you anyway. This may be because it is (a) guarding something it thinks you want to steal; (b) hungry; or (c) both.

Young heroes seem to encounter these types of monsters most frequently when they are on a quest, but not always. Monsters can be found just about anywhere, and if you stumble onto a Hydra's hunting grounds, chances are that one of seven heads would eat you

---

[4] See previous footnote re: unauthorized offspring.

before you could explain that you were merely on your way to the corner deli for a pastrami on rye.

Some monsters stay very isolated from the mortal world. Percy has to go to the Sea of Monsters to encounter Polyphemus, the Cyclops shepherd with the carnivorous sheep, and Scylla and Charybdis, who between them destroy (again) the ironclad ship, *CSS Birmingham*, and its crew. But other creatures rely on humankind for survival. In ancient times, monsters often lived off of humans by stealing their sheep and goats (or sometimes by making off with one of their maidens). In Percy's modern world, many monsters have moved into retail, making a living off of humans in an entirely different way.

This kind of magical creature doesn't mean to kill you but is simply going about its business, completely indifferent to your fate. Take, for example, the chain of Monster Donut shops. They spread across the country, each of them connected to the life force of a monster. The stores multiply like Hydra heads, but whether their success actually comes at the expense of their human customers—the modern equivalent of the stolen sheep or maiden, for example—remains to be seen.[5]

Other retail ventures are more obviously dangerous, like Medusa's shop, which Percy, Annabeth, and Grover run across in their first quest. In olden days, monsters who preyed on humans could often be found at the intersection of major roads, where there was the most traffic. Now monsters like the Medusa open shops. Mortal society used to center around the crossroads, but it now revolves around retail. Therefore, the smart hero should be careful in stores;

---

[5] If we lived in the world of Percy and the Olympians, I would definitely wonder about that coffee chain with the mermaid on its logo, for no other reason than convincing mortal society that it is reasonable to pay three dollars for a cup of coffee is surely a plot to speed the end of Western Civilization.

no one wants to pay for a cheeseburger by spending eternity as a stone lawn ornament.

Monsters don't consider death or dismemberment a flaw in their business plan. Take the Graiai, for example. Who would have thought it was a good idea to put three hags who share one eye in control of a taxicab in New York?[6] Since the sisters cannot pass the eye between them without a violent argument breaking out, the taxi's only destination seems to be disaster. Yet getting heroes on their way has been the hags' job ever since Ancient Greece.

The fact that they don't care what it does to their half-mortal passengers shows why immortal things should never be dealt with lightly. Even when a magical creature is merely going about its business—even when, like the Gray Sisters, it is technically being helpful—it can be very dangerous.

Now we come to the monster who does in fact take death very personally. In addition to the innate hatred between monster and hero, there is another reason that some fanged, winged, leather-skinned horror might want half-bloods like Percy dead. Many monsters are servants to various gods, who keep the creatures on staff to take care of odd (and sometimes distasteful) jobs, like tracking down heroes, guarding treasure, and torturing demigods who make them angry.

Which means that if you anger one of the gods, he or she is likely to send something really nasty to let you know about it. Percy Jackson angers several gods just by breathing, so he probably feels like the whole world is out to get him. But that's not actually true. Most of the time, *several* worlds are out to get him.[7]

---

[6] Though this would explain a lot about Manhattan cab drivers.

[7] By that I mean the mortal world, the immortal world, and the Underworld. Speaking of Hades, he may have a special reason to hate Percy, but all half-bloods should be wary of him. He's like that kid at your school who never gets invited to play with everyone else, but with superpowers and several thousand years for his temper to come to a boil. Hades is understandably cranky.

Whether you are dealing with the bull-headed simplicity of the Minotaur or the conniving ferocity of the Furies, if a god has sent a monster after you, there is little you can do to avoid it. So you may be wondering why I bother to mention it in a lesson about avoiding monstrous conflict.

If you are a hero, and a vengeful (or possibly just bored) god has sent a monster after you, you may not be able to steer clear of it, but early recognition of the threat will allow you to control the battlefield; wise tactics can even things out between unmatched opponents.

For instance, if you were a hero with a fire-breathing chimera on your trail, then you'd want to arrange your confrontation near a handy water source—or at least away from combustible materials. By identifying the monster early, you can lead it away from innocent bystanders, troublesome eyewitnesses, and destructible buildings. You should always try to limit collateral injuries and property damage, as it reduces the chance you will become wanted by conventional authorities.

This is a case where Percy's adventures show us how *not* to deal with monsters. Think of how much easier his life would be if he didn't spend so much time wanted by the police for blowing up cars, buses, school gymnasiums, and national monuments. Mortal law enforcement may not seem like much of a threat compared to a phalanx of bronze bulls or a pack of hellhounds, but why add unnecessary inconveniences to an already complicated quest?

Lesson Three: Spotting a Monster

Monster recognition isn't just about memorizing the names and types of creatures you may encounter, though that doesn't hurt. If you're wondering whether your algebra teacher is a Fury or just a mean old lady with a lot of cats, the most important thing is to use your head, starting with your eyes, ears, and nose.

Creatures with a nature spirit in their parentage, like nymphs, satyrs, and Cyclopes, can smell a monster easily. However, it isn't convenient to keep a nymph or satyr with you at all times. A smart demigod must learn to pay attention to his or her nose. This takes practice, since we spend a lot of our lives trying *not* to smell things. The drugstore has entire aisles dedicated to soap and deodorant, powders and perfumes and air fresheners, so that we never have to be troubled by an unpleasant scent.[8]

Fortunately, monsters don't generally worry about such things, which makes them easier to spot. Man-eating giants do not floss. While no one likes to accuse his or her classmate of having halitosis or b.o., if your new gym partner could knock over a double-decker bus with his breath, this may be a sign you need to lace up your sneakers and get ready for a fight.

Still on the fence over whether your vice principal is a Manticore? Perhaps you could "accidentally" set off the fire sprinklers in class. If he smells like the fur of a wet dog under his suit, you had better skip detention.

In the world of the Olympians, the Mist may obscure your vision, but the wise hero could use that to his advantage. If you can't remember what your lab partner looks like or have a hard time looking him in the eye, the Mist might be a factor, something that would only happen if you were dealing with a nonhuman.

Also, you can study the way the person dresses. We try to be sensitive to cultural differences in clothing, but a clever monster[9] may count on this to disguise its disguise. A head-to-toe veil may be perfectly innocent, or it may hide a face that could stop a clock— literally—by turning it into stone.

---

[8] None of which apparently changes the fact that monsters can smell heroes pretty easily.

[9] This isn't always an oxymoron, any more than "wise hero" is.

You should pay attention, as well, to fashion choices. Since monsters never die, they have trouble staying up-to-date with fads in clothes and hobbies.[10] If your new teacher dresses in a tiger-striped Hawaiian shirt every day, or the new kid in school has never heard of a PlayStation, you might not want to turn your back on them.

As long as you keep your eyes and ears open, monsters—with few exceptions—will be pretty easy to spot. Some of them are crafty, but they're really not very good at pretending to be human. Some can manage it for a little while but will usually give themselves away to a hero who is paying attention. The problem is that most heroes—not Percy and his companions, of course—may be too focused on finding the treasure or finding their quest to pay attention.

While something that is off or odd should put you on guard, no one thing—smelly breath or rude manners or bad fashion—may be conclusive by itself. It would be a shame to get expelled from school (or arrested) for trying to stab the principal with a ballpoint pen just because he doesn't use enough deodorant.[11]

This is where Percy gives us a very good example of how to deal with monsters: Look at the whole picture. The most important thing he does when he is dealing with a mythical creature is to use his brain. If nothing else, it might take his opponent off-guard. No one really expects a clever hero; the training tends to focus more on the muscles than the mind.

Remember the cardinal rule when dealing with monsters, sorcerers, and gods: *If it seems too good to be true, it probably is.* An offer of something for nothing should always put a hero on his guard, and no other sense will tell you that other than your common one.

---

[10] Or, more likely, they just don't care.

[11] Which *you* wouldn't, because you can tell the difference between fiction and reality. If you can't, then you have a bigger problem than mythical monsters.

Percy Jackson

One of the most admirable things about Percy Jackson is that he has learned from his mistakes over the course of his adventures.[12] His classical education is almost nonexistent, but he demonstrates that successfully dealing with a monster takes more than memorization of facts and history. A hero has to observe all the fine points that make a monster stand out from what passes for normal in the mortal world. A creature with an unusual number of heads is obvious. More often, what Percy notices are the many small details that add up to two things: a monster, and immediate danger.[13]

This doesn't only apply to identifying monsters and killing them but to how he interacts with all nonhumans. In his adventures, Percy uses these many details to decide how to deal with each monster on an individual basis. He rescues monsters, even protects and befriends them. Perhaps this open-mindedness is a result of having a Cyclops for a brother.

Or perhaps this is simply part of his personality and something else that sets him apart among heroes. In his encounters with gods and monsters, Percy Jackson uses not just his muscles and his mind but his heart. It makes him difficult to predict and control, which is why the gods consider him so potentially dangerous while the prophecy remains unfulfilled.

But it also makes him a hero, not just in the classical, demigod sense, but of the human kind too. That's the most important lesson we can take away from the Percy Jackson and the Olympians books. You may never have to deal with Manticores and Gorgons, and the Minotaur may not be waiting to ambush you on the way to school,

---

[12] At least in his dealings with monsters. In other matters, he still seems pretty clueless. Romance, for example (at least until he and Annabeth get together).
[13] This is, perhaps, a product of the hero's natural attention to so many details at a time, i.e., his ADHD.

but we all have to deal with our own monsters: bullies, peer pressure, stranger danger, prejudice, new kids in school . . . an endless list that makes our world challenging even if we aren't demigods.

But just like Percy Jackson, you too can achieve success in all your quests if you apply these same lessons: Avoid conflict when you can, keep your eyes and ears open, and always look at the whole picture. And like Percy, don't ever be afraid to ask for help from your friends.

•　•　•　•

Rosemary Clement-Moore is the author of supernatural mystery novels for young (and not so young) adults, including *Texas Gothic* and *The Splendor Falls*. Her books have been included on the ALA list of best books for teens and received starred reviews from *Kirkus Reviews* and *School Library Journal*. She has a long history with Greek gods, ever since she played Persephone in a musical (with singing and dancing nymphs!) that she wrote with her class in theater school. You can visit her Web site at www.readrosemary.com.

Why Do So Many Monsters Go Into Retail?

And How Come They're Never Selling Anything a Demigod Really Wants?

Cameron Dokey

Garden gnomes, waterbeds, donuts . . . it seems you can't go shopping for anything these days without running into a monster. Cameron Dokey explains why so many monsters have jobs in the service industry, and why shopping, for demigods, is a very dangerous business.

It's not easy being a young demigod.

Just ask Percy Jackson. He can tell you.

Always assuming he has time to catch his breath between pursuing a quest or being pursued by the forces of evil hot on his trail, sometimes literally breathing down his neck right behind him.

In Shakespeare, there's a stage direction that reads: *Exit, pursued by a bear*. (I am not either making this up. You can look it up for yourself if you want to. It's in *The Winter's Tale*, Act III, scene 3. And you thought Shakespeare was just some stuffy dead guy.)

But my point, and I do have one, is that the character in Shakespeare had it lucky. At least he knew it was a bear behind him. Whenever Percy Jackson flees the scene, he never knows what shape the thing after him might take. That's one of the challenges of being chased by monsters. And that's not all. Equally challenging may be the fact that Percy also never really knows what's up ahead. Friend or foe. Battle or temptation.

Which pretty much brings me to the topic of this essay: Just what is it about monsters and shopping?

There are a lot of monsters in Rick Riordan's Percy Jackson and the Olympians series. There are also a surprising number of opportunities for shopping. Action, adventure, Greek gods, retail therapy. Not your ordinary combo. Not that much about Percy falls within the realms of the usual.

An ordinary demigod? I just don't think so.

But on almost every quest Percy takes, and his first one in particular, sooner or later, some creep who definitely doesn't have Percy's best interests at heart pops up to try to sell him something. Sometimes it's something he doesn't need. Sometimes it's something he doesn't want. Usually it's both. But Percy and his pals stop to check the whatever-it-is out anyway.

Yes, that's right. Even with danger all around them, our hero and his companions take the time to shop.

What the heck is that all about?

Let's begin to answer this question by doing the same thing Percy and his quest mates Grover the satyr and Annabeth, daughter of Athena, goddess of wisdom, do in chapter eleven of *The Lightning Thief*. Which, as I'm sure I don't need to remind you, is Percy Jackson and the Olympians book one.

Like Percy, Annabeth, and Grover, we're going to kick off our monster retail tour with a visit to ATNYU MES GDERAN GOMEN MEPROIUM.

For those of us not afflicted with demigod dyslexia, that would be Aunty Em's Garden Gnome Emporium.

True confession: Aunty Em's Garden Gnome Emporium is my favorite monster retail experience of all time. Probably because I didn't have to actually experience it myself. But also because Aunty Em turns out to be Aunty "M." That's short for Medusa, who may be the original experiencer of the bad hair day.

Actually, considering she has to go around with snakes on her head where her hair's supposed to be, I think we could just go with bad hair life.

Good rule to follow, in case it should happen to come up: Never piss off Athena, goddess of wisdom, Annabeth's mom. That's how Medusa ended up as old snakehead, and now *she's* plenty pissed off. So pissed that one look at her hairdo is all it takes to turn you to stone. If you look at a reflection of her, you're good to go. But if you look at her, well, head on. . . .

That's who all the garden gnomes in the emporium are—creatures of one sort or another who looked Aunty Em right in her beady, bloodshot eyes. Grover even thinks he spots one that looks a lot like his Uncle Ferdinand. It turns out he's right. Only it doesn't just *look* a lot like his Uncle Ferdinand. It *is* his Uncle Ferdinand.

Grover gets extra points, by the way, for urging his companions not to set foot in Aunty Em's Garden Gnome Emporium. He's certain he smells monsters, and it turns out he's absolutely right. Unfortunately, Percy and Annabeth overrule him. Not necessarily because they've developed a sudden interest in acquiring yard art for Camp Half-Blood, but because *they* smell burgers and they're hungry.

Let's just re-cap the overall scenario, shall we?

Percy, Grover, and Annabeth have just begun their quest. They know there's danger all around them. In fact, they've just escaped from an attack by all three of the Furies in the back of a bus, which is no mean feat, I can tell you. So I suppose I should cut Percy and Annabeth some slack, because it does make a certain amount of sense that all that Fury-fighting would have made them hungry.

But instead of heading for a nice safe McDonald's, where you can always use the bathroom even if you don't buy a Happy Meal, what does our hero do instead? He leads his friends straight to the back of a warehouse filled with extremely odd yet lifelike statuary. Why? Because the proprietor, whose face is completely hidden from sight by a veil (did I forget to mention that?), says there's a free snackbar.

Huh?

Surely the thing somebody ought to be smelling right about now is a rat. Strangely enough, nobody, with the possible exception of Grover, does. This is monster retail at its best and brightest: side-tracking the hero and his companions, then putting their lives at risk. The fact that they all eventually escape is fine and dandy. It's also cause for alarm. Because it's right here, with the trip to Aunty Em's Garden Gnome Emporium, that a pattern starts to form.

When the going gets tough, the heroes go shopping. But some-how they never notice until it's way too close to too late that the only thing the monsters really have for sale is trouble.

Here's another case in point: chapter seventeen of *The Lightning Thief*. That's when our gang pays a visit to Crusty's Waterbed Palace.

Percy's quest to retrieve Zeus' lightning bolt has taken him and his companions from the East Coast to Los Angeles by this time. No sooner do they set foot in the city, however, than they're set on by a pack of thugs. And it is while trying to escape from them that our trio decides to pay an impromptu visit to the Waterbed Palace.

So far, so good. But wait! There's more. Because once inside the Waterbed Palace, something strange happens. Well, more than one thing, if the full truth must be told. But the *specific* strange thing I'm getting at is this: Percy and his companions stick around.

Our hero and his friends have made it all the way across the country and they're still not much closer to finding Zeus' lightning bolt than they were when they set out. Time is definitely doing that thing where it runs out. So what do Percy, Grover, and Annabeth do?

You got it. They shop.

Unlike the side trip to Aunty Em's, where he was pretty certain he could smell trouble coming, this time Grover's the one who lets the trio down. He develops a sudden, potentially fatal attraction to the waterbeds. Almost before the trio knows what's happening, Grover's tied to one of the beds, with Annabeth not far behind. Both are in definite danger of being stretched to *one size fits all.*

Unless Percy thinks on his feet pretty darned fast, not only will he fail in his quest, but he and the others are going to be extremely uncomfortable—though admittedly more likely to be picked first for basketball.

Fortunately, by the time chapter seventeen has rolled around, thinking on his feet is a thing at which Perseus Jackson is learning to excel.

He turns the tables on waterbed salesman Crusty, short for Procrustes, a.k.a. the Stretcher, a real kill-'em-with-kindness guy. Percy does this by convincing Crusty that those waterbeds look pretty good, so good that Crusty himself ought to try one on for size. The moment Crusty does this, Percy's in the clear. He dispatches the monster and rescues his friends.

The shopping trip is over. The quest is on.

But I've still got a question, and my guess is you do too: Why in Western Civilization didn't Percy walk in then walk right back out the Waterbed Palace door? As soon as the thugs had departed, of course. Fast as our hero thinks on his feet when the time comes, why does it take *the time* so long to arrive? Why didn't Percy spot that there was something weird going on right off the bat?

I mean, come on.

A guy that Percy himself describes as looking like a raptor in a leisure suit tries to sell three individuals clearly not old enough to have their own credit cards some waterbeds? Get real. Do you have any idea how expensive those things are? And I'm talking before the shipping and handling costs. No salesman is that desperate. No real one, anyhow.

It's Aunty Em's Garden Gnome Emporium all over again, when you get right down to it. Our friends end up walking right into a trap. But the thing that lures them into the trap in the first place is a front. Specifically, a store front.

So just what is it about monsters and retail? Why would monsters even pick retail in the first place? Why go to all the effort of trying to lure Percy and his friends in to shop, when it would be so much easier to simply jump out from behind the nearest available cover and wipe them out? Percy and his pals only add up to three, after all.

At least they do in *The Lightning Thief*. Our hero does get some reinforcements as his adventure moves along. Even so, monsters come in an infinite variety of shapes and sizes, not to mention numbers. Surely all they'd have to do would be to keep on coming. Sooner or later, and probably sooner, Percy and his pals are bound to get tired.

And here's another question for you: If the monsters are going to go to all the trouble of setting up the opportunity for retail, how come they never seem to be selling anything a young demigod might actually want? Like some super new weapon, the ability to shop for your heart's desire, or to travel through time.

It took me a while, but I think I've come up with an explanation.

The fact that the monsters aren't selling anything our hero and his companions really, truly want is part of the point. I'm talking about the author's point, now. And Percy not being able to spot the danger monster retail poses, at least not immediately, is the other part. Because the truth (which I put forward knowing full well that

I run the risk of pissing off any monster within earshot) is actually quite radical.

All those retail monsters Percy encounters are actually doing him a favor, whether they mean to or not.

And just what is that favor, you'd like to know? They're teaching Percy about *caveat emptor*.

You know what that is, of course.

It's Latin for "let the buyer beware." And if that doesn't apply to Percy and pals I don't know what does. Essentially what it means for them, or for any demigod and his or her quest companions, is that they need to keep their eyes open. I'm not just talking about when it comes to monster retail opportunities. I'm talking all the time.

Because when you get right down to it, almost everybody Percy meets, good or bad, has the potential to be hiding something. Half the time, it's who they really are. The other half, it's what they really want. And that's not even counting the Mist, which can enable citizens of the realm of gods and monsters to screen themselves from mortal eyes entirely, or at the very least change their forms.

Not that a character has to use the Mist to hide what they really are, of course. The most important character in the series who looks like one thing but turns out to be another is one who never uses the Mist at all. He doesn't even change shape. Not really. He simply hides his true colors until the time is right to reveal himself.

You know who I'm talking about, don't you? It's Luke, of course.

Luke, who starts out being the person Percy looks up to as a friend, then metamorphoses into an archenemy determined to bring down the gods at all costs. And he does all this without changing so much as a hair on his head.

By now, I'll bet you're beginning to see my point.

Almost *nobody* in Percy's world is what they originally appear to be, including, as it turns out, Percy himself. And if he's going to survive in this world he's suddenly discovered he's a very important part of, he's going to have to use more than his wits. He's going to have to use his eyes. What's the best way of learning to do that?

You got it. By discovering how often you just can't trust them.

That's what monster retail is really all about. It's about learning to see the difference between truth and illusion. Developing the ability to see what's really there and what is not. And as Percy's experience at Aunty Em's Garden Gnome Emporium goes to show, there's no such thing as a real bargain when you indulge in monster retail, not to mention no such thing as a free lunch.

But the thing that really makes the theory work for me is the way that Percy himself begins to catch on. He even says as much, sort of, right before he makes the stupendous mistake of stepping through the front doors of the Lotus Hotel and Casino. Why does he do this, apart from the fact that it seems like a good idea at the time?

He does it because even he admits he's learned to be suspicious. Learned to be prepared for the fact that almost anything he encounters could be either a monster or a god. But the doorman in front of the Lotus is clearly human, clearly normal. Now that Percy knows how important it is to look for stuff like this, he's able to spot it right off.

Not only that, the doorman is a *sympathetic* human, and his sympathy strikes just the right note to encourage Percy to walk through the casino doors. This turns out to be about the worst mistake he could have made and comes perilously close to derailing the entire quest.

This is seriously sneaky stuff. Why? Because the Lotus turns the tables on Percy. His decision to enter the Hotel and Casino in the first place rests on the fact that he's learning his lesson, learning *not* to trust his eyes. But who's been teaching him this? The monsters, that's who. With a little help from the people Percy actually trusts thrown in on the side.

When you look at it this way, it doesn't seem so far-fetched to suggest that all those retail monsters are actually doing Percy a favor.

You might even be able to claim that, in a roundabout sort of way, all those monsters are really on Percy's side.

Boy are they surprised.

Still not convinced that monster retail is actually a positive thing? Let's take a look at *The Sea of Monsters, The Titan's Curse, The Battle of the Labyrinth,* and *The Last Olympian* for a moment. Those are Percy Jackson and the Olympians books two, three, four, and five. Not very many retail opportunities here, you say? (With the exception of Monster Donut in *The Sea of Monsters,* my second favorite monster retail opportunity of all time, in case you're counting.)

Aha! I reply. That's just my point. By the time *The Sea of Monsters* rolls around, Percy's beginning to get the point. He's learned the lesson all those shopping opportunities were trying to teach: Keep your eyes off the merchandise and on the quest-related prize.

The fact that Percy's learned to do this makes him much more dangerous, of course. Which is also why the fighting stakes get higher as the series goes along. The monsters have learned their lesson as well. No more trying to sidetrack the hero. Luring Percy off the track just isn't going to cut it anymore. Just keep coming at him head-on until you take the sucker out.

Fortunately, they haven't managed by the end of *The Last Olympian* (not for lack of persistence). But who turns out to have been spearheading the efforts to get rid of our hero? Who is his gone-over-to-the-dark-side counterpart? That's right. It's Luke, the threat Percy almost didn't recognize in time.

This is quite a clever sleight of hand on the author's part, if you stop to think about it. Because it puts the heart of an enemy—a monster, if you will—behind the face of a friend. This makes all Percy's encounters with Luke (and Annabeth's too, come to think of it) dangerous not just physically, but emotionally as well.

When you fight a friend who's turned into an enemy, you risk destruction not just of who you are in the present, but who you've been in the past. Why? Because you have to battle both your adversary, and your own remorse for having been fooled in the first place. This is part of what makes Percy's relationship with Luke so powerful. He genuinely liked the guy, though it must be admitted that Luke wasn't always the "monster" he turns out to be. There's an awful lot of Kronos-control going on. But why does that happen? Because Luke lets it, that's why. He's got free will, but he exercises it by giving it up. And maybe that's the true definition of a monster. A being who could have been something else, then chooses not to.

It's enough to make a hero nostalgic for the days of freaky garden statuary and killer waterbeds. Surely facing a monster that can turn you into stone is easier than staring into the face of someone you used to trust and then raising your sword. Because when you do that, there's always the chance your own feelings can be turned into a weapon to be used against you.

Let's face it. Monsters who wear the faces of friends play serious hardball.

Luckily, in the end, Percy beats the pretty big odds he's placed up against. But whatever he faces next, I think we can all be certain of at least one thing: No matter where the next adventure in his destiny leads, Perseus Jackson will *not* be taking along any Ancient Greek gift cards.

● ● ● ●

Cameron Dokey has more than thirty young people's titles to her credit, including *Once*, *Winter's Child*, *The World Above*, *Wild Orchid*, *Belle*, *Before Midnight*, *Sunlight and Shadow*, *Beauty Sleep*, *Golden*, and *The Storyteller's Daughter*, all for the Once Upon a Time series. She's also proud of the romantic comedy *How Not to Spend Your Senior Year*. You can see all Cameron's titles and find out more about her at www.camerondokey.com.

Stealing Fire From the Gods

The Appeal of Percy Jackson

Paul Collins

> Would you want to be Percy Jackson? At the beginning of *The Lightning Thief*, Percy is pretty adamant that you should never wish to be a half-blood. It's simply too dangerous. And yet, don't we all wish we could uncap a pen and see Riptide appear? Don't you sometimes wish you could confront monsters as bravely as a demigod would? Paul Collins explores why this idea is so appealing and why there might be a little Percy in all of us.

Growing up is dangerous. Being yourself is dangerous.

In the classic Australian film, *Strictly Ballroom*, the chief character, Scott, wants to dance his own steps and wants to do it his way. And all Hades breaks loose!

Scott's attempts at becoming an individual, at becoming *himself*, are seen as a crime, an act of rebellion, against the social "group" of which he is a member because Scott is not fitting in; he's not *conforming*.

Well, neither is Percy Jackson.

Percy is dyslexic, has Attention-Deficit/Hyperactivity Disorder (ADHD), and is always getting into trouble. In most school systems, and society at large, that pretty much makes Percy a loser, the kid least likely to succeed, the kind of kid who'll never amount to anything and isn't worth the effort anyway. Ever heard that one before?

Rick Riordan, author of the Percy Jackson series, turns these so-called flaws on their heads.

Like many kids in his position—labeled a misfit, looked down upon, shoved to the side lines—Percy feels shut out, left behind, and is beginning to feel frustrated and anxious about it. He can't work out why some of the teachers always pick on him, why things always go wrong even when he tries his hardest to do the right thing.

Of course, once you've been stuck with a label—like dyslexic, disruptive, troublemaker—it's pretty hard to change things back, because you're dealing with people's *perceptions*. They don't see "you" anymore; they just see the label.

In its own way, *The Lightning Thief* is a classic "Rags to Riches" plot, a type of story we've heard over and over again since early childhood: *The Ugly Duckling*, *Cinderella*, *Aladdin*, King Arthur, Star Wars, *David Copperfield*, *Jane Eyre*, Harry Potter, *Rocky*, the biblical Joseph and his brothers, and many, many more. They are all essentially stories about growing up, about coming into the power and responsibility of adulthood, and about the dark forces that try to stop them. They begin, usually, with a child or youthful hero/heroine who is often an orphan or part orphan (like Aladdin, Percy has "lost" a father) and who has been marginalized, forced to live in the shadows like Cinderella: neglected, scorned, undervalued, overlooked, and mistreated.

This story is found in every culture and every time, including that of the North American Indians prior to the arrival of the Europeans and as far back as ninth-century China (and there is no reason to think that that was its first occurrence).

So why is this particular plot so important to us? What is it *really* about?

Well, I'll tell you. It's about rebellion.

It's about people growing up and becoming *themselves*. Just as Scott tries to do in *Strictly Ballroom*, just as Harry Potter tries and every person who has ever lived has tried. Just as a fair few of the heroes and heroines of Greek myths have tried.

And this is no accident.

The gods of Olympus—all-powerful, simultaneously good *and* bad, unpredictable, oddly *human* in their flaws—are stand-ins not only for the establishment (school, society, church) but also for those other godlike beings: parents.

Rick Riordan has rightly seen this and created a story about the children of the gods, who are in precisely the same power relationship to their very-much-alive-and-kicking gods as children in our world are to their parents. And this, I think, is one of the secrets to the success of the series: It mimics the experience of everyone growing up—and of every person's troublesome need to become him- or herself.

Seeing Clearly

The Lightning Thief is also about "seeing clearly": the schools Percy has attended (six so far) and the various teachers he's had, as well as his smelly unpleasant stepfather, have marked him down as a troublemaker and a no-hoper. When something goes wrong, it must be Percy's fault.

And that's because they don't see the real Percy.

Nor, for that matter, does he see *them* very clearly: He's unaware that his teacher Mr. Brunner is actually a centaur, that Mrs. Dodds is a razor-taloned Fury out for his blood, that his best friend Grover is a cloven-footed satyr, and that the three old ladies on the roadside are the Fates.

Later, he fails to see through the disguises the various gods or monsters adopt—sometimes until it's almost too late, as when the Mother of Monsters, Echidna, along with her doggie-who-ain't-a-doggie, tries to turn him into a smokin' shish kebab.

Percy's failure to "see clearly" extends to his "normal" life as well: His dyslexia, considered a handicap in our world, causes visual distortions. "Words had started swimming off the page, circling my head, the letters doing one-eighties as if they were riding skateboards," he describes it in *The Lightning Thief.* In reality, the dyslexia is the result of Percy's brain being hard-wired for Ancient Greek and is part of his uniqueness.

But most of all, Percy doesn't see himself clearly.

Like the schools and society that have labeled him as some kind of maverick and failure, he sees himself in terms of those same labels.

In the Rags to Riches story, the true focus is not so much on growing up as it is one of its chief requirements: becoming *aware*.

It is learning to be *conscious*, learning to *see* clearly and wholly, that distinguishes these types of stories. Even Peter Rabbit manages to escape the dangerous farmer and the garden in which he eats and plays to his heart's content (like any egocentric infant) only when he climbs up high to get a better view of things.

Attaining consciousness—awareness—is the true mark of the rebel, and the greatest danger for those in power, whether they be gods or parents. It is no coincidence that authoritarian regimes, like Saddam Hussein's pre-invasion Iraq, seek always to control the media and to dictate what people can and can't know.

Rags to Riches

In his astonishing book *The Seven Basic Plots*, Christopher Booker outlines and explores the fundamental stories that have entranced, and continue to entrance, the human race. One of these is the

Rags to Riches plotline. While many stories combine more than one of these plots (*Star Wars* is both a Rags to Riches story and an "Overcoming the Monster" story, as is *The Lightning Thief*), I want to concentrate on the Rags to Riches plotline, in which, as Booker puts it, "a young central figure emerges step by step from an initial state of dependent, unformed childhood to a final state of complete self-realization and wholeness"—in other words, the hero gains maturity throughout the journey, or rite of passage, that he experiences.

Why is this story, above all others, told so often?

The quick answer is that it is the only one of the seven basic plots that charts the life of a human being from the limited awareness of childhood to the discerning perception of adulthood.

The Rags to Riches story is also designed to show us the *importance* of learning through experience. It shows us the early days of life when no one in the story sees clearly; how this permits us to be easily ruled by others; how cruelty and abuse rule through ignorance; how trying to see clearly becomes a threat to this domination and in what way, by passing through various grueling tests in which a near death occurs. Throughout all this, new powers of maturity are gained, self-mastery is acquired, and a "happy ending" is defined as one in which everyone has begun to see more clearly than ever before. And as Booker points out, when people can see properly, they can move ahead and gain confidence and prosperity.

By contrast, this plot also shows how the great and fatal flaw of the dark figures in the story is always a kind of persistent or peculiar blindness, a distortion of vision, brought on by self-centeredness— that very trait that defines infancy and early childhood. The title itself tells us that the preoccupation in *The Lightning Thief* is with vision: Someone has stolen light—the very thing needed to see clearly! And the culprit? A god, of course. A god of war. A god of domination and darkness.

In this sense, we understand that the dark figures of the story are those who never grow up, who never see clearly and wholly, who remain blind and self-centered.

The Five Stages of Growth

The Rags to Riches plot generally progresses through five stages intended not only to chart the human journey but also the journey of that most rebellious of human traits: consciousness.

Stage 1: Initial wretchedness at home and the "Call"

Here we meet the young neglected hero and see the world he inhabits, a world of scorn and abuse (think of the Dursleys in Harry Potter). The importance of this stage is not just to show how things began but to draw attention to the *difference* between the hero/heroine and the darker figures around him or her—in Percy's case his stepfather, his math teacher Mrs. Dodds, the nastiest girl in school who torments him and Grover, and the school system itself. Note that in mythological terms, the lowly hero/heroine is also the "diamond in the rough," that which is overlooked and treated with contempt for appearing to be plain and inferior.

Yet what is significant here is that while the dark figures in the story rarely change at all, the hero also does not change as much as characters in other story types . . . and that's because the Rags to Riches hero *already possesses the traits that will one day make him or her exceptional.* These traits are simply buried inside him, more or less invisible to the people around the hero, and to the hero as well.

The other crucial aspect of this stage is that we see the downside of not seeing clearly, of being in a state of limited awareness: Percy buys into society's labels (believing himself to be a loser and troublemaker); he is exploited by his scumbag stepfather (he feels he has no power); he thinks there is something wrong with him, that he's bad (everything keeps going wrong); and he doesn't know what is going on or who people really are (he does not have the special knowledge or maturity he needs to "see" the bigger picture).

Stage 2: Out into the world, initial success

This is a kind of "dream stage" when almost everything goes right at last, in contrast to the next stage, though it also gives the hero time to start developing some of the skills he'll need later on. In Star Wars, Luke learns how to use the Force from Obi-Wan Kenobi. In *The Lightning Thief*, Percy Jackson arrives at Camp Half-Blood and begins his training. Like all "orphans" in Rags to Riches stories, he is also trying to find out who he is and where he came from. This search for personal identity is a powerful force and usually focuses on the hero's parentage. Here, Percy discovers he is the son of Poseidon, the lord of the ocean (interestingly, the ocean is usually a symbol of the unconscious and of the feminine).

During this stage the hero tries to grow up too quickly: becomes cocky, arrogant, or overly prideful, and thinks he is mature before he really is; he usually makes important decisions based on this false assumption. What success he finds at this point is based on some false power or outside agency (Aladdin had his genies).

Very soon he will have to go it alone, but right now he is still not seeing clearly and wholly. His relationships with others suffer. He makes enemies easily. And he does not complete crucial lessons, trying to leapfrog ahead in an impatience to prove himself—a trait that reveals to the discerning reader how unready he still is, despite the fact that he can now talk the talk and walk the walk.

Stage 3: The central crisis

Suddenly, everything goes south. The hero is plunged into despair and hopelessness, made worse by his former bravado and high hopes; he experiences a brush with death, symbolic or otherwise (E.T. "dies"; Frodo lapses into a deathlike stupor; Cedric Diggory is murdered in front of Harry while he is symbolically crucified). This stage represents the danger of discovering (or starting to discover) one's true identity: As I said earlier, becoming oneself is always seen as a crime against the masses, an act of rebellion against the establishment.

And "punishment" quickly follows.

Percy is plunged into the middle of a war between petulant gods and must set out on an almost suicidal quest for which he is far from ready. He encounters several symbolic deaths and has close shaves with real ones, as in the deadly confrontation with the Mother of Monsters, Echidna.

Here, Riordan carefully crafts the psychological development of his young protagonist: The only way to survive is for Percy to have faith in himself, or rather in the "new self" or identity that he has so recently discovered. This sudden realization that he really does have some innate power, that he really is a demigod after all, significantly occurs in a very high place, the Gateway Arch—from where he can see in all directions.

Stage 4: Independence and the final ordeal

The hero survives the central crisis, having faced "death" and emerged from it changed. This is the final test through which his transformation into his new self takes place, though this new self will still have to be tested in a climactic confrontation with the darkest figure in the story.

In all the recent stages, Percy has been discovering the importance of seeing clearly. This not only involves gaining a better understanding of what drives his two companions but also penetrating the disguises of the monsters. As each new threat unfolds, he sees through the assumed identity of the monster more swiftly than before. He is growing up.

And that, of course, makes him an even bigger threat.

Percy is now very much on his own. Like Aladdin after his princess has been kidnapped, like Harry in the cemetery, Percy must stand on his own two feet and become the master of his own powers.

To do this, he must "see" himself clearly, not just others, and know his own strengths and weaknesses.

Stage 5: Final union, completion, and fulfillment

In a series, you don't get to this final stage till the last book (unless the "completion" is to be dramatically overturned at the start of the next one). Not only can each book in a series follow the Rags to Riches plotline, but so can the series as a whole. In this sense, *Harry Potter and the Goblet of Fire* represents the central crisis of the series, which is why Harry is separated from everyone else in the maze and has a very real brush with death: his own and Cedric's (not to mention the "ghosts" of his parents and the location in a graveyard).

At this stage in *The Lightning Thief*, Percy has become more fully himself and is now seeing even more clearly. He has rebelled against the restrictions and the limiting labels that have been placed upon him, and he is ready to assume more responsibility for his own actions in the world.

But that doesn't mean everyone is happy with him.

After all, he's done what the gods could not: resolved a dangerous conflict by seeing through trickery, deceit, and false disguises. He has, in other words, rocked the boat.

Rite of Passage

So what we have here, in Riordan's *The Lightning Thief*, is the journey of a rebel, a journey toward consciousness and awareness, a journey of someone who dares to become himself and fulfill his destiny.

But, as we saw earlier, this process of acquiring consciousness, of seeing clearly, is dangerous, since it is a challenge to the established order and the powers that be. Yet everyone goes through it. And in doing so, they commit the oldest "crime" there is: trying to be an individual.

Perhaps this is the oldest of battles: the battle between the generations, reflected in the first Greek myths that tell how the Olympians threw down the older gods, the Titans, then warred with humanity, their "children," trying to keep them in darkness—a darkness that the greatest rebel of them all, Prometheus, liberated them from by stealing fire from Mount Olympus and giving it to humankind (for which he was barbarically punished by Zeus).

Just like the gods, parents—often with the best intentions—instinctively try to keep their children from growing up, because increasing awareness is always a challenge to them, a slap in the face, a rejection.

But all children grow up. Because all children are rebels, like Percy Jackson.

They are born with the seed of rebellion in them, as Booker makes clear when he notes that the young heroes and heroines of the Rags to Riches plotline are very different at the end of the story from how they began:

> What has happened to them is that they have at last revealed or developed what was potentially in them all the time. They have matured. They have grown up. They have fully realised everything that was in them to become. In the best and highest sense, they have become themselves.

● ● ● ●

Paul Collins' many books for young people include series such as The Jelindel Chronicles, The Earthborn Wars, The Quentaris Chronicles, and The World of Grrym in collaboration with Danny Willis. His latest series is The Maximus Black Files. He is also the author of over 150 short stories. Paul has been the recipient of the A. Bertram Chandler, Aurealis, William Atheling Jr., and Peter McNamara Awards and has been shortlisted for many others.

He is currently the publisher at Ford Street Publishing and runs the speakers' agency Creative Net. Visit him at www.paulcollins.com.au.

Would *You* Want to Be One of Artemis' Hunters?

Carolyn MacCullough

It's a tempting offer: Follow me, and you will live forever. But as Carolyn MacCullough explains, becoming a Hunter of Artemis is a mixed blessing. Before you decide to take that oath, you'd better read what she has to say.

If given the option of eternal youth, my guess is that nine out of ten women would take it. After all, Oil of Olay, Revlon, and Lancôme, among others, have spent millions of dollars in ad campaigns trying to convince us that we can purchase it in just one small bottle. As a society, we practically fetishize youth, craving that unlined skin and endless exuberance and effervescent energy that just seems to ooze from the pores of the very young. Most women strive to preserve youth in even the smallest of ways, no matter how many times we steel ourselves to the idea of aging gracefully.

So what if someone made you an offer you thought you couldn't refuse? An offer that seemed too good to be true (as most offers like this are)? What if Artemis herself, Greek goddess extraordinaire (also known as Diana if you happen to be Roman), mistress of the hunt, goddess of the moon, defender of all things wild and free, came down from the pearly heights of Mount Olympus and made you a proposition?

First of all, only females may apply (sorry, guys!). So ladies, the offer on the table is that Artemis will grant you eternal youth. Yes, *eternal* youth: something that people have quested for across the centuries. No need to fear the onslaught of wrinkles or the first strands of gray hair or a general diminishment of vigor and vim (two things that seem truly essential for a productive life even if most of us can't exactly define "vim" on the spot). You'll never fall victim to arthritis or memory loss or any of those other aspects of growing old that range from the merely annoying to the downright debilitating.

Okay, maybe it's a little too early for you to be worrying about all of that anyway. Your skin is unlined, and as for gray hair, that's something your mom is always moaning over, not you. But forever-firm skin and shining hair are not the only benefits of this offer. Consider that you'll also gain freedom from all the responsibilities of daily life. You'll acquire the ability to run tirelessly and the opportunity to romp with a goddess and your fellow huntresses all over the wild reaches of this world. You'll become part of a steadfast sisterhood, the ultimate zenith of girl power. You'll never have to worry about your best friend moving away and having no one to sit with at the lunch table in school, or wonder if your friends are *true* friends. And you'll never have to go through that "crisis of self-confidence" that everyone is always warning teenage girls about. Plus, no man will ever, *ever* tell you what to do or say or think, or more precisely what you *can't* do or say or think.

All you have to do is utter the words, "I pledge myself to the goddess Artemis. I turn my back on the company of men, accept eternal maidenhood, and join the Hunt."

Yes, you heard that right. Eternal maidenhood and no men. No men at all.

So therein lies the catch (I did promise one of those). In exchange for always living in the endless summer of your life, with complete freedom from everything, you must foreswear all contact with men. And I really do mean *all* contact, not just contact of the romantic persuasion. But let's talk about the romantic-persuasion kind first.

Forget about first dates. No more *should I put my hair up or down, what shoes do I wear, is this outfit okay?* No more tiny perfect butterflies in your stomach, and no more agonizing over *will he kiss me now, should I kiss him first, oh I really hope he kisses me at all!* No need for those long talks on the phone with your best friend about how he actually *looked at you in the cafeteria today or touched your hand maybe by accident, but maybe not, and how you think for three seconds he was smiling in your general direction and you know he was smiling at you because you looked behind your shoulder (in a really subtle way of course) and made sure that there was no one behind you that he could possibly be smiling at.* No need for any of that because when you're one of Artemis' maidens you really are just that: a maiden through and through. Forever. Artemis was the goddess of virginity, and while Athena was also a virgin goddess, she was known more for being the goddess of wisdom. Don't forget, Athena sprang forth fully grown from her father Zeus' head and is always depicted as a grave woman, while Artemis is always portrayed as an eternally young and carefree girl. Greek mythology tells us that Artemis made the choice to remain a virgin at a very early age (some versions pinpoint it as early as three years old). Artemis made this request, along with one for a silver bow and silver arrows, of her father, Zeus, and it was granted.

Okay, so say that you think *so far so good*. You're tired of boys anyway. Who needs them? They never call when they say they will, and when they actually do call they only want to talk about really boring things, and you don't like any of their meathead friends, and sometimes you're not sure if you even like *them*. Especially when they don't cut their hair for a while or wear that same T-shirt at least three times a week. Besides, your best friends (who needless to say are all girls) happen to understand you, really understand everything you're going through, sometimes without you even having to explain it all. So no need to stress over that part of the deal.

But consider that this contract is pretty absolute. When Artemis says no males, she really means it. This includes your father, your brothers, your male cousins and friends. No more father-daughter dances or the two of you making pancakes while the rest of your family is sleeping. No more watching TV with your brothers and fighting, in a playful way, over the remote control. No more kicking around a soccer ball in the park with your male friends. (For the record, I have never kicked around a soccer ball in a park or anywhere else, but should I ever choose to do so, it might be fun to kick the ball to a male friend or two.) Instead, you have to leave your family and begin a shiny brand-new life with your adopted sisters, your fellow Hunters.

Not so easy now, right? Remember in Rick Riordan's *The Titan's Curse*, the character Bianca is offered this choice. True, Artemis does mention that Bianca may see her brother *occasionally*, but she also quite clearly states that if Bianca swears the oath, she will have a new family starting then and there. And Bianca does end up swearing the oath and becoming one of Artemis' maidens. But her choice has some unexpected consequences that come back to haunt her.

Who cares, you say. You still want in. Your father's too strict anyway and your brothers (if you have them) are so annoying and probably wouldn't even notice if you were gone. Fine, but let's examine Artemis a little more closely to see just what you'd be getting into if you signed up for eternal youth. Artemis as portrayed in *The Titan's Curse* is a stern but fair task-mistress, willing to go to great lengths to protect her maidens. Moreover, she is a woman of extreme strength and conviction, as shown when she shoulders Atlas' burden and bears it admirably. And Riordan's rendering of her does align with the more traditional Artemis of Greek myths and legends.

Yet while Riordan's Artemis seems like the very best possible older sister a girl could ask for—daring, brave, full of vitality—the Artemis of Greek myths had a harsher side. In fact, the Artemis of Greek myths often possessed a contradictory and cruelly unforgiving nature. Although she was generally known as the protector of innocents, there are several disturbing myths that showcase her terrifying capacity for swift and brutal revenge.

One such myth concerns Niobe, the Queen of Thebes. Niobe gave birth to seven sons and seven daughters, and in a moment of hubris she bragged about her fertility at a ceremony honoring the goddess Leto. Huge mistake. Leto just happened to be the mother of none other than Artemis and Apollo. Also, she was often considered the goddess of fertility, which apparently Niobe found too much of an irony to resist. Niobe decided that she was superior to Leto, having had fourteen children to Leto's mere two.

It's generally never a good idea to compare yourself favorably to a goddess, especially at a ceremony in her honor. Furthermore, Leto was the daughter of Titans, who aren't exactly known for their easygoing nature. As to be expected, Leto didn't take the insult well and sent in her royal children, Artemis and Apollo, to exact revenge. While Apollo killed Niobe's seven sons, Artemis, an expert huntress, shot and killed the seven daughters with her deadly arrows.

In some versions, Niobe is said to have cradled her youngest daughter in her arms, begging the goddess to spare the child's life; unfortunately, Artemis' arrow had already left the bow. Niobe's husband, Amphion, was said to have either committed suicide when learning of his children's deaths or been murdered by Apollo. Niobe fled in despair to Mount Sipylus (located somewhere in Asia Minor), where she wept so much that she was eventually turned into stone (in some versions by Artemis herself).

You might ask, what was Niobe thinking to insult Leto, a goddess, a lover of Zeus, and the mother of such powerful children? It's true that back then there were very specific rules concerning honor and the right to take revenge once said honor was insulted. So let's put Niobe aside for the moment and look instead at Iphigenia, Agamemnon's unfortunate daughter. After killing a deer in one of Artemis' sacred groves (and in some versions also boasting that he was the better hunter), Agamemnon, King of Argos or Mycenae (depending on whom you're talking to), draws the wrath of Artemis down upon his head. Things really heat up when Agamemnon wants to sail to Troy with his army. Artemis refuses to allow the wind to fill Agamemnon's sails . . . until he sacrifices his youngest daughter, Iphigenia, as payback for killing one of her deer (and nominating himself as the better hunter). In some accounts Agamemnon completes the sacrifice and Iphigenia is killed, while in others Artemis relents at the last moment. In these latter versions, Artemis spirits the girl away to the island of Crimea, where she becomes a priestess of Artemis' temple. This may seem like a kinder fate, but the temple routinely indulges in the human sacrifice of strangers to the island. Not exactly the kind of career you aspire to.

Still unconvinced that Artemis might not be the most stable and considerate of bosses? What about the fate of one of Artemis' most famous nymphs, Callisto? Much like Riordan's Zoë Nightshade, Callisto was one of Artemis' favorite nymphs, who upheld her vow of chastity and hunted with the goddess frequently. Unfortunately, she caught the eye of Zeus, Artemis' own father, and once Zeus' interest is piqued there often isn't anything a girl can do. Greek mythology is full of tales of Zeus' philandering ways and the incredible lengths he goes to in order to seduce the object of his interest.

Although a few legends tell of Callisto welcoming Zeus with open arms, most of the versions have Zeus resorting to trickery. In these versions, knowing that Callisto was completely devoted to both Artemis and her vow of chastity, Zeus appeared to the nymph as the goddess Artemis herself while Callisto lay resting under a tree. Once Callisto's guard was down, Zeus abandoned his disguise and used force against her. To make matters worse, Callisto ended up pregnant from the encounter. Fearing Artemis' legendary wrath, Callisto tried to conceal her condition but finally was no longer able to one morning when all the nymphs bathed together in a forest glade. Furious that Callisto betrayed her vow (even though by most accounts Callisto hadn't done so willingly), Artemis turned her into a bear, which she then hunted down and killed. In other versions, Callisto was still allowed to give birth to her son, Arcas, who in turn encountered his mother in her bear form and killed her. In yet other versions, Artemis was on the verge of killing Callisto when Zeus interfered and placed her in the sky where she can be seen as Ursa Major. (Interestingly enough, Riordan's Artemis takes credit for placing Callisto in the sky herself.)

Callisto is not an exception to the rule, by the way. Maera, daughter of Proetus, was another of Artemis' nymphs who had the misfortune to attract Zeus' roving eye. Whether Maera was willing or not (and my guess is not), Zeus seduced her. Enraged that her nymph had "broken" her vow, Artemis killed her.

So maybe this option of eternal youth and freedom isn't looking all that attractive anymore. But what if you were a girl living in Ancient Greece, the original stomping grounds of the gods? Females in Ancient Greece, as to be expected, had very different outlooks, expectations of, and rules in their lives. Society (read: men) believed women were weak creatures who needed to be shielded from themselves as well as from the rest of the world. Traditionally, women were appointed a male guardian, usually a father or brother, though in some cases another male relative. This male guardian's, or *kyrios'*, duty was to marry off his female charge, usually when she was in her early teens. The guardian supplied the dowry and the match; the girls had very little or no say in the matter. Love or even liking was not a factor in the marriage.

Once married, a wife's main function was to reproduce. And reproduce and reproduce. Oh, and she was also supposed to spin and cook and clean. In short, she had to manage the household. But that's where her sphere of influence began and ended. A Greek wife was rarely allowed out of her own house, except to attend festivals and funerals, where a woman's presence was permitted, and even then she was never to go unattended (i.e., with a male, for her own protection). A popular belief at the time was that a good wife was an invisible wife. The less said about a married woman, the more honorable she was considered. And this extended even inside her own home. If a husband brought guests home to entertain, a wife had to make herself scarce.

And the possibilities for women who weren't destined to be wives in Ancient Greek society were even bleaker. Women who weren't marriageable were often forced to become slaves. If they were slightly more fortunate, they became courtesans or concubines. A concubine was the mistress of her own home, but, like a courtesan, her main function was to entertain men. Their lives and livelihoods depended on how well they could manage this. In fact, all of these occupations—wife, slave, courtesan, or concubine—involved a level of dependence on the good will of men that is unheard of for young women living in today's democratic societies. Given the hazardous situation of women in Ancient Greece, Artemis' proposition suddenly seems more appealing. Perhaps most out of all the goddesses, she represents all that traditional Greek women were not allowed to be: free and untamed. In fact, Artemis is a bit of a paradox. On the one hand, her commitment to purity must have been greatly admired by Ancient Greeks; yet she is also untamable and answers to no man. She is truly the eternal wild child who never has to grow up and shoulder the responsibilities that adulthood brings. She never has to compromise herself or conform to any of society's standards. No wonder she is associated with the moon—completely untouchable, forever unattainable. If offered the option of becoming one of Artemis' immortal maidens, freed forever from the shackles of marriage or slavery, I think many Ancient Greek women would have jumped on that bandwagon as it careened past them.

Ancient Greek women would have had no concept of the freedoms that are enjoyed, even taken for granted, today. Think about it: When was the last time you questioned your right, your ability really, to walk down the street in broad daylight either by yourself or with friends? Can you even imagine a world where you weren't free to choose your own friends or what subjects to study in school or whether or not you wanted to play soccer or try out for the swim team or the community theater production? There are myriad choices on our plates today and each one presents an array of exciting opportunities and possibilities.

Both Riordan's Artemis and the Artemis of Greek myth represent the ideals of freedom and independence, of glorious strength and bravery. And all of these qualities are admirable ones, ones to cultivate in our own lives. We *should* live by the principles of Artemis and all that she espoused. (Well, we should live by *most* of those principles. Maybe skip the human sacrifice bit.)

If I were given the choice of eternal freedom, I think I would have to pass. Not because I have a burning desire to kick that soccer ball around the field with a male friend or two, but because the vow's requirements are just a little too extreme for me. And even though those signs of aging are a long way off, I advise you to follow my lead, and when your time comes, put your faith in Oil of Olay, Lancôme, and Revlon.

They cost a lot less.

● ● ● ●

Carolyn MacCullough is the author of five young adult novels. Her latest two are *Once a Witch* and *Almost a Witch*, a paranormal series featuring modern day witches, dark spells, and time travel. She teaches creative writing at Gotham Writers, Inc. and lives in New York with her husband and two children. More information about her and her books can be found at www.carolynmaccullough.com.

Dionysus: Who Let Him Run a Summer Camp?

Ellen Steiber

> There's a lot more to Dionysus than a leopard-pattern Hawaiian shirt and a can of Diet Coke. As Ellen Steiber explains, the director of Camp Half-Blood has a long and complex history in the Greek myths. The god of insanity and debauchery is also the god of joy and revelry. Does this mean he's not as bad as Percy thinks? She'll let you decide.

Could there be a more bizarre choice for director of Camp Half-Blood than Dionysus?

Rick Riordan has a gift for playing with the Greek myths. He delights in taking the gods and their stories and giving them just enough of a twist to make them completely believable in our world while still retaining the essence of the ancient beliefs. His Dionysus, more safely referred to as Mr. D (names are, after all, powerful things), takes the image of the Greek god of wine and revelry and twists it into a believable contemporary portrait: If you spent most of your time drinking and partying like Mr. D, there's a good chance that by the time you reached middle age, you too would be over-weight, badly dressed, and not care a fig about anything except when you could get your next drink. You certainly wouldn't be thrilled by having a bunch of "brats" foisted on you. And there's a good chance you wouldn't be the most responsible guardian.

Certainly this is Percy Jackson's take on Mr. D when Percy first arrives at Camp Half-Blood. But first and even fifth impressions don't tell the whole story when dealing with the Greek gods, who are complex deities. Most of them are multitaskers. Dionysus is not only god of wine and the vine but also the god of fertility, who rules all growing things. (You see this side of Mr. D in Camp Half-Blood's strawberry fields, which grow so effortlessly and fruitfully that the camp is able to pay all its bills by selling its strawberries to New York restaurants.) He's also the god of madness, revelry, and theater, as well as the god of joy and divine ecstasy. In the series Riordan describes some of these facets and hints at others. How much of Mr. D, I found myself wondering, was actually part of what the Greeks believed about Dionysus? And what do the sto-ries featuring Dionysus tell us not only about Mr. D but also about Camp Half-Blood?

Percy is not impressed when he's first introduced to the camp director. Mr. D is short, pudgy, and tends to dress in either loud Hawaiian shirts or tacky running suits featuring tiger or leopard prints. Thanks to Smelly Gabe, his mother's repulsive husband, Percy immediately knows that Mr. D has a serious acquaintance with alcohol. He looks like a middle-aged drunk going rapidly to seed. What Percy doesn't immediately pick up on is that he's facing a god. He doesn't understand why Grover seems so frightened of Mr. D— until Mr. D allows him a glimpse of his true nature:

He turned to look at me straight on, and I saw a kind of purplish fire in his eyes. . . . I saw visions of grape vines [sic] choking unbelievers to death, drunken warriors insane with battle lust, sailors screaming as their hands turned to flippers, their faces elongating into dolphin snouts. I knew that if I pushed him . . . [he] would plant a disease in my brain that would leave me wearing a straitjacket in a rubber room for the rest of my life.

This is a very accurate description of some of Dionysus' favorite methods for punishing those who've angered him. These include trapping the poor mortals with suddenly sprouting grape and ivy vines, turning them into animals, and driving them completely mad. The Greek stories of Dionysus often depict a frighteningly cruel, vengeful god, yet the images of him almost always show either a beautiful youth surrounded by grapevines or a handsome man with curling, black hair and a luxurious beard. In fact, this image is so consistent that Dionysus is remarkably easy to identify on the vases and urns that have survived from Ancient Greece. The classic Dionysus looks nothing like Riordan's pudgy, bleary Mr. D. I think there may be a couple of reasons that Riordan's version of Dionysus is so unattractive. The first goes back to the myths. Like his father Zeus, Dionysus was a master of disguise and often appeared to mortals in other forms. He was known to show up as a ram, a lion, or even a young girl; he was easy to underestimate. I also suspect his incarnation as Mr. D is a warning of sorts on Riordan's part; no one meeting that unappealing little man could possibly imagine that drinking is a good idea.

You might think that the god of joy and revels would at least guarantee a good time at camp. But no. Beyond his slovenly appearance, Mr. D's also got an attitude problem. He's snarky and sullen and contemptuous of both humans and half-bloods. Though he obviously knows the campers' true names, he makes a point of pretending he can't remember them. One of the running jokes of the series is Mr. D referring to Percy as Peter Johnson. Chiron explains that Mr. D is unhappy because he "hates his job." Zeus, it turns out, is the one who ordered Dionysus to run Camp Half-Blood, as a punishment for chasing an off-limits nymph. Not only is Dionysus essentially grounded on Earth for a hundred years—though his sentence is halved in *The Last Olympian* as a reward for his bravery—but he's forbidden to drink his beloved wine. His mission is to keep the young heroes safe. And he's not happy about any of it.

On the surface, choosing Mr. D to run the camp is so ridiculous, it's comic. It may even be Riordan's sly acknowledgment of the fact that sometimes the adults who are put in charge of kids are the most inappropriate for the job. Nearly everyone has had teachers who range from inept to damaging to occasionally downright scary. Mr. D seems to be all of those rolled into one.

Percy takes an instant dislike to the whiny camp director, and you can hardly blame him. Even though Mr. D is supposed to be keeping the half-gods safe, he doesn't seem to care about any of them and he certainly doesn't bother to help or train them. All of that boring detail he leaves to the centaur Chiron. In the third book, *The Titan's Curse*, Mr. D even confesses that he doesn't like heroes. He married Ariadne after the hero Theseus abandoned her, and he's held a grudge against heroes ever since. He considers heroes selfish ingrates who use and betray others. To Percy (and yours truly), Mr. D's description of the heroes sounds more like a description of most of the gods. What Riordan doesn't tell us, though, is that Dionysus also had a bit of history with the original Perseus, the hero who defeated the Gorgons and Medusa. According to Robert Graves' *The Greek Myths*, Perseus fought Dionysus when the wine god came to Argos, killing many of his followers. Dionysus retaliated by driving the women of Argos mad, to the point that they began to eat their own children. Perseus finally had the good sense to appease the god by building him a great temple. So in addition to not liking heroes, Dionysus might simply dislike Percy because of his name.

Moody and difficult as he is, Mr. D is the first god whom Percy confronts directly, and I can't help thinking that's significant. Mr. D defies expectations. He's not beautiful or even likeable. He's the embodiment of divine indifference—a god who barely notices that mortals exist. Percy meets him at a point when he, Percy, doesn't believe in gods, and yet there's Mr. D, undeniably real and scary. The wine god is irrefutable evidence of the new truths that Percy must accept: that not only are the Greek gods real and still messing with mortals, but that one of them is his father. Shortly after meeting Mr. D, a confused Percy asks Chiron:

> "Who . . . who am I?" . . .
>
> "Who are you?" [Chiron] mused. "Well, that's the question we all want answered, isn't it?"

It is indeed. The gods want to know because they've got a prophecy to contend with, and Percy needs to know because what he discovers at Camp Half-Blood is the key to his identity. That question is really the one that Percy has come to Camp Half-Blood to answer. And the more I look at the myths, the more I believe that of all the gods, Dionysus is the perfect choice to preside over the place where questions like Percy's get resolved.

What Dionysus Did *Before* He Ran Camp Half-Blood

To really understand what Riordan does with Dionysus, it helps to look at the myths about the wine god. The most popular version of his story starts with his mother, Semele, who was not a goddess but a princess, the daughter of Cadmus, King of Thebes. Zeus fell in love with the young princess and swore by the River Styx that he would do anything she asked. But falling in love with Zeus never works out well for mortals. When Hera, Zeus' wife, found out about the romance, she disguised herself as an old woman and persuaded the princess to ask Zeus to prove his love by showing himself to her as he showed himself to Hera, in his undisguised divine form. Zeus, knowing that no mortal could survive such a sight, begged the girl to ask for something else. Semele, already six months pregnant and wanting to know the truth about her child's father, refused. Bound by his own oath, Zeus showed himself in his true form, an immense, glorious vision blazing with thunder and lightning. I suspect this was the equivalent of looking at a nuclear blast up close. Semele was by some accounts frightened to death; by others, she was incinerated on the spot. What nearly all versions of the myth agree on is that in the moment before she died, the god managed to rescue the child she was carrying. Zeus hid the unborn child by sewing him into his own thigh and only undid the stitches when Dionysus was ready to be born.

One interesting thing about Dionysus' birth is that, of the twelve great Olympian gods, only Dionysus had a mortal parent. Dionysus, though fully divine, is the only god who started life as a half-blood. Which gives him a rather unique qualification to run the summer camp.

I think it's fair to say that Dionysus had a difficult childhood. According to one version of his story, Hera, not content with destroying his mother, ordered the Titans to seize the infant. What happened next was not only violent but seriously gross. The Titans tore the baby to pieces then boiled the pieces in a cauldron. A pomegranate tree sprang from the place on the earth where the infant's blood had fallen, and Rhea, Dionysus' grandmother,[1] somehow brought the child back to life.

---

[1] Rhea, an ancient earth goddess, was the wife of the Titan Kronos and mother of Zeus, Demeter, Hades, Hera, Hestia, and Poseidon.

Realizing that Olympus was not the safest place for the child, Zeus put Dionysus in the care of King Athamas and his wife, Ino, who was one of Semele's sisters. They hid the young boy in the women's quarters, where he was disguised as a woman (which may account for some of the descriptions of Dionysus as having a feminine appearance[2]). This arrangement lasted until Hera found out about it and drove both the king and his wife mad. The king in his madness even killed his eldest son, thinking him a stag.

Zeus then put Hermes on the case. Hermes disguised Dionysus as a young ram and managed to get him safely into the care of the five nymphs who lived on Mount Nysa. They were more successful guardians, raising the young godling in a cave, feeding him on honey. Zeus, grateful to the nymphs, set their images in the sky as stars and called them the Hyades. These are the stars that are believed to bring rain when they are near the horizon. As Edith Hamilton puts it in *Mythology: Timeless Tales of Gods and Heroes*:

> So the God of the Vine was born of fire and nursed
> by rain, the hard burning heat that ripens the grapes
> and water that keeps the plants alive.

Dionysus managed to survive childhood and apparently even made his first wine on Mount Nysa. According to Robert Graves' *The Greek Myths*, soon after Dionysus reached manhood, Hera recognized him as Semele's son. Never one to give up a grudge, Hera promptly drove Dionysus mad. It was at this point that he began his wanderings, accompanied by his tutor, Silenus, and an extremely rowdy bunch of followers who terrified nearly everyone they met. These followers include satyrs and the dreaded Maenads, possessed women who worshipped Dionysus and had a nasty habit of getting

---

[2] According to the British writer Sir J. G. Frazer, there was also an ancient custom of dressing young boys as girls in order to protect them from the Evil Eye, a kind of curse.

drunk then dismembering and devouring wild animals or the occasional unfortunate human. Dionysus' followers were also known to tear apart and eat goats and satyrs, which may be why Mr. D makes Grover so nervous.

Dionysus traveled to Egypt and India and throughout the Aegean, bringing the vine with him and teaching wine-making. In most of these places he was welcomed and worshipped, which was clearly the safest approach to Dionysus.

Not everyone was thrilled to host such a riotous god. Dionysus returned to his birthplace, Thebes, because he'd heard that the king's mother, Agave, was denying that Dionysus was the son of Zeus. Essentially, they were dissing him, saying Dionysus wasn't a god. Even worse, Pentheus, the king,[3] vowed to have Dionysus beheaded if he entered Thebes. Dionysus and his followers entered the city anyway, and Pentheus ordered them shackled. But Dionysus is, among other things, a master of illusions, and Pentheus, who was already beginning to lose his mind, wound up shackling a bull. The Maenads escaped the king's guards and went dancing up a mountain where they tore a calf to pieces. Then Pentheus' mother and sisters joined the Maenads. When Pentheus tried to stop them, the Maenads, led by Agave, Pentheus' own mother, tore the king to pieces. She too was caught in the insanity of the wine god's illusions and believed it was a lion she was killing when she was really murdering her own son. As Percy discovers, the gods have a tendency to take it very personally when they're opposed.

Pentheus' attempts to protect his city from the wine god's influence were understandable but also futile. Anyone who knows anything about the Greek gods would think he should have known better. Yet others made similar mistakes. When Dionysus, disguised

---

[3] The story of Dionysus and Pentheus is told in a play by Euripides (c. 480–406 B.C.) called *The Bacchae*. My summary of it is based on a re-telling by Michael Grant in *Myths of the Greeks and Romans*.

as a young girl, invited the three daughters of King Minyas to join his festival, they refused, choosing instead to stay at home and spin wool. Again, Dionysus summoned illusions that destroyed the mind. He drove the daughters of Minyas mad by filling their spinning room with phantom beasts and turning their threads to vines. One sister, in desperation, offered her own son as a sacrifice, and all three sisters in a wine-induced frenzy wound up tearing apart and devouring the boy.

One of the best-known stories about Dionysus, and the source of those visions Percy gets when he first meets Mr. D, tells of how a bunch of sailors mistook Dionysus for a young prince. Thinking he'd be worth quite a ransom, they kidnapped him. But once they got him aboard and tried to tie him up, the ropes fell apart. Only the helmsman realized they'd captured a god, and he pleaded with his shipmates to release the young man. Ignoring him, the captain ordered the crew to set sail. Strangely, though the sails filled with wind, the ship wouldn't move. Instead, grapevines sprouted from the ship, winding across the rigging and sails; ivy covered the masts; the oars turned into serpents; and red wine streamed across the decks. At this point the captain realized something was wrong. He ordered the helmsman to return to shore. But it was too late. Dionysus turned himself into a lion, and the terrified sailors leapt overboard—where all but the helmsman were changed into dolphins.

You can't read the stories of Dionysus without noticing a few distinct patterns. One is the way that ivy and grapevines tend to spring up, trapping those who have angered him. This is a device that Riordan uses in *The Titan's Curse*, when Mr. D finally condescends to help Percy and his friends. But there are other mythic patterns, such as Dionysus' fondness for turning himself and/or humans into wild beasts, which I think speaks to the fact that humans *are* animals. For all our civilization, we're primates, and a certain primal savagery lingers beneath whatever morality and sophistication we acquire, a savagery that often surfaces in connection with intoxication. We do our best to suppress this wildness and keep it in check—that's why every civilization has laws—but it never entirely vanishes. It shows up in our crime rates and in our thirst for violent entertainment. Our species loves watching spectacles in which actors or animated characters routinely hurt and kill one another. The Ancient Greeks believed that such spectacles—for them, plays—purged these instincts. Watching the enactment of Dionysus' story was supposed to be a *catharsis*, something that would cleanse the audience of its own violent urges.

Another pattern in Dionysus' myths is the use of mind-breaking illusions. Though the wine god is capable of creating earthquakes, thunder, and lightning—all of which he does in *The Bacchae*—his weapon of choice is to bend reality in the most horrific ways possible. A more minor pattern revolves around the god's need for respect. In the myths Dionysus, the last god to join the Olympians and the only halfling among them, repeatedly insists that others recognize his divinity. This is something else that Riordan has picked up. Mr. D is always demanding proper respect from Percy, something that Percy is loath to give.

Perhaps the most dramatic and disturbing pattern in the Dionysian myths is the one in which parents go mad and tear apart and eat their young. This particular kind of insanity seems to echo the awful events of Dionysus' own childhood: being torn apart by the Titans and then all the madness that Hera caused. In a way, this is not so far from contemporary psychology that tells us that abused children can result in damaged adults. But it's also a very clear-eyed vision of the power of drink at its worst, when intoxication becomes simply toxic. I know quite a few people who grew up with alcoholic parents, and though the kids weren't literally torn apart, many of them went through a kind of emotional shredder, caught in the uncontrolled madness that alcoholism brings. When the influence of Dionysus is at its worst, people lose their sanity. Even the powerful natural instincts to love and protect one's own children dissolve in the drink.

By the time he gets to Camp Half-Blood, Percy has already had a close-up view of just how ugly and insane alcoholism can be. Smelly Gabe is a lousy human being and an abusive husband. Understandably, Percy, like those unfortunate mortals in the myths, wants nothing to do with Mr. D, and like those mortals, he underestimates him.

Fortunately, when Percy meets Dionysus, the wine god is on a kind of divine probation, not allowed to indulge in his beloved wine and doing his best not to anger Zeus again. Mr. D is a Dionysus with restraints, a highly unusual condition for the god who was also known as Lysios, the loosener. Sardonic and unhelpful as he may be, this is a kinder, gentler Dionysus than the one we see in the myths. The fact that he is trying to stay on Zeus' good side may be the only reason that Percy manages to get away with as much as he does.

Or perhaps there's an unacknowledged kinship between them. Dionysus and Percy's adventures have something in common. The stories of Dionysus might even have been an inspiration for part of what Percy undergoes. Like Percy, Dionysus made the long, difficult journey to the Underworld to rescue his mother. And like Percy, he bargained with Hades. Dionysus agreed to send Hades that which he himself loved best in Semele's place. What Dionysus most loved were ivy, grapevines, and myrtle, and he wound up giving Hades myrtle in exchange for his mother's life. He then brought his mother out of the Underworld and up to Mount Olympus. There he changed her name to Thyone, which allowed her to somehow remain among the immortals without Hera attacking her again.

The reason this myth is important is because it's tied into another one of Dionysus' many aspects. He's a god of death and rebirth. That story about him being torn apart, boiled, and reborn? Many scholars believe it's a metaphor for the process of wine-making in which the grapes are torn from the vine, smashed, and then processed into wine. Others say it's a metaphor for the grapevine itself, which is cut back to a bare trunk after the autumn harvest and yet returns to life every spring, covering itself with green leaves and sweet grapes. In either case, it's a basic pattern found in many mythologies, a belief in the immortality of the soul: Something is destroyed and from that destruction something new is born. The phoenix, for example, is a mythological creature that embodies that cycle.

When Dionysus Appears

Through Dionysus the Ancient Greeks acknowledged that humans are not wholly rational creatures. They understood that even wild, frenzied madness may be part of our nature, and they made a sacred, ritual space for those frightening impulses, channeling them into the worship of a god. But the Maenads' rites, with their crazed dancing and bloody sacrifices, were not the only way to worship Dionysus. Every spring when the grapevines began to return to life, there was a great celebration, a five-day festival dedicated to Dionysus. Despite all the madness that followed him, Dionysus was greatly loved. For centuries he was the most popular god, and this may be because he was also the god of joy, which in itself is a pretty neat thing: To the Greeks joy was sacred, a gift that could only come from the divine. His annual festival—it was believed that the god showed up and took part every year—was essentially a great party where every-one was welcome. Dionysus was the most democratic of the gods. Anyone, even the poor, could take part in his rites. (This was very different from the rites of the goddess Demeter, for example, which were only open to a select group.)

You may think partying is frivolous, but it's because Dionysus is the party god that he's able to give Percy vital information in *The Last Olympian*. Although Dionysus himself is buried under rubble in an abandoned coal mine, part of his consciousness appears in a dingy bar where there's a birthday party going on, and he's able to summon Percy. As Mr. D explains, "Wherever there is a party, my presence is invoked. Because of this, I can exist in many different places at once."

In Ancient Greece the Dionysian festivals always involved drinking wine; they were not occasions for madness or dismemberment. Instead, the festivals celebrated Dionysus as the god of theater, a source of artistic inspiration. Plays were presented, and it was believed that the playwrights, actors, and even the audience served the god by partaking in the sacred event of the play. Beyond that, it was believed that without Dionysus all of the sacred songs—all of the ways you praise and speak to the gods—would be forgotten.

The Dionysian spirit at its worst was cruel, uncontrollably violent, and flat-out insane. At its best it inspired art, joy, celebration, and a reverence for nature and the beauty of the wild. Dionysus was the life force: rowdy, chaotic, and irrepressible. Actually, one of Riordan's descriptions of the monsters is a perfect fit for Dionysus too:

> Monsters don't die. . . . They can be killed. But they don't die. . . .You can dispel them for a while. . . . But they are primal forces.

Dionysus is a primal force and though he was killed, he never really died. He can be kept down for periods, but he always resurfaces. When I was in college, one of my professors described America in the 1960s as a place and time when the Dionysian force returned—the long hair; the wildness of the music, the bands, and their fans; the explosion of color (pop art, tie-dye, and hippie garb); the political chaos; and, of course, the widespread use of psychedelic drugs.

When the 1960s began, the accepted image of the way things *should be* was neat, orderly, and squeaky clean.[4] Rock, rap, hip hop, metal, reggaeton—all of the loud, exciting stuff—none of it existed then. Most of what was on the radio was tame and boring by today's standards. And then things started to shift. Radically. My guess is

---

[4] If you want to see what I mean, take a look at any of the old TV shows from that era.

that Dionysus showed up and flowed straight through the musicians—the blues singers, Elvis Presley,[5] the Beatles, the Rolling Stones, and countless bands that followed.

Many people were scared by what happened in the sixties, and, yes, drugs and alcohol claimed many victims. That part of Dionysus has never changed. But there was also a phenomenal opening to new ways of thinking, new forms of art, and new ways of seeing. Which is where we come back to Mr. D and Camp Half-Blood.

Okay, So He Doesn't Wear a Lanyard

Traditionally, when Dionysus appears, the old rules—and all things that bind or restrict—are loosened. There's a new, intoxicating freedom in the air. Mr. D without his wine is hardly intoxicating, but I think his disinterest gives the campers a necessary freedom that allows them to develop into heroes. He isn't very protective and he isn't controlling. The kids are not kept dependent in any way. Mr. D allows them to take serious risks and make near-fatal mistakes. In fact, if what he says is to be believed, more often than not he's hoping they'll fail. But heroes can't be coddled. You can't expect kids to go on quests and survive monsters if they don't know how to rely on their own resources. Mr. D is running an odd kind of boot camp in which he's sort of the reverse of a drill sergeant, basically saying: "Do what you want and what you can. That's the training you need."

And yet when Percy, whom he seems to loathe, needs him most, Mr. D comes through. In *The Titan's Curse*, against all expectation, Mr. D not only saves the heroes from certain death but also calls Percy by his rightful name. I'm still not sure why he does it. Is it because Percy finally humbles himself and asks for help? Or is it

---

[5] Though the blues and Elvis' music predate the sixties, both channeled a kind of freedom—pure, unrestrained soul—that could be said to be aligned with Dionysian energy.

a response to the Manticore, who taunts Percy by saying that the half-gods don't have any "real" help? It seems possible Mr. D isn't about to let a monster diss him and that he enjoys proving both the Manticore and Percy wrong. Or perhaps Mr. D is just doing his job and he's a better guardian than Percy gives him credit for. After all, almost as soon as the Manticore and his henchmen are taken care of, Mr. D focuses on Thalia. He knows she nearly accepted the Manticore's offer and he chides her for it, making it clear that he too knows how tempting power can be.

In *The Last Olympian*, Mr. D is back in hilarious form, calling Percy by any name except his own and oblivious to Percy's problems. But again Mr. D comes through for the demigods. He not only warns them of what's really at stake if the Titans take Olympus and Kronos casts off his human form, but also admits that the gods need mortals to rescue Olympus and that they've always needed heroes. His true reason for summoning Percy may be his request that Percy try to keep his son Pollux alive, proving that even the snarky Mr. D cares about his halfling son. This, too, is vital information for Percy, because part of what he's trying to resolve in this book is the gods' seeming indifference to their mortal offspring.

There's also the fact that though he seems to have no respect for kids or mortals, Mr. D is curiously fair. When Grover first brings Percy to camp and Percy is nearly killed by the Minotaur, Mr. D, who heads the Council of Cloven Elders, refrains from passing judgment on Grover. He gives him another chance. Twice Percy confronts Mr. D, even calling him a jerk and furiously demanding to know why he doesn't help. Mr. D could kill Percy instantaneously, and yet he spares him. Though Mr. D may enjoy playing with Percy's head—he's sarcastic and insulting—he refrains from actually doing harm. This may be due to his punishment or to some condition we haven't learned about by the end of *The Last Olympian*.

There's an interesting scene at the end of *The Titan's Curse*, where Percy and his friends are on Mount Olympus facing the judgment of the gods. Percy pleads for his life and the lives of Anna-beth, Thalia, Grover, and the Ophiotaurus. In the argument that fol-lows—whether the heroes should be destroyed or honored—Mr. D aligns himself with Ares and Athena as one of three gods who abstain from the vote. He points out quite reasonably that Percy may be the godling in the Oracle's prophecy, the one who will destroy them all. Ares' decision to abstain seems to stem from the fact that Percy's made an enemy of him, but Mr. D, surprisingly, seems far more aligned with Athena. He isn't being vengeful or mad. Instead, he seems calm, clear-sighted, and of all things, reasonably cautious.

For most of *The Battle of the Labyrinth,* Dionysus is offstage. When Percy initially returns to Camp Half-Blood he's delighted to find that Mr. D is away recruiting other gods for the coming battle with the Titans. True to form, Mr. D doesn't show up until neces-sary, at the very end when Grover is trying to persuade the Council of Cloven Elders that he found Pan and that the great god is truly gone. Except for Chiron, the council isn't having any of it—until Mr. D appears, this time wearing a suit and truly sober. He's griev-ing for his son Castor and he brings bad news: the minor gods are siding with the Titans against the Olympians. Still, despite being in a particularly bad mood, he tells Silenus that Grover is right and when the council vote is tied, he dissolves the council, settling the matter once and for all. This isn't truly surprising; for all the madness, illu-sion, and intoxication, Dionysus has always been clear-sighted and strangely honest. It makes sense that he, a god of the wild, would sense the truth about Pan and know that Grover fulfilled his search.

What is surprising is that Mr. D then invites Percy to take a walk with him and admits that Percy and Annabeth saved the camp. When they reach the amphitheater, Percy finds that Mr. D has healed Chris Rodriguez, the half-blood who went insane in the Labyrinth. Being a god who causes madness, Dionysus is also able to heal it. Percy can't quite believe that the wine god is actually being nice. A sardonic Mr. D assures him that he oozes niceness. As if to prove it, he delivers a very uncharacteristic message: "a kind act can sometimes be powerful as a sword." And for the first time he tells Percy a bit of his own history as a mortal, how he was mocked for being a mere winemaker and yet became an Olympian. So what gives? Is Mr. D actually encouraging Percy, the camper who so deeply annoys him? I think we can only take Dionysus at his word, and believe that he's offering Percy, and the rest of us, a genuine bit of hope—that acts of kindness matter, and that we may all have the potential to be greater than others think.

One of the things I find so intriguing about Greek mythology is that the Greeks saw the positive and the negative in everything. They embraced opposites. I doubt it would have occurred to them to have a divine figure who was purely good and compassionate, like the Buddha or Jesus Christ. The Greek gods always seemed to have dual natures. They were all capable of tremendous good and tremendous harm. They were dangerous gods, whose natures may have been much closer to our own human nature than we'd like to admit. Dionysus is neither good nor bad but spans the entire spectrum of behavior. As one of the Greek gods, he represents an ancient way of looking at things: that all of Creation, cruel and kind, orderly and chaotic, destructive and creative, is part of the divine.

Why Is Wine Such a Big Deal?

Wine, in and of itself, is also neither good nor bad. Riordan makes it clear that alcoholism, or an excess of drinking, is not a good thing or in any way attractive. But there's another side to the fruit of the vine. What Riordan doesn't really address—probably because these books are written for readers under the legal drinking age—are some of the ancient ritual uses of wine. It was in these rituals that Dionysus was known as the god of divine ecstasy, a usually blissful state in which normal limitations disappear and one is united with or open to the divine. And without understanding that aspect of the god, you can't really understand Dionysus.

One thing to keep in mind when we talk about the Greek myths is that these were not just a bunch of stories made up to explain natural phenomena like sunrise and thunder to people who didn't have our current understanding of science. The myths tell the stories of gods whom the people worshipped. The Ancient Greeks built temples to these gods and prayed to them and followed specific rites or rituals, asking the gods to aid and protect them. One of the things I love about the Greek pantheon is that they had specialists. You prayed to Artemis if you wanted a good hunt, to Ares before you went into battle, and to Dionysus if you wanted a healthy orchard or a good crop of grapes. Wine was part of many of these rituals, which shouldn't surprise anyone. It's been a sacrament (part of sacred ritual) for millennia and is still part of many ceremonies both in Judaism and Christianity.

Why wine? It relaxes. It loosens the grip of the ordinary world, the clutter of everyday life: thoughts about what you have to do, where you have to go, what someone said. Wine dissolves inhibitions, freeing people from worry and fear. It makes people feel good and even empowered. It's used as part of religious rituals for the very deliberate purpose of preparing the worshipper to forget about the ordinary world for a while and to open to the divine powers. Wine is a kind of intermediary, or medium, that allows you to communicate with the deities. When worshippers went to a Dionysian festival they weren't just letting loose; they were opening themselves to the truths of the gods. This state of intoxication was called divine ecstasy. It was in this state that the messages from the gods—even prophecies—came through. It was also a state of divine inspiration, from which songs or stories or ideas would arise. Inspiration is another word for breath, and creative inspiration was said to be the gods breathing through you.

Wine was considered to be part of Dionysus, literally. It was believed that if you drank his wine, you took a bit of the god inside you. He was, as Edith Hamilton points out, the only god who existed both outside and *inside* his worshippers. The Maenads, the most extreme of his devotees, believed that when they drank his wine, they were possessed by him. Dionysus bridged what Michael Grant describes in his book, *Myths of the Greek and Romans*, as "the sharp gulf between human and divine."

There's a lovely symmetry in the myths of Dionysus. His mother, Semele, died because she wanted to see a god in his full glory. Her son allows humans to see the gods through him, and even to take the divine inside them. It's as if he's still working on his mother's problem, saying, "Okay, maybe you can't look at the gods full on, but there *is* a way you can experience them, and I'll let you do it."

So the underlying assumption in the use of wine as part of religious ritual is that it's hard to access the gods in our usual distracted state of mind. Or put another way, one of the trickiest things about having religious faith is that most of the time we can't see the divine. Like Homer, Riordan uses the device of the Mist to explain why mortals are usually so blind to the presence of the gods. Historically, just about every religion has dealt with this problem: What is it that you have to do to actually experience the divine? There are nearly as many answers as there are religions. Some faiths say that prayer alone is the way. Others transcend—go beyond—the everyday state of mind through entering a kind of trance. This can be done through meditation, chanting, drumming, dancing, singing, fasting, yogic practices, and the use of psychoactive drugs. Alcohol, of course, is one of these drugs.

But there's another idea about how we can access the divine that has to do with place. As the writer Alain Daniélou explains in his book *Gods of Love and Ecstasy: The Traditions of Shiva and Dionysus*:

> There are places where the visible and invisible worlds are very close to each other. . . . They are a sort of door, through which it is a little easier to pass from one world to another.

I think Camp Half-Blood is one of these sacred places, which is why Dionysus, the god whose rites allow people to communicate with the deities, is the perfect god to run it. He's the gatekeeper, the one who lets mortals in to meet the gods, whose presence ensures that the boundaries between the divine and the mundane remain in place, and who admits the half-bloods to experience their own semi-divine inheritance. When Percy leaves Camp Half-Blood without permission in *The Titan's Curse*, it's Mr. D who comes after him. In his own self-centered way, Mr. D is completely aware of who enters and leaves the camp. With his strange indifference, Mr. D allows the kids the freedom to shrug off their old confining identities—for example, Percy as a problem student with ADHD—and find their new true identities as half-gods and heroes. It's in Camp Half-Blood that the Mist vanishes and one can see the supernatural. Creatures such as the centaurs and satyrs reveal themselves in their true forms. Here, even monsters, like the Minotaur, appear. It's the place where the kids meet the divine (Mr. D himself, for starters) and realize that they each have the gods inside them. And it's Dionysus, the god of all growing things, who allows the half-gods to fully grow into themselves. In Camp Half-Blood, the campers don't have to drink or enter a trance in order to partake of the wine god's blessings. They merely have to be in his baffling and amazing presence. Rick Riordan's portrayal of Mr. D pulls off a bit of magic that I think even the gods would envy. He's given us Dionysus without his wine and yet with all of his power and mystery. God of the vine, fertility, wildness, drama, and joy. Master of madness, magic, and illusion. The gatekeeper who gives mortals entry to the divine.

Great Books on Greek Myth

Daniélou, Alain. *Gods of Love and Ecstasy: The Traditions of Shiva and Dionysus*. First published in French as *Shiva et Dionysus* 1979. Reprint of 1982 translation, Vermont: Inner Traditions, 1992.

Grant, Michael. *Myths of the Greeks and Romans*. 1962, Reprint, New York: A Meridian/Penguin Book 1995.

Hamilton, Edith. *Mythology: Timeless Tales of Gods and Heroes*. 1940. Reprint, New York: A Meridian/Penguin Book 1989.

● ● ● ●

Ellen Steiber lives in Tucson, Arizona, where she writes and edits books. She has always loved mythology and thinks that there's a good chance that the Greek gods are still around. While she was writing this essay, Iris appeared in a gorgeous double rainbow right outside her office.

Other essays she's written appear in *The World of the Golden Compass*, edited by Scott Westerfeld; *A New Dawn*, edited by Ellen Hopkins; and *Nyx in the House of Night*, edited by P.C. Cast. She is currently finishing the sequel to her novel *A Rumor of Gems* and blogging about jewelry and gemstones at www.houseofgems.com. Please check out her Web site: www.ellensteiber.com.

The Gods Among Us

Elizabeth M. Rees

Are heroes a thing of the past? Elizabeth M. Rees doesn't think so. Sometimes all it takes is a monster rearing its ugly head for the gods and heroes of the modern world to reveal themselves. Maybe the person sitting next to you on the bus is actually a demigod. Or maybe the demigod is you. . . .

> When the gods come among men, they are not known.
>
> —RALPH WALDO EMERSON

What You Can't See Might Harm You

Living in New York City, just under two miles from what became Ground Zero, I witnessed the events of 9/11 all too close to home. It was a scene to gladden the war-mongering heart of Ares, the Greek god of war. The smoky, fiery image of the Twin Towers was surely one lifted straight from Hades' wildest dreams.

Although I am old enough to know Superman is make-believe and that James Bond is just a character in books and film, I actually found myself wondering, "Where are they?" Why didn't Superman soar onto the scene and snatch a plane in each fist a second before they struck? Why had James Bond's trademark derring-do failed when his valiant deeds were most crucial?

What a foolish part of me expected was larger-than-life action taken by one of our own pop culture demigods (Clark Kent) or heroes (Bond). What I and the rest of the world got instead was a reality check: heroes and demigods sure don't exist in real-life New York.

But subsequent events proved me wrong. Mr. Emerson says if divinities are here, we don't know it, but he might better rephrase it: We just don't *recognize* the gods and demigods and heroes that surround us in our daily lives.

Every emergency worker who raced into those buildings that terrible day or worked to help victims or labored over recovery of any possible survivors was a hero ten times over. It was as if they reached inside the deep pocket in the overalls of their souls and pulled out the equivalent of Percy Jackson's penknife in Rick Riordan's series, Percy Jackson and the Olympians: a great weapon with which to combat evil. Our twenty-first-century heroes' weapons were courage and strength beyond any ordinary mortal's wildest expectation, courage and strength on the scale of those exemplified by those old Greek gods.

According to Riordan in his quintet of books, the gods are indeed among us, and they can be *known*: that is, if you happen to be half-blood like Percy Jackson and many of his friends.

But like Percy at the start of the series, you've probably never given much thought to Greek gods—or their complicated lives and carryings on—outside of the classroom. And again like Percy (and later in *The Titan's Curse*, both Bianca and Nico di Angelo), you'd certainly never imagine that immortals might be living right down the block in your own neighborhood.

Who even bothers to give a second glance to the extensively wired guy riding the city bus? While he messages someone on his Blackberry, Mr. Motor Mouth is babbling nonstop on his cell and tapping his foot to an upbeat tune playing on the iPod plugged into his free ear.

Or how about that leather-jacketed biker roaring by on his Harley? What gives him the right to curse *you* as he nearly wipes out at the crosswalk? You glare after him, but I bet you don't wonder—or even care—who he is.

Then there's that panhandler who has staked her claim on your corner—she's homeless, and you want to feel sorry for her, but she doesn't smell so great, and there's something scary about her sunken eyes and that weird knit jester's hat she wears even in mid-summer. If you're like me, you scurry past, pretending not to see her, not wanting to think where she came from or who she might be or even if she has a name.

Or did you even wonder why that amazingly beautiful girl stopped to preen and fix her makeup at every cosmetics counter in Macy's en route to the exit? Maybe, maybe not.

But since I entered the world of Percy Jackson and the Olympians, I find myself thinking that, just like Percy, I might have encountered Hermes, or Ares, Medusa, or even Aphrodite on a shopping spree, and not even known it!

Although come to think of it, just once, maybe I did.

Late afternoon winter sunlight slanted from west to east across from Grand Central Station as I waited to cross the street. It was the height of rush hour and hoards of commuters hurried down the sidewalk to get into the station. In the crowd I spotted a matted-haired man. He was walking the head-down, shuffling walk of the homeless and looked half-crazed. But New Yorkers, as is their wont, took no notice of him.

Suddenly he looked up and a radiant smile crossed his dirty face. Walking in front of him was a young woman. He could only see her from the back but her long blonde hair shimmered like spun gold in the sun. He reached out with one hand and touched it. From across the street I gasped, fearing she was in some kind of danger. But the smile on his face was so joyful, and his touch must have been gentle because she never noticed—nor did any of the milling crowd, intent on getting somewhere fast. It was a moment's vision, but it has never left me.

Since reading Percy Jackson and the Olympians, I've wondered: Was the woman a demigod? Was she a child of Aphrodite, lighting the world with her beauty? Was the homeless man a half-blood like Tyson, unclaimed, unloved, and lost in a world that could never provide him with shelter or understanding? And, if indeed I was treated to a glimpse into Percy Jackson's universe, how come no one else noticed? If these demigods inhabit my hometown, how come I don't see them more often?

Pulling the Mist Over Our Eyes

In Riordan's world, the gods themselves and their half-blood children, as well as the occasional ordinary mortal, can see through what Riordan dubs "Mist," a brilliant invention that makes the whole premise of gods among us possible. Mist is the phenomenon that veils gods, as they go about their own twenty-first-century lives, from the view of ordinary mortals. Because I'm not a half-blood, or at least I don't think I am, I'm not supposed to recognize a god even if he or she were standing next to me. The Mist obscures the identity of the gods so people (or ast least *most* people) can't see them for what they are.[1] Occasionally, however, the Mist suffers a major-league breakdown.

---

[1] One important exception to this rule is Rachel Elizabeth Dare, who encounters Percy at the Hoover Dam in *The Titan's Curse* and sees right through the

Like during Percy's gym class at Meriwether College Prep in downtown Manhattan, when all Hades breaks loose and a gang of man-eating giants called Laistrygonians attack Percy during a dodgeball game. Suddenly all the kids in the gym find themselves in an explosive, deadly *mêlée* while their coach fiddles with his hearing aid and never looks up from his magazine. Mist renders the coach oblivious, but Mist everywhere else in the gym dissolves, and reality abruptly breaks down. Prompted by Percy, the kids dash for cover. But the bloodthirsty monsters have magically sealed all the exits, barring all hope of escape. Eventually Percy, his half-brother Tyson, and Annabeth manage to flee onto the streets of lower Manhattan. Fire engines roar to the scene of the explosion. And ordinary mortals had witnessed the whole thing, because, for a moment, the Mist had lifted.

But though Mist may lift in a moment like that, it can and must descend again. Exactly how Mist works or why it breaks down at times is a bit unclear in the series—at least to this reader. Nevertheless, we do learn that, when it comes to gods moving among ordinary mortals, Mist seems to generate itself and always has, as Chiron explains to Percy:

> Read *The Iliad*. It's full of references to the stuff. Whenever divine or monstrous elements mix with the mortal world, they generate Mist, which obscures the vision of humans. You will see things just as they are, being a half-blood, but humans will interpret things quite differently.

Mist, much to Percy's shock. Her ability is not just a one-time aberration due to failure of the Mist itself, either. In *The Battle of the Labyrinth*, she sees through the Mist at Percy's new school as a pair of empousai (vampire-like servants of Hecate) attack him. Her vision is even clearer than our half-blood hero's: whereas Percy is mesmerized by one empousa's blonde cheerleader charms, it's Rachel who sees the empousa for the monster she really is and has to pinch Percy's arm to snap him out of his illusion. Rachel's remarkable ability to see through Mist even helps her locate an entrance to the Labyrinth as well as to negotiate its perilous twist and turns. And her unique abilities, though she is mortal, allow her to eventually take on the soul of the Delphic Oracle in *The Last Olympian* and utter the next Great Prophecy.

And though Mist does break down from time to time, apparently the gods (and demigods) have ways of playing Mr. or Ms. Fix-it. In *The Titan's Curse*, the Mist seems not to be working properly when Percy and his friends enter Westover Hall. But with a snap of her fingers, Thalia manages to restore the Mist enough to allow Mrs. Gottschalk to believe that Percy, Thalia, and Annabeth are students at the school. Thalia's ability surprises Percy, who learns that restoring Mist is a skill Chiron could have taught him. Thus we learn that Mist can indeed be manipulated.

For instance, no one present during the giants' attack at Percy's gym remembers what really happened once the crisis is over. Mist's intervention restored order and translated the chaotic events into ones ordinary mortals could comprehend: namely, that Percy was some crazed bomb-wielding maniac who tried to blow up his school. Bad for Percy, but good for the psyche of the mortal witnesses.

Mist lifts or fails or only half-works several times during the series (one particularly dramatic instance is at the St. Louis Gateway Arch in *The Lightning Thief*), but for the most part the Mist holds fast, gods and their shenanigans remain invisible, and the system works.

Why Some Days Just Feel Like They're Going to Be *Very* Bad Days

Even with the Mist in good working order, the presence of any one of at least the big-league gods (Zeus, Poseidon, Ares, or Aphrodite, for example) does seem to affect the general atmosphere and moods experienced by mortals.

And they affect Percy. When Ares first encounters Percy in the Denver diner in *The Lightning Thief*, Percy tells us "bad feelings started boiling in my stomach. Anger, resentment, bitterness. . . . I wanted to pick a fight with somebody. Who did this guy think he was?" Interestingly, the presence of the god awakens subconscious emotions, fears, or tendencies. Violence is, after all, said to beget violence—or at least feelings of revenge.

In our world, it's hard to know where some moods—particularly the bluesy, down, or bad ones—actually come from. We all know what it's like: Some days you wake up feeling particularly glum or angry or annoyed for no apparent reason. Your mom says, "Hey, did you get out on the wrong side of the bed or something?" (I, myself, have never figured out exactly which is the "right" side of the bed!) Everything from that first buzz of the alarm clock to the last few minutes before you go to bed that night just seems to go from bad to worse. You get to school with mismatched socks (or shoes—believe me, that happened to a friend of mine once!); you leave your fave lunch box on the bus; you forget to bring your homework or you discover the cat really did eat that book report; to top it off, the class bully starts a text message smear campaign making fun of your mismatched socks!

Whatever it is that's gone wrong, I suspect that what side of the bed you got out on has little to do with it. In Riordan's world at least some of it could be chalked up to the presence of Hermes—a prankster if there ever was one. And Ares might be prodding that bully to nastier exploits than usual. If he needles him hard enough, those text messages might turn into a physical pummeling during an afterschool scrimmage session right under the eyes of a conveniently distracted coach. But there is an upside or two. Maybe Apollo decides to help you wreak revenge on the bully. Or the sun god, who is also the god of poetry, wafts into English class on a beam of sunlight and inspires Mr. Bully to jump up and recite a really, really bad haiku—in praise of *you*!

If you don't know what's going on, it can be confusing. Percy experiences this himself when he enters the Tunnel of Love, touches Aphrodite's scarf, and momentarily turns to mush.

The Greek gods have always reveled in the joys, sorrows, and tragedies of mortals. The atmosphere we breathe is charged with their qualities, good and bad, the love as well as the hate. Just read *The Iliad* and *The Odyssey*. Sometimes, however, the gods don't just change the atmosphere by their presence. Often they instigate all sorts of trouble and human upheavals. Homer sure knew what he was talking about: His gods regularly fall in love with humans, battle over humans, and, over eons, promote terrible rivalries and wars between bands of humans. It's not out of the question that they would continue to do so.

The stories recounted in *The Iliad* and *The Odyssey* illustrate some particularly annoying habits of these deities, habits that make them less than good neighbors. After all, their favorite pastime seems to be interfering in human affairs. Twenty-first-century America provides ample fodder for playing out—through human or half-human pawns—their eternal family spats and feuds. And perhaps the supersized negative feelings the activities Riordan's transplanted gods generate also spawn much of the violence in our world today.

Could it be that Ares was frolicking amid the carnage in Percy's hometown on 9/11? Which brings up the question, why might Ares be in New York, as Riordan suggests, to begin with?

New York, New York: Great Place to Visit, But Why Live Here?

The simple answer is that all the gods in Percy Jackson and the Olympians have, like hoards of others, immigrated to America, and their headquarters is New York City. Why New York? I doubt it's because they are either Mets or Yankees fans.

Riordan's explanation is in keeping with his mastery of Greek mythology and the culture of Ancient Greece. As Chiron tells Percy when he arrives at Camp Half-Blood, New York is simply their home base. Today's Mount Olympus is on the 600th floor (right, that's not a typo) of the Empire State Building. The divine abode hasn't been in Greece for millennia. Chiron explains that Western Civilization is "a collective consciousness that has burned bright for thousands of years. The gods are part of it." The whole Western worldview *first* flowered in Ancient Greece, then moved to Rome and eventually beyond as time passed and the center of power moved. Since gods are immortal, they don't die out with the passing of civilizations or kingdoms. Instead as power shifts in the Western world, they are forced to relocate to the empire or country that's currently dominating the scene—which in the twenty-first century is the good old USA. And the only place to set up their home base is the nexus of that power—in this case, the Big Apple.[2]

New York City happens to be the best location for those gods to settle for many reasons. First of all, it's one of the most high-energy places on the planet—some would say too high-energy, since the city is purported never to catch a night's sleep. Nothing in New York City seems to move slowly enough to be brought into focus—walking the streets and avenues of this town, there's a distinctive feeling that everything's caught in fast-forward. The gods seem to thrive on this frenetic energy, even if most of the mortals don't, and the half-bloods among us no doubt walk around distracted and endlessly confused. All this excess energy is readily available to fuel family feuds, and certainly must help power up the strife the gods continue to sow among humans.

Now another reason New York, New York, would feel like home-sweet-home to these Ancient Greek deities: New York isn't just frantic, it's over-the-top wealthy—the perfect place to indulge in all the heady high-end perks of the high life.

Personally I suspect that while the gods are the very bedrock of Western Civilization and need to settle in its power-base, they also can't stomach anything less than living the good life in ultimate

---

[2] As I read the books and grew increasingly fond of loyal Grover, I thought how delighted he must be that the logo of New York was one of his favorite snacks. Okay, New York City is not the Big Enchilada—but Grover does favor apples as well. At least it's not the Big Tin Can.

luxury. I can't picture Aphrodite in a third-world country, can you? Now Saks Fifth Avenue is another thing.

The idea of the gods living among us mere mortals is scarcely new, at least as far as the Ancient Greek deities are concerned. Look up Mount Olympus in the dictionary—it is indeed "home of the gods," but it also has a real geographic location: Northern Thessaly.

Michael Grant points out in *Myths of the Greeks and Romans* that though the gods don't live *with* ordinary people, they do live "on, or not too far from the earth." And in *Mythology: Timeless Tales of Gods and Heroes*, Edith Hamilton says, "The exact spot where Aphrodite was born of the foam could be visited by any ancient tourist; it was just offshore from the island of Cythera." She also says that Pegasus lived in a real stable in Corinth.

Similarly, Percy and his friends finally locate Nereus in San Francisco in *The Titan's Curse*. The ancient sea god is disguised (of course) as a homeless man, fishing on a wharf. So if you want to find the old man of the sea himself, book a vacation in the Bay Area and check him out while you're there.

Much like the immortals of the Greek era, Riordan's deities have a home base on Mount Olympus but can basically hang out anywhere they want. So Percy's first encounter with Ares occurs outside a Denver, Colorado, diner. Ares, as far as we know in the series, doesn't live in Denver. His presence in the Mile High City has one purpose: to talk to (and trick) Percy.

Do We Really Want to Bring Them a Housewarming Present?

While wondering why these divinities have deigned to grace us with their presence, we might also ask ourselves if we should really welcome their presence here.

The gods do provide convenient scapegoats. It would be nice to be able to blame all contemporary conflicts and injustices on the whims of disinterested gods. Maybe the violence that bloats our cable news channels is not triggered by acts of ordinary mortals: Maybe monster hags and raging war gods are causing the whole mess to begin with. After his bus to the West Coast blows up not far from the George Washington Bridge in *The Lightning Thief*, Percy voices just this sentiment in his narration: "It's nice to know there are Greek gods out there, because you have somebody to blame when things go wrong."

When the gods moved to New York, they came with plenty of baggage: their feuds, their wars, their Olympian-sized dysfunctional families, their inability to keep promises and vows (particularly of matrimony). Like true rock stars they've paraded onto the scene with their entire entourage: monsters in the form of Furies, Cyclopes, the Hydra, the Ophiotaurus; various spirits (naiads, dryads, and satyrs, among others); magical beings like the Gray Sisters and their taxi service; and let's not forget the Oracle. In fact, the whole assortment—or at least a generous sampling—of weirdoes that populated the mythical realms of Ancient Greece turn up in the course of the series.[3] And these weirdoes don't just "turn up" and make cameo appearances. Far from being window dressing or sidekicks, this motley crew provides much of the action on all of Percy's quests.[4]

---

[3] Some of the spirits and monsters in the series remain true to their origins, but not all. *Most* Cyclopes are to be feared, but Tyson is a loveable baby who is one of the really good guys, as is Grover, and the Ophiotaurus, though it might be used for ill, is an innocent being. He saves Percy and relates well to Tyson, but the gods fear him, because he could bring an end to their existence. Possibly. Because no one really knows what would happen. Last time the Ophiotaurus was murdered, Zeus thwarted the final deed predicted to demolish the immortals for good. He sent an eagle to grab the poor dead creature's entrails before they could be cast into a fire.

[4] In *The Sea of Monsters*, Riordan cleverly recreates some of the most memorable episodes in Odysseus' journey with just those monsters and other mythical creatures. Percy assumes the role of hero doing the rescuing, though in some cases he's rescued (by Clarisse of all people!) himself. The sirens, who in

In light of all the baggage these gods bring with them, I find myself wondering, is the presence of these gods such a good thing? The answer is, that's a really bad question. First of all, in the world of Percy Jackson and the Olympians, they are already here and are having too good a time to plan on leaving soon. Secondly, when it comes to sending these inconvenient neighbors back to where they came from, we can't. We, and possibly those very gods themselves, just don't have the choice.

It All Boils Down to This Thing Called Free Will

Freedom of choice is something we usually take for granted—until we look a little more closely at what it, and free will, really means. At first glance it means you can decide to take this road or that; you can do your homework or not; if you're Percy, you can decide to search for Zeus' lightning bolt or not.

But as it turns out, the whole idea of freedom of choice and free will is one of those things that philosophers have pondered probably since the first cavemen gathered around the campfire and began to chew over life's important questions—the kind of questions with no definite answer, like what came first, the chicken or the egg? No one really knows.

Do we have the ability to choose our direction in life or does fate or destiny choose our path for us? The answer is both. We almost always have a choice about what we do, but at the same time we are usually making that choice in a situation that we have no power to change.

The idea of being free to choose what happens to you sure seems simple enough. You choose to do your homework or to play a video

---

ancient times seduced Odysseus' crew with song, lure Annabeth with visions befitting a twenty-first-century half-blood: She sees her mortal dad and goddess mother picnicking with Luke in Central Park. Later Riordan reprises Jason's ancient quest with his Argonauts.

game. But if you're a student, do you really have a choice? In one sense you do. You can choose to skip your homework assignment. But if you do choose not to finish that book report due at 9 A.M. tomorrow, you still have to deal with the consequences, and those consequences—be they detention or a bad grade—limit your freedom of choice. You definitely have no choice about being a student going to school—your age and your circumstance are not under your control.

So the situation we are put in—like being in school or being born a half-blood—is something we generally have no ability to change. How we deal with that situation—that's another story.

Throughout the Percy Jackson series, time and again, Percy finds himself in dire straits (mostly) not of his own choosing. It's how he chooses to deal with it that makes his story a real page-turner.

Percy didn't choose to be a half-blood. But he does choose to go on all those quests that keep almost getting him killed, right? Take the quest to retrieve Zeus' lightning bolt: He could have said no. Or could he? Part of the reason he went was to see his mother again; could he really have chosen not to go, given who he is?

Another question: Sally's "death" at the hand of the Minotaur on the outskirts of Camp Half-Blood *seems* unavoidable while it's happening, but I wonder, was it really?

There are two ways of looking at Sally's (apparent) death. There were two possible outcomes to the standoff with the Minotaur: Either Sally would survive and Percy would die, or Sally would die so Percy would live. You could say she chose to sacrifice herself for Percy of her own free will. On the other hand, perhaps the gods put her in that very situation where she would be *forced* to make that choice, a situation where she *had* no choice but to act as any mother would, and sacrifice her own life to save her son's. When you look at it that way, the gods may have been using a mother's love to propel Percy into a situation where he was forced to go on a quest and do their bidding.

But why would the gods even bother to lure Percy into their world and make him their own go-to guy?

The gods have a problem. As Chiron tells us, they can't cross certain borders or trespass on one another's realms; heroes, however, can go wherever they want. So when the gods' squabbles lead them into other gods' territories, they need heroes to do their dirty work. Heroes are made weapons of the gods, vehicles through which the gods wreak their vengeance. Keeping that in mind, it makes sense that the gods would throw Percy and his mother into a no-win situation if they thought it would motivate Percy to help them out.

So the gods saved Sally at the last moment in order to motivate Percy, whose love and loyalty to those closest to him underscore almost every crucial decision he makes—whether it be brilliant or disastrous. Does Percy have a choice when it comes to what Athena tells him is his fatal flaw—personal loyalty? All of us have flaws, though maybe all aren't exactly fatal. Fear, pride, over-optimism, jealousy, greed, a too-trusting heart—these are all flaws I know I've glimpsed some in family and friends. (As for myself, I'll take the Fifth.) The problem is these flaws limit the range of choices we can make, and so the gods can use them to manipulate us.

No One's Perfect, Especially Not the Greek Gods

When it comes to flaws, the Greek gods themselves seem to be full of them. Unlike the Egyptians or Babylonians, "the ancient Greeks made the gods in their own image," Edith Hamilton tells us. And since these gods were supposed to resemble mortal everyday Greeks, gods are far from perfect. In fact they often behave like noisy, sometimes nasty, mortal neighbors.

If Mr. Greek Everyman and his wife had a particularly loud marital spat, they'd shout accusations and threats at each other. Maybe the guy was as capable of domestic abuse as Percy's creepy stepdad, Gabe. Gods made in the image of the guy-next-door mirrored the same set of seriously bad but woefully familiar very *human* behaviors. Except if Hera caught Zeus on a date with his latest fling and hurled threats at him, he could choose to hurl his thunderbolt back, or remind her of how he punished her once by dangling her upside down in the clouds. Same spat, but on a mega-scale.

Though the Greek gods were basically souped-up versions of Ancient Greek mortals themselves—warts and all—those warts generally were on their characters and souls, NOT on their faces. The Greeks saw their gods as *more*—not only more violent or vengeful, but also more beautiful or brave or fierce or powerful versions of themselves. The mortals always gave the gods physical, and sometimes psychological, qualities that they admired and to which they could also aspire. The gods were not there just to entertain and instruct through bad tabloid-worthy antics but to inspire their devotees to reflect the occasional divine goodness in their own mortal lives.

One of the "better" qualities of the Greek gods was their extraordinary physical beauty. This should not surprise us—after all, everyone loves looking at a pretty face. However, as much as (if not more than) our own modern Hollywood-inspired culture, the Ancient Greeks valued a beauty crafted from ideals of physical human perfection.

Whereas divinities of other ancient cultures are often depicted as fantastic semi-monstrous figures made up of creative assemblages of animal parts, the Greek gods were depicted as extremely beautiful (in the case of the goddesses) or well-toned and muscular (in the case of gods). I bet they would have laughed the goddess of wisdom out of town if she'd looked more like a goddess of another, perhaps earlier, culture. Imagine their reaction if, instead of the elegant, self-possessed Athena, wisdom manifested itself as a cross between a crocodile and a koala bear. (I know—there were no koala bears anywhere near Greece. Still, it's an interesting combo!)

If you tried to imagine a super-hyped version of you now, in the twenty-first century, you'd probably picture a supermodel or pop star or big-screen hunk. Today we expect our own small- or big-screen "gods" and "goddesses" to reflect our current standards of beauty. Perfect features, glowing tresses, complexions to die for, and physiques that are—well, let's just say they are generally the source of elite personal trainers' fame and fortune. We call these stars "screen idols" and even talk about *worshipping* them.

It's not too often, unfortunately, that our own subjects of worship are good behavior models, either (except maybe the stars, starlets, and rock musicians who lend their names, efforts, and finances to support and publicize worthy national and international causes). But there are moments at least when the gods of Riordan's series act in ways that should inspire us. Like the Ancient Greeks we joke and giggle and sneer at some of the immoral and outrageous actions they take in Percy Jackson and the Olympians, but we also find ourselves surprised at the gods' better qualities. Who would have believed after Dionysus' consistently negative attitude toward Percy that the god would come to our hero's aid and actually save him by destroying the Manticore in *The Titan's Curse*?

Also, in spite of his conflicted reactions to having Percy as a half-human son, Poseidon frequently helps our hero: He stirs up the ocean waters several times during Percy's adventures, saving Percy from certain death. When he begs his father for help, though Percy is never sure Poseidon will come through, he usually gives it.

Toward the end of *The Lightning Thief* we are given two glimpses of gods not just helping mortals but also being genuine good guys. Poseidon takes Percy aside on Mount Olympus and with a "fiery pride in his eyes" tells Percy outright that he's done well. A few pages earlier, all-powerful Zeus softens his attitude toward Percy, thanks him, and spares his life—with conditions, of course.

So even if those Ancient Greeks and their gods could be as mean-spirited, bullying, or prideful as anyone we know today, they could also be as kind, loving, joyful, forgiving, and compassionate.

When we read stories from *The Iliad* and *The Odyssey* and re-read the Greek myths, we find ourselves recognizing the good and bad qualities possessed by gods, demigods, and heroes alike. Their flaws are not mysterious but disturbingly familiar. We sometimes feel as if by looking at their exploits we are looking into a mirror, and when we do, a hazy distorted version of our own selves looks right back at us.

Because, as we learn from reading myths, the qualities, good and bad, possessed by the gods are part of our own nature. We may share their flaws, but we also partake of their amazing powers and goodness.

Indeed, the gods are always among us, whether we are in the world of Percy Jackson and the Olympians or not. And those gods are not just hovering over, eavesdropping on, or wiretapping the phones of the half-blood next door. Veiled to our sight they dwell in our world and within ourselves. Thanks to them we have within us strengths (and maybe some weaknesses) we don't even suspect.

Sure, the gods often toy with us by throwing us one or more of life's wicked curve balls. But in the quirky way of those old Greek gods, they don't necessarily leave us to flounder on our own. . . . Even if they are the source of some of our troubles, they never really abandon us: Those same nosy, interfering, annoying gods are also on standby, ready to inspire us, bolster our resolve, and lend us courage, much as 9/11 emergency workers were inspired to superhuman efforts to rescue the thousands of people who escaped those Twin Towers. The news and current history tend to focus on the tragic souls who didn't survive. But due to the deep inner strength and courage of those who rushed into buildings to help, many more lives were saved than were lost. Superheroes and demigods in the guise of ordinary very brave men and women walked the city that day, and I am sure they still do.

Great Books on Greek Myth

Hendricks, Rhoda A., ed. and trans. *Classical Gods and Heroes: Myths as Told by the Ancient Authors.* New York: Morrow Quill Paperbacks, 1974.

Grant, Michael. *Myths of the Greeks and Romans.* New York and Scarborough, Ontario: New American Library / Mentor, 1962.

Hamilton, Edith. *Mythology: Timeless Tales of Gods and Heroes.* New York: New American Library / Mentor, 1942.

● ● ● ●

Elizabeth M. Rees is a visual artist as well as an author of numerous middle grade and young adult novels, including Heartbeats, her original six-book series published by Aladdin from 1998 to 1999. Her latest work of fiction, *The Wedding: An Encounter with Jan van Eyck*, was published by Watson-Guptil in 2005 and was listed on the New York Public Library's Best Books for the Teen Age, 2006. She lives and works in New York City. She is currently working on a fantasy novel about a fat fairy, as well as a series of short stories about the afterlife. Her essay, "Smoke and Mirrors," appeared in *The Girl Who Was on Fire*.

Percy Jackson and the Lords of Death

J&P Voelkel

Percy's been dealing with the Olympian gods for a few years now, and everybody needs a break once in a while (even from their own family). Maybe it's time for a vacation. Lucky for Percy, there's a whole world full of gods and monsters he hasn't yet encountered. J&P Voelkel suggest a trip to Central America and share some surprising similarities between Greek and Maya mythology.

Once Percy Jackson has vanquished all the foes that Greek and Roman myths can throw at him, what's next? Sure, his old adversaries could re-materialize and attack at any moment, but like a video game you've already beaten, the second time around would be so much ancient history. Yawn.

And what's the point of spending all your summers at Camp Half-Blood if you have no new challenges to train for? There are only so many sword practices, mock battles, and games of Capture the

Flag you can play before your hyperactive demigod brain starts itching for some real-life action.

So it seems like only a matter of time before Percy would be hounding the Oracle for a new prophecy and begging Chiron for a new mission to sink his celestial bronze sword into.

Something huge. Something different.

Something extraordinary.

Something even a battle-hardened demigod has never faced before.

No problem.

It's a big world out there and every culture has its own myths and legends, all brimming with new allies to bond with and new bad guys to subdue. For example, Percy could head to Scandinavia, land of the Vikings and home of the Norse mythology that inspired Tolkien's tales of Middle Earth. Here, the sun is pulled across the sky by horses, and the gods live not on Mount Olympus but across a rainbow bridge in a walled kingdom called Asgard. Here, too, is Valhalla, the feasting hall for fallen heroes, with a celestial goat grazing on its roof. (A new BFF for Grover perhaps?)

In Asgard, the most obvious opponent for Percy would be Thor, the storm god (whose name gave us Thursday). They're evenly matched as Thor's weapon is a hammer called Mjölnir that behaves a lot like Percy's sword, Riptide. Wherever Thor tosses his hammer, it finds its way back to him like a magic boomerang. Yet when its owner is on the move, it shrinks small enough to be carried in his tunic. Also—Percy beware!—Thor's hammer always hits its target.

Let's just hope that Thor's all-knowing father, Odin (whose name gave us Wednesday and whose wife Frigg's name gave us Friday) does not enter the fray. With his spear that never misses, his eight-legged horse, and his severed giant's head that foretells the future, he's a daunting adversary. He also gave his right eye for a drink from the Well of Wisdom, so he's got brains as well as brawn (if slightly limited vision).

Of course, meeting Odin might remind Percy of his previous experiences with monocular beings. He might remember, with a shudder, his hair-raising ride in the taxi of the three Gray Sisters (who only had one eye between them). Or he might think fondly of Tyson the Cyclops, one of Percy's best friends and his half-brother.

As the general of Olympus' army, Tyson is a very useful person to have around. But he wouldn't be in Asgard to help Percy and neither would their father, Greek god of the sea, Poseidon. In their absence, perhaps Percy could count on a little family support from Njord, one of the Norse gods of the sea.

Njord's son Freyr has a magnificent, magical ship that folds into a pouch when he's not using it. Unfortunately, he's lost his magic sword, but he's still pretty lethal with a deer antler. Better still, Percy could call upon Njord's daughter, Freyja. When she's not riding her battle pig or being pulled in a chariot by two large cats, she wears a feathered coat that turns her into a falcon. She and Annabeth Chase would get on like a Viking longhouse on fire. And while the two were swapping battle stories, perhaps Percy could borrow Annabeth's baseball cap to outwit one of the most powerful weapons of the Norse gods, the Tarnhelm, or helmet of invisibility.

So things are shaping up for an excellent grudge match. And even if Percy loses, he can expect to be selected by the Valkyries, Odin's battle maidens, for a coveted place in Valhalla. It's not winning the battle that gains you entry into this hall for heroes but how bravely you fought the fight.

There's just one problem: no matter how impressive their weapons and gizmos, the Norse gods aren't that into sparring with mortals. They're generally friendly and helpful. They're not even immortal themselves unless they eat the golden apples of the goddess Idun. Plus, they're all going to die along with mankind in the final battle between good and evil. So you can't blame them for having other stuff on their minds.

True, Norse myths offer a supernatural smorgasbord of evil supporting characters to keep Percy on his toes, including trolls, elves, shapeshifters, witches, wolves, and beserkers (men who could turn themselves into bears). But that's just another day in the woods at Camp Half-Blood. Our jaded demigod deserves some worthier opponents: a pantheon of peril and a vanguard of villains, all set in a horribly hostile habitat, where even the environment is an enemy.

So call us biased—we write books about the Maya—but we think Percy would have the most fun in Central America. Here in the tropical rainforest, he'd discover an ancient people who stared into the night sky and saw crocodiles, macaws, snakes, and turtles in the twinkling stars. He'd explore the ruins of towering pyramids carved with mysterious glyphs. And he'd run into enough myths, monsters, and magical beings to keep him busy for a whole new series!

Warning: if you're not familiar with new world mythology, prepare to have your mind blown. Although less is known about the Maya gods than their Greek, Roman, or Norse counterparts, it's safe to say that they're the most hilarious, moody, fun-loving, bad-tempered, ghoulish crowd you've ever met.

For example, there's a god of sacrifice who cuts his own head off, a god with a leg like a spinning snake, a cross-eyed sun god, a god with a snout like an anteater, a goddess of the hanged, a howler monkey god, a maize god with a head like a corncob, a god of tattoos and body art, a black jaguar god with a screech owl on his head, a goddess with a headdress of snakes and a skirt of crossed bones . . . and let's not forget the most evil of them all, the twelve Lords of Death, whose job it is to spread misery, disease, and death in the world. There are dozens of Maya gods and each one played a vital role in the everyday life of Ancient Maya city-states. Moreover, many of them have multiple personalities, being both good and bad, young and old, male and female.

Where the Greek gods are embroiled in family feuds and affairs of the heart and the Norse gods are fighting among themselves, the

Maya gods seem to be more single-minded. For better or for worse, their focus is on interacting with humans. Indeed, they require the regular spilling of high-born human blood to keep the wheels of the universe turning. And you don't get much more high-born than a demigod like Percy . . .

But we get ahead of ourselves.

First, we need to set the scene.

As anyone who's ever read a middle grade adventure knows, there are three essential rules:

1. Ditch the parents.
2. Get rid of the cellphones.
3. Take your main character out of his or her comfort zone.

Now that Sally and Paul know that Percy can look after himself, it's unlikely that his mother and her new husband would insist on accompanying him. And cellphones can't spoil the plot where we're going as you rarely get a signal in such remote areas. So all that's left is to whisk Percy out of New York City and drop him in the teeming rainforests of Central America.

Surviving here would be his first challenge.

Rainforests are damp, hot, sunless places, home to half the world's plant and animal species. Life here is a constant battle for food, light, and water. Particularly food.

Hear that terrifying roar? It sounds like a hungry jaguar in search of a demigod lunch. But Percy can relax. It's just a howler monkey, the loudest land animal on the planet, proclaiming his territory. The only thing dangerous about howler monkeys is the way they pee on you if you stand beneath their tree.

More of a threat is the constant buzzing in your ears. The rainforest is swarming with vicious biting insects, from tiny no-see-ums to mosquitoes and assassin bugs. Some of the creepiest creepy-crawlies include scuttling cave spiders with pincers like crabs, huge jumping spiders, and big, hairy tarantulas. (We wouldn't blame arachnophobic Annabeth for skipping out on this adventure!) Percy should also watch out for leeches, ticks, and a delightful little insect called a botfly, whose larva hatches under your skin and grows into a maggot that feeds on your flesh. (Don't worry, it's harmless and will pop out a few weeks later.) There are also toxic frogs, venomous scorpions, and some of the deadliest snakes in the world.

You get the picture. It's a perilous place.

On the bright side, it rains a lot. So, with a daily downpour of healing water, Percy stands a better chance of surviving wounds and snakebites than the average New Yorker plunked down in the rainforest. Maybe he could even make himself some aquatic weapons.

On the down side, all that water coupled with heat creates mist. Not the Mist that makes mortals see things differently but the ordinary kind that makes things foggy, even for demigods. Percy would need to keep his wits about him—which is why Grover would be his ideal companion on this quest.

As a creature of the wild, Grover would be in his element. There's no wilder place on Earth. In fact, what's left of the spirit of Pan might well be living in what's left of the rainforest. While he's here, perhaps Grover could even place a satyr's sanctuary on all the endangered animals.

When he's not repelling bugs with his pan pipes, Grover would be busy sniffing out unseen dangers. Just as the woods at Camp Half-Blood are home to dryads, so the Maya jungles are alive with mythical creatures. But unlike the friendly nymphs at Camp Half-Blood, most of the Maya spirits are bent on causing harm.

Two of the most commonly seen are the alux, pronounced *al-oosh*, and X'tabay, pronounced *eesh-ta-bye*.

Aluxes are wild-energy sprites that like to play tricks on humans. Sometimes they're invisible; sometimes they take shape as little people. The aluxes are famous for having a sweet tooth, so Percy might want to bring along some blue candy to keep them sweet.

Less easy to win over would be X'tabay, a deadly spirit of the night. She's a fallen Maya goddess who takes the form of a beautiful woman. Like the Sirens' call in Greek mythology, men find her voice irresistible. Few have encountered X'tabay and lived to tell the tale. Most victims are found wrapped in thorny branches with a look of terror on their faces.

Also lurking in the shadows might be Che Uinik, a savage giant who preys on travelers. (Not too much of a threat actually because his feet are on backward and he has to lean against the trees because he has no bones—so if you make him fall over, he can't stand up.) Or is it Ek Chapat, the monstrous seven-headed, man-eating centipede? Or Mesa-hol, the demonic bird that flies upside down when the moon is full and shakes your whole house when he lands on your roof? Or Ekuneil, the fat gray snake that tries to slide the twin tips of its poisonous double tail up your nostrils? Or Kakasbal, a hairy monster with horns, big ears, and a body made out of the organs of different animals that hate one another? Or Ua Ua Pach, the giant who has three tongues like knives and wears three large necklaces of human kidneys? Or Xhumpedzkin, a lizard-like creature that kills you by biting your shadow?

The list goes on . . .

But no matter how gross their monsters, the gods of the Maya are more fearsome still. Here are some of the major ones that Percy might encounter.

Most famous is Kukulkan, the feathered serpent, an evil, monstrous snake that brings winds and earthquakes. A very ancient being, he may be even older than the drakons, those giant armor-plated serpents in *The Sea of Monsters*.

If Kukulkan arrives, Chahk is said to follow. Chahk is a god of storms, rain, and warfare. With bulging eyes, a large upturned nose, and a seashell through his ear, he is not an attractive fellow. But he *is* a formidable warrior. Chahk wields the god K'awiil as his fiery lightning axe, so he's like an even more terrifying combination of Thor and Zeus. What's more, Chahk sometimes appears as four separate but identical versions of himself, each dressed in a different color like a one-man squad of Power Rangers.

Scary, huh? But maybe Chahk and Percy would join forces. Water was the most valuable commodity in the Ancient Maya world, which made Chahk—as a bringer of rain—one of the most important gods. He would surely be intrigued by Percy's ability to control water and manipulate storms.

But how would Chahk's lightning axe, K'awiil, feel about an alliance with the son of Poseidon? K'awiil is the god of lightning in his own right and patron of lineage, kingship, and aristocracy. With his reptilian face, a smoking mirror embedded in his forehead, and a long snout that bursts into flames, he's another ugly customer. But Percy's pedigree would surely pacify him. It was K'awiil's job to verify the divine ancestry of kings, so he should be thrilled by Percy's direct blood ties to one of the Big Three.

By far the most unpleasant Maya god is the ruler of the underworld, Ah Pukuh. As the god of violent and unnatural death, he's the Maya equivalent of Hades but without the good looks or the charm. Percy could recognize him instantly by his death collar of disembodied eyeballs dangling on their optic nerves. Ah Pukuh is usually pictured as a bloated, decomposing corpse or a dancing skeleton smoking a cigar. As if those guises weren't stinky enough, Percy would certainly smell him coming as his nickname is Kisin, which means "flatulent one."

Ah Pukuh's henchmen are the twelve Lords of Death, led by One Death and Seven Death. The other ten are violent demons who work in pairs to inflict human suffering. Scab Stripper and Blood Gatherer sicken people's blood, Demon of Pus and Demon of Jaundice make people's bodies swell up and die, Bone Scepter and Skull Scepter kill people and reduce them to skeletons, Wing and Packstrap cause people to die coughing up blood on the road, and Demon of Filth and Demon of Woe hide in dirty houses and stab the owners to death (a powerful incentive to keep your room clean if ever there was one).

So Percy would have to make a decision: be content to skirmish with a few deities or take on the greatest Maya myth of all—the story of the Hero Twins who overcome the Lords of Death?

It would be no easy job.

Like the skeleton warriors in *The Titan's Curse*, the Death Lords are probably immune to Riptide's blade because they're already dead. So, assuming that Nico de Angelo's power does not extend as far as the Maya underworld, Percy would have to follow in the footsteps of the Hero Twins and outwit the Death Lords with stealth and cunning.

He'd have no trouble finding them. Just like the domestic arrangements of the Olympians and the Norse gods, you go up for the good guys and down for the bad guys. In fact, the Norse underworld and the Maya underworld are similar in that they are both cold and wet. The name of the Maya underworld is Xibalba, or "well of fear," and it is accessed through deep, dark, water-filled caves. Given Grover's terror of underground places (which smell to him of death and monsters), this may be where he and Percy would part company.

When he arrives at the entrance to Xibalba, Percy would be faced with three rivers to cross—not rivers of sacred water like the River Styx but a river of scorpions, a river of pus, and a river of blood. As his ability to increase surface tension probably doesn't work on these substances, he might want to conjure up a boat for himself. Or perhaps he could hitch a ride from the Paddler Gods, one with a jaguar headdress and the other with a stingray spine through his nose, in their hollowed-out canoe.

Percy would then go from the disgusting to the disorienting: a speaking crossroads that would attempt to send him in the wrong direction. Boy, those Death Lords love their practical jokes. Similarly, when Percy first meets them, they'd offer him a seat on a bench that is really a red-hot griddle. Percy's immunity to heat should carry him through this test, but it would infuriate the Death Lords when he didn't fall for their prank.

Like Camp Half-Blood, Xibalba provides accommodations for its visitors. But these are no ordinary bunkhouses. Each conceals a trial designed to humiliate or even kill the unwary guest. Like the stable-cleaning, hydra-fighting type of missions given to Hercules (and Percy), they are tasks that would be considered impossible for ordinary mortals but which—with a little luck—could be overcome by a determined demigod.

First, Percy would be shown into the Dark House. As its name suggests, it is pitch black inside, but the Death Lords are kind enough to provide a flaming torch. The only catch is that a visitor must keep the torch alight all night but return it unused in the morning. The Hero Twins used macaw feathers and fireflies to simulate flames; maybe Percy could work an illusion with Greek fire.

Next, he'd face a house colder than the Hubbard Glacier in *The Son of Neptune*, followed by one hotter than the fiery forges of Hephaestus in *The Battle of the Labyrinth*. Having survived the ice fortress of Alcyoneus and the molten lava of Mount St. Helens, we figure Percy would keep his cool and not break a sweat. Which is just as well, because he'd need all his energy for his next challenge: the Jaguar House.

This, you guessed it, is filled with hungry, man-eating jaguars. Percy's ability to communicate with sea creatures and horses wouldn't help here. (Horses didn't arrive in Central America until the sixteenth century, so they are unknown in Maya myth.) Assuming again that he'd come prepared, he could copy the Hero Twins and bring something juicier for the jaguars to eat (maybe some of those cheeseburgers that Thalia promised him). Or perhaps he could repeat his performance with the Nemean Lion and distract the jaguars with astronaut food.

In the fifth house, Percy would be pitted against Camazotz, the monstrous, bloodsucking queen of the vampire bats. She has leathery wings and glowing eyes like the Furies, and tries to decapitate people with her massive claws. One good thrust from Percy's sword should put an end to her evil ways. But even Riptide would be powerless against all the little scalpel-sharp obsidian blades that fly around the Razor House. The only way to save himself would be to reason with them, like the Hero Twins did, and convince them they'd be happier cutting something else.

It seems fairly clear that Percy wouldn't get much sleep at night in the Maya underworld. Which is a shame, because during the day he'd be challenged to endless ballgames. Bear in mind that the Maya ballgame as played by the Death Lords is about as close to our idea of a ballgame as Capture the Flag at Camp Half-Blood is to the playground version. In other words, it's a fast, no-holds-barred, violent game full of cheats and fouls. The Death Lords have even been known to use a player's severed head as the ball.

Yuck.

But the good news for Percy is that, like baddies the world over, the Death Lords are not as clever as they think they are. For all their scary appearance and love of gore, they're just like little children. They're easily distracted, extremely gullible, and they fall for the same tricks over and over again. Percy would soon work out how to bamboozle them and return to the mortal world. (No pearls of passage here. Even the dead had to bamboozle the Death Lords if they were to stand a chance of reaching the Maya heavens.)

And do we really believe that Percy would be victorious? Yes we do.

Because Percy Jackson is a true hero.

And heroes always win through.

But Percy's demigod powers could not save the day without his mortal intelligence, courage, and fast-thinking ingenuity. After all, the monsters of mythology were created by mankind in the first place. The role of the supernatural was to embody human fears, explain the inexplicable, and impose a sense of order on a chaotic universe. (The threat of monsters has also always been an effective way to ensure the good behavior of small children.) The Maya gods, just like the Greek gods and the Roman gods and the Norse gods, drew their power from humans. The type of myths that ancient people invented for themselves tells us a lot about how they lived and thought and dreamed.

But Percy is a modern kid. He knows that bullies at school can be sharper tongued than any snake-headed deity. He knows that a drought is more likely to be caused by climate change than a lack of human sacrifice. And he knows that, for all the passions and egos and tantrums of the gods, the strongest emotion in his world is the love of Sally Jackson.

And that's what the gods can't handle.

The thing about being a mythological god, no matter which mythology, is that you're focused on your own little department, your own selfish desires, your own warped logic.

It's like the absolute opposite of life in the rainforest, where the creatures have to work together to share their resources and adapt to one another's foibles.

If Percy didn't get that already, he'd get it from his trip to Central America.

It's all about the team.

And we'd back Percy Jackson's team against the biggest, ugliest, craziest, meanest villains in the whole world of myths and monsters.

• • • •

Jon and Pamela Voelkel spend a lot of time in the jungles of the Maya, researching their fast-paced and funny Jaguar Stones series (Book One: *Middleworld*. Book Two: *The End of the World Club*. Book Three: *The River of No Return*. Book Four is coming soon). Like Annabeth Chase, the only thing Jon's scared of is spiders. Like Grover Underwood, Pamela's scared of pretty much everything including caves, darkness, deep water, bats, rats, heights, and snakes (but not spiders, and especially not tarantulas because they're soft and fluffy like kittens). When not traveling or writing and illustrating their books, J&P are visiting schools, choosing prizes for Jaguar Stones Club giveaways, or working on their Web site at www.jaguarstones.com.

Eeny Meeny Miney Mo(m)

Picking Your Very Own Godly Parent

Jenny Han

> Rule Number One: You don't get to choose your parents. But what if you could? We've all fantasized about our "real parents" at some point in our lives. If you discovered you had an Olympian mom or dad, who would you want it to be? Jenny Han offers some important advice for making your choice.

The lives of half-bloods in Greek mythology usually end in blood and guts and fire—we're talking vengeful gods, three-headed dogs, monsters, ancient curses. It's all very dangerous and life threaten-y. If you were the child of a really powerful god like Percy is, you'd have to stay at Camp Half-Blood all year long, for fear of attracting monsters in the real world. You could never really go back home. Your life would be forever changed. If not over. If you're lucky.

And yet . . . the thought of having that powerful blood surg-ing through you, of having access to a whole other kind of magi-cal world, one that defies reason and gravity, even—it might just be worth it. I know I for one would just love a taste of ambrosia and nec-tar. I'd jump at the chance to learn Ancient Greek, practice archery, take swordfighting lessons, play Capture the Flag with real armor. But before I could sign up for all of that at Camp Half-Blood, I'd have to actually be a half-blood. I'd have to have a parent who was a god.

The thing is, you can't pick your parents. Not in this life and not in Percy's. But if you *could* choose, who would you pick? Clearly, there are pros and cons to having each god for a parent. Nobody's perfect, especially not in Greek mythology. So you must choose carefully. You have to really do your homework in order to make an informed deci-sion. So let's get to it—we won't only look at Percy Jackson's world, we'll look at the Ancient Greek myths for reference too. We want a complete background history. After all, this just isn't the kind of deci-sion you rush into haphazardly. You've got to have all the facts.

"The Big Three": Potential Dads

We'll start at the top, with Zeus, ruler of Olympus, lord of the friendly skies. Powerful, impulsive, and passionate, Zeus rules with his mas-ter bolt. To be a child of Zeus is to be a child of the sky, which basi-cally means I could fly, if he willed it so. Everyone knows that flying is pretty much the coolest kind of power any person could have. Ever. Not much can top flying as far as powers go. And I would be a princess, because Zeus is the king; he rules over Mount Olympus. What girl wouldn't want to be a princess? There's a certain kind of caché associated with being a daughter of Zeus—you're at the top of the food chain, you might say. You're so popular, you're prom queen, quarterback, and valedictorian all rolled into one. I probably wouldn't have to worry about who I'd sit with in the cafeteria, if you know what I mean.

But being at the top of the food chain comes with a price—with great power comes great responsibility, right? As Zeus' child, all the eyes of Olympus would be on you. They would be expecting nothing short of greatness from the kid of the thunder god. That's a lot to live up to.

And then, there is the matter of his jealous wife, Hera—something tells me she wouldn't exactly be a nurturing stepmom. She might turn me into a cow or something, just to spite Zeus for cheating on her again. When Zeus fathered the hero Hercules with a mortal woman, Hera put snakes in the baby's crib! She did everything in her power to make life hard for Hercules. And this was even after Zeus named the kid after her to appease her (the Greek version of the name is actually spelled *Hera*cles)! So while I would love to be a flying princess, the thought of hoofing around in a field chewing cud or being strangled to death by snakes isn't so appealing. Hera just isn't the kind of goddess you can win over so easy. If ever.

Next we have Hades, god of the Underworld. As such, Hades controls all the earth's precious metals. I would be decked out like Princess Grace of Monaco, and I would in fact be a princess, Princess of the Underworld. Princess of the Dead. But not princess-y in a prissy way. No, I would be a total badass, with a long black leather coat and a diamond scepter that doubles as a weapon. Yeah, a weapon!

If Hades were my dad, I wouldn't be afraid of death. Death would be like my British manservant, my very own butler. I would say, "Serve me," and Death would. I could even bring back my loved ones from the dead—not without a heavy price, but still. That's quite the perk.

I might even learn to like living in the dark, without sunlight or flowers.

No monster would ever mess with me—in fact, they'd have to protect me, follow my orders, be my minions. Cerberus would be my pet: I could train him to attack bad guys. (Though my dad would kind of be a bad guy.)

Not all bad though—after all, there is honor in death, and Hades does have some sense of honor. Interestingly enough, he is the only one of the Big Three who doesn't break the sacred pact and father a mortal hero in the Percy Jackson series. And when Percy returns Hades' helm of darkness, Hades returns Percy's kidnapped mother. He didn't have to do that. The guy has a sense of fair play, even if it is kind of twisted—after all, he did kidnap his wife to get her to marry him. Further, while Hades does sit by during most of the battle against the Titans in *The Last Olympian*, he comes through when it really counts. If he hadn't helped the half-bloods fight Kronos, who knows whether they would have been able to save Olympus. You can't say he doesn't have any honor after that.

What Hades doesn't have is a comfortable home. He gets a cabin at Camp Half-Blood by the end of the Percy Jackson series, which means I might be allowed to live there during the summer. But what would I do for the rest of the year? I'd probably have to stick with my dad Hades in the Underworld and sit on my own throne made out of kitten bones or something equally ghoulish. Hell would be my playground. But who wants to play in hell? Not me. I'd rather stay clear of it altogether; diamonds aren't worth living in a mine.

Plus, what if I inherited my father's looks the way Nico di Angelo did? Percy describes Nico's eyes as having that "intense, manic fire that made you suspect he was either a genius or a madman." Somehow, I don't think crazy eyes would look good on me.

And finally, there's Poseidon, Percy's dad. Chiron calls him "Earthshaker, Stormbringer, Father of Horses" in *The Lightning Thief*. He is all of those and more—he is the god of sea. I do love the ocean. I'm sure that if I wanted, I could be part mermaid and spend half the year in the water with my merman boyfriend, freeing dolphins from tuna nets and riding on the backs of humpback whales. Oh, to have my own seahorse! And when I was on land, I would still be one with water. When I got hurt, all I'd have to do was hop into the shower and I'd be all healed up. I could make fountains and waterfalls wherever I went, and I bet I'd be a really good surfer. I wouldn't even need a board. Maybe I'd be an Olympic swimmer, or a captain of my own ship, or a horsewoman—since Poseidon is the lord and creator of horses, I figure they'll listen to me too. With the sea god as my dad, the world would be my oyster!

But Poseidon isn't perfect either. He doesn't have the strongest relationship with his family—he once defiled Athena's temple by bringing a girl there for a little afternoon delight, and he is too proud to convince Zeus he didn't steal his master bolt, thus resulting in Percy's dangerous quest. And though Poseidon does love Percy, which he shows warmly with a hug, even, in *The Last Olympian*, he's also not above using him for his own purposes.

He's a prideful god, that Poseidon. Just imagine what it would be like to have a dad who never says sorry, always thinks he's in the right—not too much of a stretch for most people, which is kind of the point. Having a god for a dad is supposed to be fun fantasy; it isn't supposed to be just like real life.

All in all, I wonder—would it be so great to have a godly dad as opposed to a godly mom?

Potential Moms

At the top of the goddess food chain is Hera, queen of Olympus, wife of Zeus. She's probably the most powerful goddess in all of Olympus. And every century, Hera is allowed to grant one wish. Surely she would grant that wish to her own daughter. Wishes aside, it would be an incredible honor to inherit some of that power. The thing is, I wouldn't want to inherit her jealous tendencies or her vengeful nature.

Hera is the goddess of marriage, so it's extremely unlikely that she would stray—and even if she did, she seems kind of boring to me as far as godly parents go. Hera doesn't have many of her own interests. She's too busy running around turning Zeus' girlfriends into cows and weasels to be a good mom.

And while we're at it, let's take a look at her mothering track record. When her son Hephaestus was born, she thought he was so ugly that she pitched him right off of Mount Olympus. Nice. And her other son Ares, god of war, is pretty much a creep. It's kind of ironic that the goddess of marriage and childbirth isn't such a great wife or mom.

Then we have Artemis, goddess of the hunt and the moon, and all-around warrior woman. To be a daughter of Artemis is obviously impossible. She has sworn to be a maiden forever—in other words, no kids and no family, just her pack of loyal huntresses. If she *were* my mother, well, it would have to mean that I was the product of an immaculate conception. Just call me baby Jesus, version 2.0—not outside the realm of possibility in the world of Greek mythology. I'd be really good at archery and hunting—although I have to say, I'm not into the whole killing animals thing. I don't wear fur, unlike Artemis, who runs around wearing animal skins—head, hooves, and all.

Artemis would at least be a loyal mom; she's a woman of her word. It is Artemis who defends Percy, Annabeth, and Thalia at the Olympian council when her fellow gods want them punished in *The Titan's Curse*. She says, "If we destroy heroes who do us a great favor, then we are no better than the Titans." What a classy lady!

She doesn't discriminate against mortal or immortal. All are welcome (though it's true she isn't too crazy about boys joining her band of Hunters), so long as you choose her path: to never grow up and be young forever, just like Peter Pan. That sounds nice but also awfully permanent. I don't know that I'd want to be a girl forever. I wouldn't want to be disowned just for choosing true love and a grown-up life. I would want to follow my own path, not my mother's.

I highly doubt Artemis would be in favor of frivolous things like the prom, or nail polish, or boys. If I got dumped, I can just imagine her reaction: She'd tell me that men are scum anyway and she'd turn the guy into a boar (because all men are pigs, get it?). While there have been times in my life when I've been mad enough to wish I could turn a guy into *worse* than a wild pig, having a mother who could do it—and actually would—is a bit much. I don't need that on my conscience. Sometimes all a girl really needs from her mother is a shoulder to cry on.

Then we have Demeter; not a very powerful goddess but a semi-important one nonetheless. Demeter is the goddess of nature and the outdoors, and I have to say right off the bat, I'm not a camping kind of girl. I do like flowers though. As Demeter's daughter, I could grow wheat and flowers and all sorts of pretty things.

Only thing is, Demeter's other daughter Persephone ended up kidnapped and living in the Underworld, and that's not where I'd want to be. Even if I didn't end up Hades' second wife, Demeter would probably be suffocating and overprotective because big sis Persephone is gone half the year in hell. I would probably be sitting around in my room tending to my plants and wishing I was allowed to go out at night like all my friends. And I could forget about dating— after what happened with Persephone, I'm sure Demeter would veto any kind of boy action. What fun is it being a half-blood if I'm not even allowed to be out and about using my powers? And speaking of powers, growing flowers isn't the flashiest of magical abilities. If I wanted to be a gardener, I'd be a gardener.

With Aphrodite, the goddess of love and beauty, the perks are pretty obvious. If I were her daughter, I bet I would be so unspeakably beautiful boys would forget their own names. They would forget place and time all because of my pretty—no, dazzling—face. That's tempting. But then again, I wouldn't want to be so wrapped up in my looks I didn't care about anything else—Percy describes Aphrodite's children as just sitting around admiring themselves and gossiping all day long. Physical perfection can be boring too.

And what if I didn't turn out gorgeous like her? That can happen, you know. I might not inherit her beauty genes. I might turn out ugly, or worse—mediocre. That would be devastating. If Aphrodite were my mother, I bet she'd be one of those pageant moms who pressures her daughter to be physical perfection—tan skin and white teeth and bouncy blonde hair. If I didn't live up to her expectations of what beauty looks like, she might not want to claim me as hers. She might even throw me off of Mount Olympus just like Hera did to Hephaestus.

But apart from the vanity factor, I don't know that I'd want a mother who claims to hold love above all else but then turns right around and treats her own husband so shabbily. She is cruel to Hephaestus, and she flouts her relationship with Ares in his poor homely face. Speaking of Ares, what does she see in him anyway? Even if she is the goddess of love, she doesn't seem terribly wise about it. We're talking about a woman who started the Trojan War over a golden apple. She seems a lot like those moms who stay with deadbeat dads, hanging around in a dead-end relationship. Wake up and smell the ambrosia, Aphrodite—your man Ares is a creep. Watching her hang out with that guy would get really frustrating, I'm sure. She's a goddess, millions of years old; she should have outgrown that whole bad-boy complex by now.

When it comes to wisdom, there's no one wiser than the goddess Athena. As her daughter, I too would be so wise. Also, I'd have cool gray eyes just like my mom. I would always have a plan, always know just what to do. I would certainly be good in a crisis, just like Annabeth. If I chose to live in the mortal world, I could be the secretary of state, or Scrabble world champion.

I can tell that Athena is a good mom by the way she looks out for Annabeth's best interests. Right off the bat she says that Percy is bad news and could mean danger for her daughter, and even though that kind of thing is hard to hear, she's just trying to be a good mom. But it could also get annoying having a mom who knows everything, sees everything. A girl should be allowed to have a secret or two.

Other Potential Dads

Ares is the god of war, and he thrives on rage and aggression. Ares is the adrenaline that pumps in your veins when you're hopping mad and looking for a fight. If Ares were my dad, at least I'd know how to handle myself in a brawl. I'd be so tough, nobody would try to mess with me. Toughness can be a good thing. I'd like to be tough. But according to Percy in *The Lightning Thief*, Ares' kids are some of the "biggest, ugliest, meanest kids on Long Island, or anywhere else on the planet." Big, ugly, and mean? No thanks. Apparently, they aren't too smart either. Ares is known for his brawn, not his brains. And as Annabeth says in *The Lightning Thief*, "Even strength has to bow to wisdom sometimes."

I can only imagine what it would be like to have the god of war for a dad. Forget about organized sports: Ares would be the dad running along the sidelines screaming at the referee and cussing other parents out. Forget about bringing a boyfriend home: Ares would probably beat him to death with a mallet for even thinking about dating his daughter. And the fights we would get into! Ares and I would battle all the time over my curfew and my lack of killer instinct.

Then there's Artemis' twin brother, Apollo, the sun god, god of order and reason. Apollo has proven he's loyal to his sister, which is a plus. And I could ride around in his fiery chariot, sitting shotgun, and make the sun rise. The sun would rise and fall on my shoulders. Well, on my dad's shoulders. Also, I'd be excellent at archery, most likely, and possibly the lyre. Apollo is also the god of poetry, which is cool. I have a feeling, though, that I might get tired of his reciting bad poetry all the time like he does in Percy's books.

Apollo is also prophetic, meaning he knows the future. It'd be pretty sweet if that talent was passed on to me. I'd know my whole life before I even lived it. I'd know everybody's life. I could have my own hotline where people called me for advice. I wouldn't want to end up like Cassandra though—Apollo gave her the gift of prophecy, but when she didn't return his love, he made it so no one would ever believe her predictions. That would pretty much suck. What's the point of being a know-it-all if no one ever believes you?

And let's not forget Dionysus, god of wine and fertility. He is Apollo's brother and his opposite in nature. Instead of reason and moderation, Dionysus is all about pleasure and chaos. Hence the wine. Let the good times roll, that's what Dionysus would say.

How amazing would it be to conjure up beverages whenever I wanted? A chocolate milkshake or Cherry Coke slushee right out of thin air. Not a bad trick. It would certainly make me popular at parties and weddings. But Cherry Coke doesn't quite outweigh flying, riding in a chariot over the sky, or even talking to horses. If I want a Cherry Coke slushee, I can just go buy one. Maybe that's why Dionysus is so cranky; his abilities do seem to pale in comparison to the rest of his family's. No wonder he's got such a chip on his shoulder.

Then there's Hephaestus, and, well, there's not a whole lot alluring about Hephaestus. Not much at all. Not to be shallow, but he's not exactly known as the most attractive guy on Olympus, and I'm sure his kids aren't winning any beauty pageants either—they're all burly from working in the metal factory. Yes, he could teach me how to be a mason or a weapons builder, but I have zero interest in being a blacksmith. What I do have an interest in, however, is magical tools. Every cool magical tool in Olympus was forged by Hephaestus. He made Hermes' winged helmet and sandals, Cupid's bow and arrow, and Apollo's chariot. Maybe he'd make me a magic typewriter or something, or a golden pair of sunglasses that turns me invisible when I put them on. That'd be cool.

But it would be depressing to have a dad whose wife runs around on him all the time. His life is kind of depressing, period. There's the whole   being-thrown-from-Mount-Olympus-by-his-parents   thing, which is why he's crippled. He's had some tough breaks, which is sure to affect him as a father—maybe he's been hardened, but maybe not. Maybe he's a compassionate father because of everything he's had to endure. Then again, maybe he's bitter because of his hard-knock life. I don't know if I want to find out.

Since Hermes is the god of travelers and mischief, if I were his kid I could do all the traveling and mischief-making I ever wanted to do and know that my dad is watching over me, really proud. I could be the next Amelia Earhart, the next Marco Polo. But then, look at the way Luke turned out. He's no Amelia Earhart. I know it's unfair to do like the Oompa Loompas do and automatically blame it on the parents, but abandoning your son to be raised by his crazy mother doesn't sound like something a great dad would do. Still, after all Luke has done, Hermes cares for him and wants him saved. I'm not sure a lot of the other gods or goddesses would do the same for a wayward child.

Hermes encourages Percy and his friends to take risks, to carve out their own paths—to not always obey rules but to make their own. He doesn't talk down to Percy the way some of the other gods do; he treats him like an actual person. And for a god of mischief and thievery, he's pretty wise.

Who's Your Daddy? Or Rather, Mommy?

Now, who to pick? There are some good options here: mermen, flying, Cherry Coke slushees. It's a hard decision to make. Of everyone, Poseidon sounds like the best bet, a sure thing. He's proven himself a good dad to Percy, and he has enviable powers. I'm pretty sure he'd be a good dad to me. I bet he'd give me a pearl tiara on my sweet sixteen.

But he's not the parent I would pick. No, of all the gods and goddesses in Olympus, I would have to pick Artemis. With Artemis as my mother, the night sky and moon and stars would be mine. Who needs pearls when you can wear a strand of stars around your neck?

She would teach me bravery and independence and pride. She would teach me to respect nature and animals. She also seems like the most humble of the gods, the most willing to learn from others. Maybe it's because she is the most childlike. Artemis is fearless and brave, yet she is also willing to take on other people's burdens. She holds the world on her shoulders just as Atlas did, and of her own will. Artemis is a class act. With her as my mom, maybe I'd be one too.

But here's the other reason I'd pick Artemis. When I die, I'd become a star just like Zoë Nightshade. I'd become my own constellation. People would wish on me before they fell asleep at night, and I would twinkle for all eternity. Travelers would be guided by my light, ships would follow my course. I'd pick all of that over being turned into a cow or a tree.

There are worse ways to go than by being turned into a shining star by your mother. In fact, I can't think of a better way for a young hero to go. They all strive to prove their worth, to really make a name for themselves. That's why everyone wants to be a hero in the first place—to do the right thing, but also to become immortal, to become a legend people talk about forever and ever. To be important, to their parents if no one else. Because in the end, that's what all the kids at Camp Half-Blood really want: to be the twinkle, the star, in their parent's eye.

* * * *

Jenny Han is the author of *Shug*, a coming-of-age story about a twelve-year-old girl who learns about love the hard way. But then again, is there any *other* way? Jenny was born and raised in Richmond, Virginia, and now lives in Brooklyn, New York, where she writes books and also works at a school library. Her other books include *The Summer I Turned Pretty*, *It's Not Summer Without You*, *We'll Always Have Summer*, and *Burn for Burn*.

Percy, I Am Your Father

Sarah Beth Durst

> At one time or another, who hasn't wanted to assign their parents a letter grade? "I'm sorry, Mom, but you get an F for not letting me go to that party." Or, "Dad, good job showing up for my baseball game. You get a B+." Sarah Beth Durst takes us on a tour of the good, the bad, and the really bad parents of the Percy Jackson series. One word of warning: If you give your godly parent a failing grade, don't tell him or her. You're liable to wind up as a tree or a smoking crater.

Note to self: Do *not* become a parent in a fantasy novel.

Seriously, have you ever noticed how disturbingly often parents in fantasy novels are dead, kidnapped, missing, clueless, distant, or unknown? Kind of makes me want to round up all the authors, sit them on those pleather psychiatrist couches, and say, "Now, tell me about your mother . . ."

On the other hand, it works very nicely as a storytelling device: Get the parents out of the way and then something interesting can happen. I think of it as the *Home Alone* technique. You see it in books by C. S. Lewis, Lemony Snicket, J. K. Rowling . . . and you definitely see it in Rick Riordan's Percy Jackson and the Olympians series. All the kids at Camp Half-Blood, including the protagonist, Percy, are separated from their parents.

But are the parents really gone from the story? True, they don't have much screen time, but in Rick Riordan's books, the influence of these seldom-seen parents is so profound as to be (brace yourself—there's a pun coming) mythic.

The parents in the Percy Jackson books run the gamut from very cool to extremely evil. To facilitate our discussion of them, I'd like to introduce: Sarah's Sliding Scale of Parenting Skills.

Okay, so it's not actually a sliding scale. It's more of a report card. But that just doesn't have the same ring to it. After all, what's more important: accurate use of vocabulary or catchy alliteration? Don't answer that.

Worst Parent Award (Grade = Instant Expulsion)

Let's begin with the worst of the worst, the absolute bottom of Sarah's Sliding Scale of Parenting Skills, the parent who is so bad that he has won the Worst Parent Award for three millennia in a row. (Several years running, he also won Worst Dressed too, when he showed up to the awards ceremony in bell bottoms and suspenders. . . . Okay, I'm just making that up. Dionysus always wins Worst Dressed for his tiger-stripe Hawaiian shirts.) The recipient of this award is directly responsible for the central conflict of the Percy Jackson series. If he had cultivated better relationships with his children, the entire series would have been different. He is the Big Bad, the primary villain. He's also a lousy father.

I'm not talking didn't-attend-his-daughter's-piano-recital lousy, or even forgot-to-pick-the-kid-up-from-soccer-practice lousy. No, this paragon of parental virtue began his parenting career by eating his own children.

Yes, that's right. He *ate* them. Swallowed them whole. No ketchup. No marinade. No mercy. He would have gotten away with it too, except that his wife tricked him into swallowing a stone instead of the baby Zeus. Zeus then grew up to free his siblings from his father's stomach, slice his dear papa into pieces, and toss the pieces into the deepest pit in Tartarus.

I'm talking, of course, about Kronos, the evil Titan Lord who wants to rain death, destruction, and chaos on the world. In what is perhaps the largest understatement of the series, Percy says, "Kronos didn't care for anyone, including his own children."

To be fair, Kronos does have other children who he did not eat. But he's not BFF with them either. We learn in *The Titan's Curse* that Chiron, the wise and kindly centaur who trains and befriends Percy, is also Kronos' son. He wants to accompany the heroes on their quest to save Artemis and Annabeth, but he believes that if he does, his father will kill him (thus fulfilling the Oracle's prophecy). Regardless of whether Chiron is right or not, that's not what I'd call a healthy relationship. To quote Percy again: "I've met plenty of embarrassing parents, but Kronos, the evil Titan Lord who wanted to destroy Western Civilization? Not the kind of dad you invited to school for career day."

Failures (Grade = F)

Moving up Sarah's Scale of Parenting Skills, we find the failures. These charmers include Ares, Smelly Gabe, and Atlas.

Atlas is easy. Killing one's own child = an automatic failing grade. In the climactic battle in *The Titan's Curse*, Atlas' daughter Zoë Nightshade shoots arrows at Atlas to protect Percy, and then leaps between Atlas and Artemis to protect her beloved goddess. Atlas knocks her aside without a moment's hesitation. She dies, in part from the dragon Ladon's poison, but mostly, Percy believes, from her father's final blow. "Atlas' fury," Percy thinks, "had broken her inside." I don't care how many archery competitions Atlas sat through or how many times he stayed up late worrying while she was out on dates with Hercules. He killed her. 'Nuf said. "She started it" is not an excuse.

Next, let's look at Smelly Gabe, Percy's stepdad. Unlike Atlas, he is actually responsible for *saving* Percy's life. You'd think this would boost his grade, but according to the strict rules of Sarah's Sliding Scale of Parenting Skills, intentions matter. Gabe protects him by smelling so overwhelmingly human that he masks the magical "scent" of a demigod, hiding Percy from the mythical monsters who hunt the children of gods. (I'm thinking this isn't a literal smell, but maybe I'm wrong—Percy says "the guy reeked like moldy garlic pizza wrapped in gym shorts." Yum.) This protection is in no way intentional on Gabe's part. As are most people who have not encountered deodorant, Gabe is unaware of the power of his scent, magical or otherwise.

If we look at Gabe's intentional acts, we see he emotionally abuses Percy, physically abuses Percy's mom, and gambles and drinks away the family's money. When his wife and stepson disappear in *The Lightning Thief*, he accuses Percy of foul play and milks the situation for personal gain. So while he performs a valuable service for the series (preserving the protagonist = good), as a parental figure, he fails.

Our final failure is the god Ares. Ares is the epitome of all bullies, and that translates directly into his parenting style. Look at the exchange between Ares and Clarisse in *The Sea of Monsters*. "You're pathetic," he tells her. "I should've let one of my sons take this quest." She swears she'll succeed and make him proud. He says, "You will succeed. And if you don't . . ." He raises his fist, and Clarisse flinches. Like Gabe, he's an abuser. Clarisse embarks on her quest in book two in large part to please and impress her dad, but she won't get the support and praise she needs from Ares. He's a failure as a father.

(Incidentally, he's also a failure as a son and brother. He thinks a war between relatives is the best kind of war. "Always the bloodiest," he says. "Nothing like watching your relatives fight, I always say." He must be such a joy at family reunions. Just imagine what Thanksgiving is like.)

Unsatisfactory (Grade = D)

Only mildly better than the actively evil parents are the negligent ones. Thalia's mom falls into this category. All we know about her is that she was an alcoholic who died when she drove drunk. But that's more than we know about the other D-grade parents. The other near-failures are the scores of deities who fail to acknowledge their offspring as their own. Cabin eleven at Camp Half-Blood is filled with Undetermineds (kids whose parentage is clearly divine but unknown). Percy describes them in *The Lightning Thief* as "teenagers who looked sullen and depressed, as if they were waiting for a call that would never come. I'd known kids like that at Yancy Academy, shuffled off to boarding school by rich parents who didn't have the time to deal with them. But gods should behave better."

Because of this parental negligence, the Undetermineds are left to feel bitter and angry—and are therefore vulnerable to manipulation by Luke and Kronos. Thanks to these D-grade parents, Kronos' army grows. And that's just inexcusable. Maybe gods aren't into the whole introspection thing, but you'd think that after several centuries of parenthood, they'd absorb a few tips, perhaps read a few self-help books (*Men Are From Mars, Women Are From Venus* . . .). I'm with Percy—the gods should know better, and Percy shouldn't have to use his wish in *The Last Olympian* to force them to recognize their own children.

If it weren't for the fact that all of Western Civilization would be destroyed in the process, I'd say these deadbeat moms and dads deserve the walloping that, in *The Last Olympian*, they narrowly escape.

Satisfactory (Grade = C . . . ish)

Four divine parents fill out the center of our bell curve. Some rate high C's, and some rate low C's. They are occasionally negligent (though this can, in part, be excused by the rule against direct interference) and occasionally manipulative (Percy calls it "treating their children as chess pieces"), but they do show some hints of parental competence.

Let's begin with Poseidon, Percy's father. On the plus side, he does claim Percy as his own shortly after Percy arrives at camp, which is more than many other divine parents do. (I really wish he'd said, "Percy, I am your father," in a deep James Earl Jones voice. How awesome would that have been? That said, an elderly teacher figure does give Percy a pen that transforms into a magic sword, not unlike a light saber, and says that his father wanted him to have it when he was old enough, so my inner Star Wars geek is appeased.)

Also on the plus side: Percy's dad is there for him every time Percy calls for help. For example, after the Chimera bites him in book one, Percy calls on his father to save him as he falls into the water, and his father not only saves him but sends someone to dispense helpful advice for completing the quest. (Looks like someone is angling for extra credit. . . .) In book two, Percy calls for help, and his dad sends hippocampi. (Hippocampi are so my newest favorite mythological creature. I keep asking my husband for one. He keeps saying no, the griffin wouldn't like it.)

On the downside, like most of the gods, Poseidon is a rather absent father. In *The Sea of Monsters*, Hermes asks Percy if he ever feels abandoned by his father, and Percy thinks, "Only a few hundred times a day." He wishes his father were with his mother, he wishes his dad would make contact more often, he wishes he'd given him more warning that he has a half-brother, and he wishes his dad would acknowledge him more. Like Clarisse, Percy craves parental approval, even if he won't admit it. As Grover says, "You're glad your dad is alive. You feel good that he's claimed you, and part of you wants to make him proud. That's why you mailed Medusa's head to Olympus. You wanted him to notice what you'd done."

Unlike Ares with Clarisse, Poseidon does acknowledge and compliment Percy. More than that, his dad vouches for him and places an enormous amount of trust in him, betting that his son won't turn evil and destroy the world—and he turns out to be right. (Okay, for most parents, this isn't really a stretch, but gods have to worry about stuff like that.) He also manages to show up at Percy's birthday party in *The Battle of the Labyrinth*, despite being in the middle of an ocean war, and tells Percy he's his favorite son. As Percy recounts, "He smiled, and at that moment, just being in the kitchen with him was the best birthday present I ever got." Hmm . . . maybe Poseidon should really be upgraded to a B. The only thing that keeps him from a higher score is that fact that he left his son Tyson (the Cyclops) to live on the streets of New York in a cardboard refrigerator box. Granted, he later grants Tyson's prayers by giving him Percy as a brother and finding him gainful employment. . . . Okay, he's a C+, but with some grade grubbing, Poseidon could move up the Scale of Parenting Skills to a B-grade parent.

Hermes is another C-grade parent who also has the potential to move up the Scale of Skills. His heart is in the right place: He wants to save his son Luke. Luke has turned out rather badly. Possibly due to lack of parental guidance, he has fallen in with a bad crowd. The evil Titan Lord who wants to overthrow civilization can't be a good influence on a still-forming mind and body. (I keep thinking there should be some kind of public service announcement: Don't smoke, don't drink, don't plot world destruction with the aid of ancient mythological monsters. . . .) But despite Luke's dastardly deeds, Hermes refuses to give up on his son. "My dear young cousin," he says to Percy in *The Sea of Monsters*, "if there's one thing I've learned over the eons, it's that you can't give up on your family, no matter how tempting they make it." After Luke's death, it becomes especially clear how much Hermes loved his son and how much Hermes wanted Luke to love him in return. Percy's assurance of Luke's love seems to bring him some comfort.

But up until the end of the series, Luke clearly has father issues. (Seriously, just look at his boat—it's named after Andromeda, a girl who was chained to a rock by her parents to be eaten by sea serpents. Talk about family problems.) You see his bitterness about his father right from the first time Percy meets him in *The Lightning Thief*, and that bitterness fuels his betrayal of Percy in book one, his actions on behalf of Kronos in book two, his role in Annabeth's imprisonment in book three, and his donation of his body for use by our chief bad guy. So even though we only see him for a few scattered pages throughout the series, and even though he means well and believes that Luke will make the right decision and save Olympus in the end, Hermes is also the driving force behind Luke's destructive behavior.

Another so-so parent-god is Athena, Annabeth's mother. We don't see her much throughout the series. She does help out her daughter on occasion—she gave Annabeth her cap of invisibility (hey, that's what I should ask my mom to get me for Christmas!), and she gives Percy advice while on his quest to save Annabeth in *The Titan's Curse*. She also offers Percy and Annabeth some crucial advice in *The Last Olympian* during the battle for Manhattan. But she's not exactly having mother-daughter pizza nights with Annabeth. I'd rate her a flat C. She's a neutral force in Annabeth's life.

Zeus is a low C. Yes, he saves his daughter Thalia from death by transforming her into a pine tree, but is life as a tree really such great shakes? Couldn't he have intervened a wee bit sooner or more effectively? How about turning her *enemies* into trees? (I know, I know, no direct interference, but isn't he already breaking the rule with the tree-transformation thing?) He also supplies angels to help our heroes escape from the skeleton warriors at Hoover Dam, but he's not so quick to answer her other prayers (for instance, in *The Titan's Curse*, she prays for a thunderstorm with no more effect than my chanting "rain, rain, go away . . ."). So he's there for her when things are at their most dire, but he's not a day-to-day kind of dad.

It doesn't make for a built-on-trust kind of relationship. When lightning nearly hits her in *The Titan's Curse*, Thalia thinks her dad is trying to kill her, but it's actually Kronos using her parental hang-ups to try to manipulate her. Dr. Thorn later tries to lure her to Kronos' side by talking about how her father abandoned her, and Luke gets her to hesitate by mentioning her dad. To be fair, Zeus does acknowledge and compliment her at the end of the quest—more than just "Hi, kid. Nice hair." But his unreliability makes Thalia a wild card for much of book three, so that's not enough to boost Zeus to the next grade level.

One thing that can be said about these C-grade parents: They at least sometimes try. They don't always succeed, but at least they occasionally care. "Families are messy," Hermes says in *The Sea of Monsters*. "Immortal families are eternally messy. Sometimes the best we can do is to remind each other that we're related, for better or worse . . . and try to keep the maiming and killing to a minimum."

Most Improved (Grade = B)

The Most Improved Parent of the Year Award belongs to Dr. and Mrs. Chase, Annabeth's father and stepmother. When Annabeth talks about her dad and stepmom in *The Lightning Thief*, she is far from complimentary. She complains that they treated her like a freak who endangered her stepsiblings and made her feel so unwanted that she ran away. She paints them as such ogres that when Percy meets her stepmom in book three, he says, "I half expected Mrs. Chase to turn into a raving lunatic at the mention of her stepdaughter, but she just pursed her lips and looked concerned."

Clearly the Chases failed in some way to connect with their daughter, or else she wouldn't have run away at age seven and been nearly squashed by the bad guys—tough to get a perfect score on Sarah's Scale of Parenting Skill with that on your record—but I think Annabeth is wrong about them. Think about it: Whenever she's home, monsters attack. Can you blame her parents for being a wee bit tense around her? Other kids bring home problems with bullies or grades or smoking, but heroes bring home problems with teeth, claws, swords, and way too many arms. You don't find info on how to deal with that in any parenting advice book ("Just say no to monsters!" "I don't care if that hellhound followed you home, you can't keep it unless you promise to walk it every day . . ."). Despite this, the Chases keep trying. At the end of *The Lightning Thief*, Annabeth takes Percy's advice and writes a letter to her dad. He responds instantly with an invitation for her to move back home. Give the man a gold star.

In *The Titan's Curse*, Dr. Chase takes "trying" to a whole new level. When Annabeth is kidnapped and her friends need transportation to reach her, Percy and Thalia turn to Dr. Chase for help. Dr. Chase and Mrs. Chase loan them a car without much argument. In fact, Dr. Chase wants to do more, but Percy and Thalia refuse. As they leave, Mrs. Chase tells them to tell Annabeth she still has a home with them. But that's not the last of it. Just when things are bleakest, Dr. Chase flies in on his plane, machine guns down the monsters, and saves the day.

I think all the parenting advice books would agree: Gunning down an army of evil monsters to save your daughter's life is good parenting.

Best Parent Award (Grade = A)

And the envelope, please. . . . Winner of the award for Best Parent in the Percy Jackson and the Olympians series is . . . Sally Jackson! [Insert sound effect of wild applause. Sally smiles, waves shyly at the audience, and makes her way to the stage. Her son, Percy, toasts her with a cobalt blue Cherry Coke.]

Sally loves her son. She is willing to sacrifice her happiness for his safety. As Percy learns in *The Lightning Thief*, she married the odious Smelly Gabe in order to protect Percy from the monsters who hunt half-bloods—or at least that's Grover's theory: "Gabe has been covering your scent for years. If you hadn't lived with him every summer, you probably would've been found by monsters a long time ago. Your mom stayed with him to protect you. She was a smart lady. She must've loved you a lot to put up with that guy." (Given Sally's previous taste in men, I'm inclined to believe Grover. Plus, as soon as Percy proves he doesn't need protection, Sally rids herself of Gabe, and finds the much-nicer Paul.) Regardless, Sally does her best to give Percy a normal life for as long as possible. Okay, yes, she nearly gets him killed by not sending him to Camp Half-Blood sooner (details, details). She makes up for it by insisting that he leave her and save himself when the Minotaur attacks. He doesn't, of course (again, details).

She also scores extra points for sheer coolness. Look at the beginning of *The Titan's Curse*: "The Friday before winter break, my mom packed me an overnight bag and a few deadly weapons and took me to a new boarding school." Unlike parents in other fantasy stories, who either are an impediment to or are ignorant of their child's responsibilities as Chosen One (or superhero or nice vampire or whatever), Percy's mom drives him and his hero friends to battle.

Instead of blocking her son's heroics, Sally encourages him. She pushes him to defy the camp director (who incidentally is a god, so this is no trivial act) and rescue his friend Annabeth in *The Titan's Curse*. "As much as I want you to come home," she says, "as much as I want you to be safe, I want you to understand something. You need to do whatever you think you have to. . . . I'm telling you that I'll support you, even if what you decide to do is dangerous." Okay, how awesome is that? Just for that statement, I think Sally Jackson deserves Best Parent in a Fantasy Series Ever. Seriously, name one other parent in a fantasy novel who says something like this. (Um, that's a rhetorical dare. Please don't go research it. Point is that it's unusual.) And she doesn't just say it once, she repeats the sentiment in *The Battle of the Labyrinth* after Percy and Annabeth tell her Percy's plan to navigate the Labyrinth. She loves him, she trusts him, and she supports his decision to face mortal peril.

Percy loves her too. The very first time he describes her, he says, "She's the best person in the world." He treasures his memories of summers spent on the beach in Montauk, and his favorite taste in the world is her homemade blue chocolate chip cookies. (She has an obsession with blue food. But really, who doesn't?) He misses her while he's at school and at camp. About fifty pages into the first novel, during the fight with the Minotaur, Sally dissolves into shimmering golden light (ooh, shiny!). Percy believes she's been killed, and he accepts the quest to retrieve Zeus' master bolt from Hades in the hopes of bringing her back to life. He says point-blank to Grover, "I don't care about the master bolt. I agreed to go to the Underworld so I could bring back my mother." Percy is willing to travel to hell and back (literally) for his mother. He loves her so much that when the Oracle prophecies that he will "fail to save what matters most in the end," he knows this means his mother, but he hopes to hell (sorry—couldn't resist the pun) that the Oracle is wrong and continues on anyway. His love for his mother inspires the quest that drives the entire plot of *The Lightning Thief*.

His devotion isn't exactly news to the other characters. Ares successfully dangles information about Percy's mother as bait to lure Percy into a trap, and Hades uses her as his hostage. But the bit that *is* news to Hades, the part that he couldn't predict (perhaps because he doesn't understand it), is that she inspires Percy to heroic action. Because of her, he makes the heroic choice *not* to rescue her from the Underworld. He believes that she'd never forgive him if he failed to stop the gods' war for her, and his belief in her goodness shapes the outcome of the novel.

In other words, if not for the awesome parenting skills of Sally Jackson, *The Lightning Thief* would have been a very different and very sad book.

Instead of a war between gods and the catastrophic end to life as we know it (which would have been a downer), Percy gets a happy ending: His heroism is rewarded by the return of his mother. In fact, he has a reunion with his mother at the end of each of the first four books. In *The Lightning Thief*, he decides to return to live with her. In *The Sea of Monsters* and *The Titan's Curse*, he calls home after he finishes with his adventures, and in *The Battle of the Labyrinth*, he returns home so his mother can throw him a birthday party. How many other heroes do that? Not many. Clearly, Percy and Sally have a strong and positive relationship, which makes her a shoo-in for the Best Parent Award, as well as one of the most important and influential characters in the series, despite her limited screen time.

Parents: Can't Live With 'Em, Can't Live Without 'Em

So what do all these parents up and down the scale have in common? Some are human; some are gods. Some are decent; some are the embodiment of all evil. Some never appear; some swoop in at the last minute to play pivotal roles in climactic scenes.

All of them, though, exert a profound influence on their children—and therefore on the course of the stories. Percy, Luke, Clarisse, Annabeth, and the other wonderful characters in Percy Jackson and the Olympians are constantly trying to live up to, get revenge against, gain approval from, get close to, get away from, or save the lives of their parents. We may not see the parents on stage often, but god or not, good or not, they are omnipresent.

And now, if you'll excuse me, I have the sudden urge to call my mom. . . .

• • • •

Sarah Beth Durst is the author of young adult novels *Vessel; Drink, Slay, Love; Enchanted Ivy; and Ice;* as well as middle grade novels *Into the Wild* and *Out of the Wild.* She has twice been a finalist for the Science Fiction & Fantasy Writers of America's Andre Norton Award, for both *Ice* and *Into the Wild.* Sarah lives in Stony Brook, New York, with her husband and children. Visit her at sarahbethdurst.com.

As Bad as They Wanna Be

Hades, Nico, and the Underworld

Hilary Wagner

It's hard to find a badder bad boy than the Lord of the Underworld. But is Hades really bad or just misunderstood? Hilary Wagner professes her love for Hades and Nico and explains why, though someone's clothes might be black, his or her heart may not be.

I ♥ Hades

I'll admit, all the gods get decent marks on the "coolness scale," but in my book, Hades is top dog, or top hellhound in his case. Sure, he's a little bit on the brooding side and in need of a quality self-tanner, but still, the dude sports some serious swagger. Percy may have no love for the guy, but even he admits in *The Lightning Thief* that Hades was the only god he'd met so far that appeared godlike.

Think about it—he's the essence of cool, clad in black, long-haired and lanky, hanging out in his alternative night-clubby underworld palace. Sure, there's that raging smell of sulfur and those bothersome bloodcurdling screams, but I'd imagine that's easy for Hades to stomach with his glitzy goddess wife Persephone at his side. To boot, he's richer than all get-out, making Zeus and Poseidon look like minor players on the who's-who-of-godly-wealth list. I mean, no wonder his family doesn't like him. He's the quintessential bad boy.

Now I'm not going to run out and buy a Hades lunchbox or furiously scribble Hilary + Hades in my notebook 100 times over, but I've *always* had a thing for the bad boys. Hopefully we all outgrow it, but at some point in our lives, most of us want to either date a bad boy (or girl) or be one. Don't get me wrong; when I was little, I loved the fairytale prince and princess movies like *Snow White* and *Sleeping Beauty* with their guaranteed happy endings, but man, wouldn't it have been a lot more exciting if the evil queens actually won and didn't plummet to their deaths? (As it turns out, evil queens plummet a lot.) Or what if Shere Khan from *The Jungle Book* stories actually got his fangs into poor little Mowgli? I guess the reviews might not have been as favorable for that version. When I first watched the epic movie *Titanic*, I secretly wanted Billy Zane (you know, Rose's wealthy, super-great-looking boyfriend) to beat the living daylights out of Leonardo DiCaprio. I know that sounds harsh, or maybe you're thinking I'm a little touched in the head, but that's not the case. No offense to nice guy Leo, but bad boy Billy was . . . well, just plain cooler.

Okay, so it probably sounds like I think the good guys are about as thrilling as an acne cleanser infomercial, but I *do* have love for them. Percy Jackson frankly amazed me—this confused kid from New York who thinks he can't do anything right was in fact on a path to save the entire world. Yes, PJ rocks some swagger too, but the bad boys tend to intrigue me just a little bit more. Why? It's not that they do bad things, exactly. It's *why* they do those things.

What's behind their rebellious natures? When it comes to Hades, you have to ask yourself, *what makes him so bad?*

Can We Blame the Guy?

So, what does make Hades so bad? Was he born to be a baddy, like our friend Voldemort in Harry Potter, or was Hades made bad because of his circumstances? Sure, we could call it a convenient catchline, but I think there's a lot of truth to "nature vs. nurture" when it comes to Hades. If we humans have family hang-ups (and we're generally here less than a century), why can't a god be affected by some serious family scars when he's left to stew for centuries about them?

As the ancient myths tell it, Hades didn't exactly *ask* to be Lord of the Underworld. After kicking some Titan backside, Hades, Poseidon, and Zeus drew lots for their respective kingdoms. Hades drew the crummiest lot, sticking him with the dark, depressing, and otherwise terrifying Underworld . . . and there's even a rumor that Zeus tricked him into picking it, ensuring he and Poseidon wouldn't get stuck with the joint.

Throughout his godly tenure, Hades was about as well liked as a bad drachma. He was said to be grim and morose and just being around him made people squeamish, giving them a serious case of the willies. Even when making a sacrifice to him, people would avert their eyes in fear, using only their creepiest of black animals to guarantee something really, really bad would happen to the neighboring farmer that might have been filching their sheep or eyeing their wife—that's how much he freaked people out. In a nutshell, Hades puts the dead in deadpan.

So, he was brooding and moody and gave folks an overall icky feeling. I get it—but you'd be moody too if your entire family thought you were the king of creepy and your job stuck you in the Underworld twenty-four/seven. You've heard of Seasonal Affective

Disorder, right? In short, it's when darkness and the lack of sun affects us mere mortals negatively, making us bummed out and otherwise grumpy. Well, why can't it affect a god too, especially after thousands of years? I mean, he's perpetually surrounded by millions of dead souls, many looking pretty Night-of-the-Living-Deadish, and his only buddies are slathering demons, drooling hellhounds, and weapon-wielding skeletons dripping with rotten flesh. He gives the phrase "I see dead people" a whole new meaning. That's got to get to a guy!

Let's be honest—it's not as though Hades had a great role model for a dad either. Sure, demigod Luke got the short end of the stick in that department too, but *nothing* like Hades. Plenty of people have horrible fathers and turn out all right, great in fact, but how many of us can say our dad swallowed us whole, due to his own insecurities, only to be literally regurgitated up later on? Because Hades and his siblings were gods, they actually *lived* in Kronos' stomach (which is super gross), maybe doing the backstroke in gastric juices or playing dodgeball with half-digested grapes. That had to do something to the guy. I suppose, psychologically, he could try to turn it around, be grateful his dad puked him up and he was still kicking, but if that happened to me, not to mention being stuck for all time ruling the ultimate house of horrors, I might be a bit surly too.

Not His Brothers' Keeper

Okay, yes, Hades is sometimes more than just a little surly. He's made some bad choices in his otherwise godly life. There's that whole issue of Hades trying to murder Percy and kidnapping his mom (but in his defense, in that situation his crimes were based on misinformation. He was led to believe that Percy had stolen the master bolt and his helm—the very symbol of his power). And, fine, he sent some drooling monsters after Zeus' daughter Thalia (luckily her dad took pity on her and turned her into a tree—nice gesture). And I'm sure Persephone wasn't a happy goddess camper when he kidnapped her and then tricked her into eating some pomegranate seeds (I guess Hades has a thing for abduction), trapping her in the Underworld for part of each year. Boss man Zeus even frowned on that move. But Hades' misdeeds are child's play compared to his lightning bolt and trident brandishing brothers' transgressions.

Both Zeus and Poseidon take their badness *way* beyond the classic bad-boy persona. For god's sake (no pun intended), Zeus *devoured* his first wife, Metis (I'm thinking that's a crime), so his own daughter Athena couldn't be born and usurp his power. He's said to have forced himself on Hera before marrying her—always an effective way to kick off a loving marriage—and numerous others, including Io, Callisto, and Electra, to name a violated few. Oh, and let's not forget that pesky Trojan War many claim he's responsible for—apparently old Zeus' way of controlling the problem of overpopulation . . . and he's got an issue with Hades tricking Persephone? All I've got to say to that is pot, meet my buddy kettle.

Poseidon's no better. He dwells in the sea, wielding his mighty trident (among *other* things) and pretty much doing as much bad as his skyward brother. Now, there are a couple versions of this myth, but it is believed that Poseidon forced himself on the then-beautiful Medusa and let her take the rap, claiming she seduced him. This caused a ticked-off Athena to turn Medusa into a hideous gorgon because it happened on her turf. That's pretty cold-blooded, even for a god. Poseidon also had his unwanted way with Amphitrite, Demeter, and scores of other females.

What's more, both gods were *notorious* cheaters, fathering many children (most of whom they abandoned) and exemplifying the phrase *male chauvinist pig*. Apparently, neither brother was around the day Daddy Kronos planned on giving them the "no means no" speech. So if Zeus and Poseidon are the ones who should be doing life sentences in San Quentin about a million times over, why is

Hades the one getting dumped on—blatantly shunned by his family and even we humans?

The Good, the Bad, and the Downright Despicable

Okay, so, clearly, comparing Hades to his brothers is like comparing a paper cut to a severed arm, but what about the books' other bad apples, gods and otherwise?

Let's face it: when we think of the Underworld, it's easy to remember everything that's bad about it—Tartarus, for one, the pit hidden in the deepest depths of the Underworld, where Kronos dwelled, among other big baddies. We also have the Fields of Punishment, where the rotten apples who aren't quite as rotten as Kronos wind up. Next, there's the Asphodel Fields, where all the run-of-the-mill souls land. As Annabeth explains to Percy in *The Lightning Thief*, "Most people, well, they just lived. Nothing special, good or bad, so they go to the Asphodel Fields." Admittedly, that doesn't sound too great, not really what you'd consider a reward or even a pat on the back for playing by the rules. I suppose it's better than eternal damnation, but perpetually drifting in an overcrowded field, as though ceaselessly waiting at the DMV, sounds about as fun as repeatedly stabbing yourself in the eye with a fork.

But that's not the only place dead souls end up, and that's significant. Hades is Lord of the Underworld, right? The guy can do what he likes, sending anyone and everyone to the Fields of Punishment, Tartarus, or whatever ghoulish eternity he might think up in his twisted godly head. Well then, if he's such an old sourpuss, why does he allow extraordinary souls, those who did something awe-inspiring with their lives, to spend eternity in Elysium—the Greek version of Heaven? Granted, it's near impossible to get in the joint (think of the ultimate A-list Hollywood party), but maybe, in his way, Hades was just trying to up our game. If we knew Elysium was waiting for us, wouldn't we *all* strive to be extraordinary—not just play nice in the sandbox? Hmm . . . wandering aimlessly for all time in an endless field of nothingness or living in a swanky Elysium villa, surrounded by joyful laughter, pool parties, and everlasting cookouts—you decide.

And forget comparisons with his brothers; was Hades even all that bad in comparison with other villainous characters in the Percy Jackson and the Olympians series? I'm not so sure. After all, it was Luke and Ares who brought Hades to the boiling point in *The Lightning Thief* by tricking him into believing Percy had stolen Zeus' master bolt and Hades' precious helm. Slimy Ares had the chance to turn Luke in; he could have ended the whole thing right then and there, but he chose, to put it mildly, a more destructive path. Ares, who's pretty much a jerk throughout the entire series, did it because he thinks war is about as cool as a vintage Ferrari Testa Rossa, and what would be cooler than a war of godly proportions—the Big Three pummeling one another into oblivion?

Luke, on the other hand, had much darker motives, making him far more dangerous and, in my eyes, almost as evil as Kronos. Luke had it rough, but that's no excuse to join the dark side. His plans were all about power and vengeance—taking control that was not his to take and giving payback to those he thinks wronged him. When Hades wanted to vaporize Percy, he had a reason. A reason to actually *kill* him, I'm not so sure, but a reason all the same. He thought he was a thief. He thought Percy was the one who'd started all the godly drama, causing all kinds of mayhem. Murderous or not, Hades' motivation to go after Percy was a fair one (at least a god's version of fair). Luke's reason was purely selfish. He wanted personal glory.

Now, Kronos' wicked ways are a bit baser than Luke's and even warmongering Ares'. In *The Lightning Thief* we learn that, in the old days, Kronos and the other Titans kept humans ignorant, using us as tasty hors d'oeuvres and cut-rate entertainment (oh, how funny, human finger puppets!). After Zeus chops Kronos into itty-bitty pieces and takes over, Kronos *still* finds a way to invade men's nightmares and twist their thoughts to his evil will. Throughout the series, many lives are lost due to Kronos and his sick need to be all-powerful. In the end, even Luke loses his life to Kronos, the one guy he thought he could count on. Never thought I'd say this, but somehow Hades is looking more and more like a pale shrouded teddy bear of doom than the big bad Lord of the Underworld.

Daddy Dearest vs. Dad of the Year

Okay, I'll admit, I hate to second guess myself, but once we found out Hades was a daddy, I got a little worried. Maybe the misunderstood-bad-boy theory was just that—a theory.

I mean, Hades may have broken with family tradition and not swallowed Nico, but unless he has some intense parenting classes, Hades will *never* score a Dad-of-the-Year award anytime soon. Sure, Hades has some good qualities, like not condemning every human to Tartarus or making us pooper-scoop Asphodel Fields after the hellhounds have had a potty break, but he was downright cruel to his demigod son, Nico. In *The Last Olympian*, he belittles him, habitually comparing him to his dead sister, and otherwise screwing with the poor kid's already screwed-with head. I was actually upset when I read this, just waiting for Hades to evoke the ghost of the hanger-wielding Mommy Dearest, but instead, he did something truly remarkable. He listened. He came through in the end—when it mattered most. In *The Last Olympian*, when New York is under attack, he could have ignored Nico's pleas for help, but instead, he rose to the occasion and ultimately became a key player in saving the world from Kronos' gluttonous Titan hands. How would it have all panned out if Hades had done nothing, something he'd grown quite good at when it came to helping out his family? After all, he was practically a hermit, staying in the Underworld and generally wanting to be left alone (typical bad boy loner). Could his motives have been purely selfish? If Kronos and his goons *hadn't* been sent packing, Hades would have been in as much trouble as his brothers. But if that was the case, why would he risk his own godly skin? He could have easily sent up the Furies and scores of dead minions with lots of gooey flesh and innards hanging off them, but instead he put his life on the line. *He* led the charge. Did Nico change his mind or did some fatherly instinct kick in, forcing Hades to finally realize there was more to life (or death) than himself?

In *The Last Olympian,* we learn Hades *did* have a soft side—dare I say a loving side? We discover he loved Nico, Bianca, and their mother, Maria. Hades literally begs Maria di Angelo to go with him to the Underworld, where she and their children can be safe from Zeus, but Maria refuses, unable to believe Zeus would actually hurt children. Hades knows his little brother a bit better:

> Zeus has decreed that the children I currently have must be turned over to Camp Half-Blood for proper training, but I know what he means. At best they'll be watched, imprisoned, turned against their father. Even more likely, he will not take a chance. He won't allow my demigod children to reach sixteen. He'll find a way to destroy them, and I won't risk that!

Does that sound like a dad who hates his kids? Admittedly, when Maria is killed, Hades loses it on the Oracle, cursing her for all time, though she was only the messenger. And when Bianca dies in *The Titan's Curse,* Hades blames Nico, the one left alive, resenting his only son and turning his pain into wrath. If you haven't noticed, the gods aren't exactly good at saying things were their fault, and this was no exception. Hades plays the blame game just like the rest of his family and I doubt he'll outgrow that any millennium soon. It's a character flaw, sure. But it's not exactly *evil.*

Like Father, Like Son?

Speaking of Nico: We see glimmers of his personality in *The Battle of the Labyrinth*, but it isn't until *The Last Olympian* that we start to understand who Nico Di Angelo really is. Frankly, I want to know more—as in a three-book series more. I'm not trying to drop hints or anything—and no, that *wasn't* me camped out on Rick Riordan's lawn with the "Write a series about Nico" sign (at least you can't tell from the security cameras). I just think this kid has a lot more to say.

What I love about Nico is that he doesn't start off dark and gloomy. When we first meet him in *The Titan's Curse*, he's this cute talkative kid who loves regular kid-type stuff—nothing dark about him—but then, his whole world is upended. The untimely death of his older sister, Bianca, seems to be the point when his doom and gloom sets in. All at once, he loses his sister, finds out his father is the mayor of scary town, and journeys (all by himself, mind you) down to the Underworld. Your average kid would never knowingly set foot into the Underworld, but Nico is willing to do it. As his life falls apart and his anger and sadness set in, he begins to come alive, as if all things horrible and cheerless make him who he is, not to mention trigger his morbid powers . . . remind you of any tall, dark, and pale gods you might know?

In *The Battle of the Labyrinth*, a storm cloud seems to form over Nico (think of the cloud of dust over Pigpen, only this one's filled with rancorous ghosts and screams of tortured souls). Nico becomes morose and sulky, which may sound typical for a kid his age, except a normal teen can only summon up some killer burps with cola and French fries, not crowds of dead dudes—which is just one of the reasons you don't want to get on Nico's bad side. For another, he can sense when you're dying. (Not sure I'd want to have that precious nugget of knowledge hanging over my head.) And just like his dad did in the first book, Nico holds a lethal grudge against Percy, blaming him for his sister's death. It's not until he summons up

Bianca that he truly understands it was not Percy's fault . . . and even then it takes a good amount of time to sink in.

Percy was lucky he was dealing with Nico and not his dad in this situation. Nico was just beginning to grasp his powers at that point . . . or maybe Nico *did* have a hold on them already and he just wasn't quite willing to use them. Nico is not physically tough like Percy or Annabeth, but he realizes his powers at a very young age, and is able to harness them much quicker than Percy or Annabeth did. Nico sure does open up that massive fissure at the end of the book. But remember, when he did that, it was to help *save* Percy, the very person he hated, so maybe, just maybe, Nico is already fighting his godly genetics, knowing that's not who he wants to be, even if that is who he is.

Just like Luke had a choice to do the right thing, Nico does too. Possibly it's because he wasn't raised by Hades, but Nico seems to be turning out, well . . . *good*. Even a little Percyish—if Percy had black eyes, wore a skull ring, and made people, satyrs, and pegasi jumpy and slightly queasy in the stomach.

Nico bravely stands with the other gods and demigods, and defends the human world from Kronos when he has every reason not to. Let's not forget it was Nico who told Percy to bathe in the River Styx, giving him godlike powers so he had a fighting chance against Kronos. We can only guess what might have happened had Nico not come up with the idea. In that regard, Nico is just as much a hero as Percy.

Nico is daring too. He boldly faces down the Lord of the Dead, basically calling out a god on his warped way of thinking when Hades refuses to join the other gods in fighting in *The Last Olympian*.

> "Maria died!" Hades reminded him.
>
> "You can't just cut yourself off from the other gods!"

"I've done very well at it for thousands of years."

"And has that made you feel any better?" Nico demanded. "Has that curse on the Oracle helped you at all? Holding grudges is a fatal flaw. Bianca warned me about that, and she was right."

"For demigods! I am immortal, all-powerful! I would not help the other gods if they begged me, if Percy Jackson himself pleaded—"

"You're just as much of an outcast as I am!" Nico yelled. "Stop being angry about it and do something helpful for once. That's the only way they'll respect you!" Hades' palm filled with black fire. "Go ahead," Nico said. "Blast me. That's just what the other gods would expect from you. Prove them right."

Umm . . . sorry, Hades, we know you're the big bad ruler of the dead and all, but you just got served by someone who doesn't even have a license to drive a chariot yet. Put that in your pipe made of human bone and smoke it!

Nico has the courage to stand up to his dad, but he also has self-awareness. He tells Hades off but admits he's an outcast too. He doesn't fit in at Camp Half-Blood, just as Hades doesn't fit in at Olympus, but unlike Hades, Nico doesn't use that as an excuse to become a bad guy. He accepts the fact that he's different, and fights tooth and nail to use his powers only for good.

That Pesky Fatal Flaw

Nico is already proving he is powerful, clever, loyal to his Camp Half-Blood buddies, and clearly courageous. It's hard enough for a regular kid to stand up to a human dad, but to stand up to a god— one of the Big Three—who could incinerate said kid with a minor swish of his condemned-soul-stitched cloak, is darn well fearless.

My question is . . . can it last? When Nico speaks to his departed sister in *The Battle of the Labyrinth,* she explains their fatal flaw is holding grudges. Even with all the good in Nico, can he fight his godly traits—his fatal flaw—any more than Clarisse can control her urge to rip your throat out if you look at her funny or any more than Percy can control his overwhelming sense of loyalty? After all, Nico's resentment ran deep when he thought Percy was to blame for Bianca's death. It might just take one more devastating event to send him tumbling over the edge, permanently tipping the scales—turning him into his bitter, grudge-holding father for good. Nico realized his powers when everything in his life turned bad. What if that negative energy actually makes him stronger—what if his rancor is a conduit of power? He's already mastering the powers he *knows* he has. What about the powers yet to come?

So, what *does* the future hold for Nico long-term? Maybe Hades will be forced up to Olympus or maybe Persephone will convince him to take her on a romantic cruise of doom. Nico could step in as ruler of the Underworld, starting all sorts of demigod disobedience once in charge. When he grows up, he could become the president (a known path for demigods), giving him hold over the world of the living *and* the dead! Or maybe he could start a killer rock band, touring across the world with Jimi Hendrix, Kurt Cobain, and a backup band of bone daddies, but of course we measly mortals wouldn't know we were in the presence of long-dead musical legends. With that tricky Mist in our eyes, we'd just pretty much worship Nico and his band. When it comes to Nico's future, if he can control his fatal flaw, the sky might just be the limit—quite literally, since that's Zeus' turf, but you know what I mean.

There's nothing more fascinating than the mysteries behind the bad boy, but the best kind of bad boy is the one who's trying not to be bad. The more serious one's fatal flaw, the more challenging the fight against it is, and with the complicated Hades as a father, Nico has a more compelling fight than most. It seems much of Hades' loathing is rooted in pain, not an innate desire to be bad. The mere desire to be bad is too easy of an answer, and Hades and Nico are far more profound than that.

For Nico's sake, let's hope the roots of the family tree, at least from his father's side, don't run too deep. For our sake as readers, though—let's hope they do.

●   ●   ●   ●

Hilary Wagner is the author of the middle grade fantasy series The Nightshade Chronicles (Holiday House). The first book in the series, *Nightshade City*, is a CBC Best Book of 2011 and winner of the Westchester Fiction Award. The third book in the series, *Lords of Trillium*, will be released in 2013. Hilary also writes for National Geographic School Publishing and speaks at schools around the country. She believes Hades' Underworld palace might be a cozy place to write, especially if she could cuddle up with Mrs. O'Leary. Find out more about Hilary and her books at www.nightshadecity.com and www .hilarywagner.blogspot.com.

The Greek Hero—New and Improved!

Hilari Bell

We usually think of heroes as being good people. They're not just handy with swords; they're also first-rate friends and nice to puppies (even hellhounds). But back in Ancient Greece, things were a little different. A lot of its heroes were, well, jerks. Hilari Bell compares those original demigods to Percy and friends and shows just how much our heroes, and our definition of heroism, have changed.

The older generation always claims that the world is getting worse. (Every older generation, from time immemorial. Young people, they say, have no manners. And their music . . . horrible! Things were *much* better when *they* were young.) But despite what the older generation claims, the world gets *better* over time. And nowhere does this trend show more clearly than in the qualities people give their heroes—because heroes embody the virtues the rest of us aspire to.

This means that the virtues heroes possess change from culture to culture and age to age. Think about Superman and Captain America, their quiet heroism and modesty—because in the '40s and '50s modesty and quiet heroism were valued. Then think about what Tony Stark's flamboyant egotism says about the time he came from. The '60s had a lot going for them, but quiet modesty . . . not so much.

As our modern superheroes reveal the values of the society that created them, so do the Ancient Greek heroes. If you read Greek myths, you soon realize that those Ancient Greeks put family loyalty first—anyone in those old myths who harms their family, the gods destroy. Patriotism to your city was also valued, though it's less important than family. But aside from those virtues, a lot of the ancient heroes were pretty much looters, brigands, and bullies. Or, as Dionysus puts it in *The Sea of Monsters*:

> My point is you heroes never change. You accuse us
> gods of being vain. You should take a look at your-
> selves. You take what you want, you use whoever
> you have to, and then you betray everyone around
> you. So excuse me if I have no love for heroes. They
> are a selfish, ungrateful lot. Ask Adriane. Or Medea.
> For that matter, ask Zoë Nightshade.

The gods in Rick Riordan's books haven't changed much since Ancient Greece—they're still capricious, callous, lying, weak-willed bullies. (And yes, they're still vain too.) But the Percy Jackson series is set in our times, with a new set of heroes who grew up with modern values. And whether or not Dionysus admits it, heroes have improved a lot, as taking a look at some of the older heroes will show!

Let's start with Percy's namesake, the original Perseus.

Both Percy and Perseus encounter the Gray Sisters, or Graceae, three old women who have only one eye and one tooth between them. But Perseus went looking for them, stole their eye and tooth, and threatened to leave them blind and starving unless they led him to the Hesperides. And he didn't even try to ask them for the information first—he hid and watched them till he saw his chance, and then snatched their eye and tooth before they even knew he was there. Straight to extortion for Perseus.

Percy Jackson doesn't start out wanting anything from the sisters except a taxi ride to Camp Half-Blood. It's the old women who reveal that they know where he's supposed to go. And Percy doesn't steal the eye from them either—they're struggling for it, and it falls into his lap. He does threaten to throw the eye into the traffic if they don't tell him where he needs to go—not much better than his namesake, in some ways. But not giving them back their eye, as they drive faster and faster through busy roads, risks Percy's life as much as it does theirs. Perseus never risked himself when he dealt with the Graceae.

When Perseus went hunting for Medusa, in the original myth, he had a good reason to start with—he was trying to save his mother from being forced to marry a king she didn't like. The king demanded Medusa's head as ransom for Perseus' mother, and, well, her appearance did turn people to stone. But in the myth, Medusa didn't go out hunting for victims—in fact, she and her sisters moved to an isolated cave to *avoid* killing people! There were a lot of statues of stone warriors outside her cave, but it's pretty clear that all those warriors went there to kill her. In that ancient time, if you left Medusa alone, she wouldn't bother you.

Perseus went after her anyway. He flew to her cave and slaughtered Medusa in her sleep. And I have to admit that if you're going to kill someone, this is the practical way to go about it . . . but it's not exactly heroic.

Percy Jackson doesn't start on any of his quests intending to kill anyone—not even Kronos. He goes to Aunty Em's Garden Gnome Emporium not because he's hunting monsters but because Medusa lures him and his friends in. There's plenty of evidence that she's killed *a lot* of innocent people over the years who were no threat to her. And it's only because she's trying to kill all of them that Percy is forced to slay her.

Although killing Medusa wasn't his greatest moment, the ancient Perseus isn't entirely a villain. He rescued Andromeda on his way home—a good deed by anybody's standards. But when Andromeda's fiancée tried to claim her hand, Perseus turned not only him but all his innocent soldiers into stone. And when he finally got back to the evil king with Medusa's head, Perseus not only turned the king to stone—which might have been justified— he also turned all the king's family and followers into stone too. Granted, the king had thrown Perseus' mother into a dungeon or made her a slave, depending on which version of the myth you read. But none of those myths say the king's followers did anything worse than "mocking" Perseus.

I believe I mentioned that the gods haven't changed? They probably intended for modern Percy to use Medusa's head as a weapon . . . but modern heroes are no one's pawn. Percy ships the head back to the gods, where it will do no harm to innocent mortals. And if the gods think that's "impertinent," he doesn't care.

As Ancient Greek heroes go, Perseus wasn't the worst. Hercules was probably the most violent of the ancient heroes, but that was mostly because Hercules had too much muscle for his own good— along with *serious* anger management issues. As a child, he killed one of his tutors; later, he started a war by maiming representatives from another city when they dissed his hometown.

It's not like Percy Jackson never loses his temper. I don't think there's any moment in the series when Percy is more angry than he is at Nico when Nico betrays Percy and hands him over to Hades in

The Last Olympian. If he'd had the chance, Percy might have emulated Hercules and taken a swing at Nico then. But even at the height of his fury, Percy refuses to endanger Mrs. O'Leary by telling her to attack Nico. And when Hades is cruel to his son . . .

> Next to me, Nico knelt. I wished I had my sword so I could cut his stupid head off. Unfortunately, Riptide was still out in the fields somewhere.
>
> "Father," he said. "I have done as you asked."
>
> "Took you long enough," Hades grumbled. "Your sister would have done a better job."
>
> Nico lowered his head. If I hadn't been so mad at the little creep, I might have felt sorry for him.

Percy is angry enough to want to kill . . . but at the same time, he sees Nico's pain. He may be too angry to admit it, but he feels sorry for him. And when he does get a chance to kill Nico . . .

> I lunged out blindly. Before I was fully awake, I had Nico pinned to the floor of the cell with the edge of my sword at his throat.
>
> "Want . . . to . . . rescue," he choked out.
>
> Anger woke me up fast. "Oh, yeah? And why should I trust you?"
>
> "No . . . choice?" he gagged.
>
> I wished he hadn't said something logical like that. I let him go.

Percy can certainly get angry, but unlike Hercules, he controls his actions. As he tells Zoë Nightshade in *The Titan's Curse*: "I'm not Hercules."

The qualities that make someone a hero do vary from culture to culture, but it's not like those Ancient Greek heroes didn't know better! We know this because there are several heroes who *weren't* brigands and bullies.

Look at Jason, who was probably the best of the ancient heroes. He started out with a worthy goal: to get back the throne from King Pelias, who murdered his family. And he didn't even plan to kill Pelias; he was going to win the throne by doing heroic deeds— mostly by fetching back the Golden Fleece, something Percy steals from the Cyclops Polyphemus in *The Sea of Monsters*.

When Jason went after it, the Golden Fleece was owned by a human king instead of a Cyclops. But instead of just waltzing in and stealing the fleece, Jason went to the king and asked for it. The king gave him tasks to let him earn the fleece—and for once, none of those tasks involved committing crimes! No one ever said that the king's daughter, Medea, couldn't help Jason.

Unlike Jason, Percy actually steals the fleece—but Polyphemus is trying to kill Percy and all his allies. (Not to mention that he'd kidnapped Grover.)

In fact, the only horrible thing Jason did was to fall in love with a homicidal psychopath. As Medea and Jason sailed away with the fleece, Medea chopped up her brother and threw him overboard to stop their father's pursuit. I think this should at least have given Jason pause. Made him stop and think a bit before he went and married this woman. But no, he kept his promise and married her on the voyage home. And when King Pelias refused to give up his throne in exchange for the fleece, Medea tricked his own daughters into poisoning him—which should have made a sensible man start thinking about divorce. But no, Jason stayed married to Medea for ten more years before he finally "put her aside" to marry a hot young princess. He really shouldn't have been surprised when Medea murdered the princess, and all of her own and Jason's sons, and then fled.

Speaking of relationships, Percy Jackson treats his girlfriends better than those ancient heroes did, too. Annabeth isn't even his girlfriend, officially, when he meets poor Calypso in *The Battle of the Labyrinth*. And when he has to leave, he cares about Calypso's heartbreak: "'I would never do anything to hurt you,' I said. 'But my friends need me. I know how to help them now. I have to get back.'"

Because Percy is the only one who knows how to navigate the Labyrinth, he does have to return. But he acknowledges Calypso's feelings, his own, and the cruelty of the Fates.

> As I sailed into the lake, I realized the Fates really were cruel. They sent Calypso someone she couldn't help but love. But it worked both ways. For the rest of my life I would be thinking about her. She would always be my biggest *what if?*

Jason dumped the woman who helped him without a backward glance. (Though in Jason's case, it's not so much callous ingratitude. It's more, "What took you so long?") So did Theseus; he dumped Adriane after she'd betrayed her father to help him kill the Minotaur. And when you consider how much value those old Greeks placed on family, that was a particularly rotten thing to do.

Let's look at one more of those old heroes—Odysseus. I don't have much of a problem with Odysseus' actions during the Trojan War; it's in the land of the Cyclopes, with Polyphemus, where Odysseus started behaving badly. As home invaders, Odysseus and his men put Goldilocks to shame, breaking into Polyphemus' cave and eating all his supplies. When Polyphemus came home and found them cleaning out his larder, he was understandably upset—though I have to admit, eating two of Odysseus' men was a bit of an over-reaction. On the other hand, blinding the homeowner you'd been robbing was pretty unfair. And that "my name is Noman" bit was pure snark.

After Percy gets into Polyphemus' cave in *The Sea of Monsters* using the same hanging-onto-the-sheep trick Odysseus and his men

used to get out, they have to fight Polyphemus for their freedom . . .
and, with Tyson's help, Percy wins.

> Polyphemus was sprawled on his back, dazed and
> groaning, and I was standing above him, the tip of
> my sword hovering over his eye . . .
>
> "Please, noooo!" the Cyclops moaned, pitifully
> staring up at me. His nose was bleeding. A tear
> welled in the corner of his half-blind eye. "M-m-my
> sheepies need me. Only trying to protect my sheep!"
>
> He began to sob.
>
> I had won. All I had to do was stab—one quick
> strike.
>
> "Kill him," Clarisse yelled. "What are you waiting
> for?"
>
> The Cyclops sounded so heartbroken, just like . . .
> like Tyson.
>
> "He's a Cyclops," Grover warned. "Don't trust
> him."
>
> I knew he was right. I knew Annabeth would
> have said the same thing.
>
> But Polyphemus sobbed . . . and for the first time it
> sank in that he was a son of Poseidon, too. Like Tyson.
> Like me. How could I just kill him in cold blood?
>
> "We only want the fleece," I told the monster.
> "Will you agree to let us take it?"

Where Odysseus maimed without mercy, Percy tries to spare his
enemy—even though he knows Polyphemus can't be trusted.

There's no place in the stories of their youth where it talks about
the old heroes befriending or scorning anyone, but I have a hard
time seeing any of them making friends with a big, ugly homeless kid who was scared of everything. Percy befriends Tyson, and

stands up for him against the bullies at his mortal school. And Tyson returns the favor by defeating Polyphemus.

Odysseus doesn't behave much better, from a modern point of view, in his dealings with Circe. Because his own men had been turned into pigs, I have no problem with him forcing Circe to turn them back into men. But Odysseus never even thought about trying to rescue Circe's other victims. He left them all in their animal forms. In fact, Odysseus and his men stayed with Circe for a year after that, and they all became good buddies. I wonder how often they ate pork?

When Annabeth dumps the vitamins into the cage to save Percy in *The Sea of Monsters*, it may not be a conscious attempt to save Circe's other victims. But it does. And it seems like simple justice that those victims turn out to be some of the worst pirates of the ages and are more than capable of distracting Circe while Percy and Annabeth make their escape.

There are many places in the series where you can directly compare Percy's reaction to a challenge with that of the ancient heroes, but there are other places—like when he befriends Tyson—where there can't be a direct comparison, because Percy does things that most ancient heroes simply wouldn't do. In the bad old days, a monster was a monster and an enemy was an enemy. The idea of understanding or compassion for them never entered an ancient hero's head.

Percy Jackson sees monsters and enemies as people, who might deserve compassion even though they're on the other side. And it's not just Tyson and Polyphemus or Nico. Even though he's had bad experiences with hellhounds, Percy is willing to give Mrs. O'Leary the benefit of the doubt. He lets Nereus think he was close to winning their fight, to spare his feelings. Percy feels understanding, if not liking, for Clarisse—and he gives her the credit for the quest they ended up undertaking together, which is something no ancient hero ever did.

Percy offers a monster, Eurytion, career advice that will make his life better, and that turns him from enemy to ally. In fact, over the course of the series, Percy develops quite a knack for keeping people from becoming enemies—so he doesn't *have* to kill them. Percy tries not to kill whenever he can avoid it, even if it imperils his mission. When he and Beckendorf are trying to blow up the *Princess Androm-eda*, Percy spares the twelve-year-old hero who serves Kronos. And later, when Kronos' cavalry is attacking the Empire State Building, he disintegrates their horses instead of killing the riders. Once they've dismounted, he tries to wound instead of slay.

Percy also shows compassion for lesser creatures. I don't remem-ber any ancient hero worrying about his horse getting tired, as Percy does with Blackjack, or his dog getting hurt, as Percy does with Mrs. O'Leary. And I don't remember the ancient heroes wanting simply to help creatures like the Hippocampi. Or standing up for an innocent, like Bessie.

The concept that other people might have rights is a modern one—but look how Percy deals with the naiad in *The Battle of the Labyrinth*, even though he has a stable full of manure to dispose of:

> ". . . you're not going to ruin my river."
>
> She looked like she was ready for a fight. Her fists were balled, but I thought I heard a little quiver in her voice. Suddenly I realized that despite her angry attitude, she was afraid of me. She probably thought I was going to fight her for control of her river, and she was worried she would lose.
>
> The thought made me feel sad. I felt like a bully, a son of Poseidon, throwing his weight around.
>
> I sat down on a tree stump. "Okay, you win."

The Ancient Greek's definition of a hero was mostly about physi-cal strength and courage. Poseidon puts it pretty well in *The Titan's*

Curse when he's talking to Percy about his having taken Atlas' burden to free Artemis, so she can defeat the Titan: "Only a hero, someone with great strength, a true heart, and great courage would do such a thing. No one in Kronos' army would dare try to bear that weight, even upon pain of death."

But as Percy points out, by that definition, *Luke* is a hero! And so are all the other Ancient Greek heroes, with their violence, bragging, theft, and betrayals.

Athena, a goddess of the old school where enemies are enemies, tells Percy: "Your fatal flaw is personal loyalty, Percy. You do not know when it is time to cut your losses. To save a friend you would sacrifice the world. In a hero of the prophecy, that is very, very dangerous" (*The Titan's Curse*). But ultimately, it's Percy's ability to see Luke clearly, to understand, to trust, to *befriend* his enemy, that lets them all defeat Kronos. And I don't think any of the ancient heroes would have been able to do that.

Those ancient heroes weren't villains. They lived according to the rules and values of their society and times. And Chiron is probably right when he says in *The Sea of Monsters*, "Heroes embody that struggle. You fight the battles humanity must win, every generation, in order to stay human."

But modern heroes fight those battles with more grace, dignity, and compassion than the ancient heroes ever could—which says good things about the state of humanity in *our* time.

● ● ● ●

Hilari Bell writes science fiction and fantasy for kids and teens, including the Farsala Trilogy, the Knight & Rogue series, and the Raven Duet. Her favorite hobby is "decadent" camping, because that's the only time she gets to do enough reading—though when it comes to reading, there's no such thing as enough. Her Web site is www.hilaribell.com.

Not Even the Gods Are Perfect

Disability as the Mark of a Hero

Elizabeth E. Wein

No one is untouchable. Superman has his Kryptonite. Achilles has his heel. Percy Jackson has ADHD and dyslexia. Why make a hero with learning disabilities? As Elizabeth E. Wein points out, there is a long literary tradition of imperfect heroes. Sometimes our weaknesses are actually marks of greatness.

Maybe your brain is hardwired to read Ancient Greek. Maybe you're struggling to read this book. You wish it was in an alphabet you recognized. You wish the words didn't look like brain-teaser puzzles.

It's far more likely that if you're reading this, reading comes easy to you. Maybe you look at the kid in your class with learning disabilities and you think, "Must be stupid—he can barely read."

Maybe you feel sorry for him. Maybe you're interested in finding out more, but you're shy and embarrassed and avoid making eye contact or talking to him, because he's so different and you don't know what it's like and you don't want to say the wrong thing.

Maybe you make fun of him. Maybe behind his back, so he won't know.

Maybe to his face. "Hey, here's a hard one for you, what's two plus two?" It's got nothing to do with reading, but it'll still hurt. It's an easy insult.

I wish I had made it up for this essay. Unfortunately, someone said it last week to a dyslexic sixth grader at our local school.

Now, what if that kid had the power to sweep you off your feet with a wave of water, dump you upside down in a fountain, and leave you drenched, without ever touching you?

It's less likely you'd do any more easy teasing.

And maybe more likely you'd want that kid on your side.

— — —

In the Percy Jackson books, the half-blood children of the Olympian gods are almost always marked by learning difficulties, specifically dyslexia and ADHD (Attention-Deficit/Hyperactivity Disorder). It turns out that these distinctive problems, which society normally labels disabilities, are really signs of talents closely related to the hero's divine origins. If you're a half-blood, these apparent defects can also do two very useful things: They can reveal your true nature in the world of the gods and disguise it in the world of mortal men.

Percy's dyslexia is caused by the fact that his "mind is hardwired for Ancient Greek" (*The Lightning Thief*). His ADHD, which makes it hard for him to pay attention in school, is due to his ability to see and sense more than normal mortals. When the disorder seems to make him impulsive and edgy, this is his "battlefield reflexes" kicking in. Most other half-bloods suffer from the exact same combination of disabilities, which is why, in their guardian roles as keepers, satyrs always look for dyslexia when they're scouting out potential Camp Half-Blood campers.

Why should Riordan choose to use disability in this way, as the mark of potential heroism—indeed, as the mark of the children of gods?

In fact, this idea is not a new one. There are several conventions at work here. The first is a literary convention called a *motif*. A motif is a theme or image in a story that has been used many times in fiction or myth. The helpful, speaking horse, like Blackjack the Pegasus, is a traditional motif—it even has a catalogue number in an oversized book called the *Motif-Index of Folk-Literature* by folktale scholar Stith Thompson. The idea of the hero having a disability is not listed in the *Motif-Index*, but it is still a recognized literary theme. It's also a historical one: Great people with disabilities have always inspired awe and admiration. Think of Admiral Horatio Nelson, the great English naval hero who was missing an arm; or President Franklin D. Roosevelt, confined to a wheelchair because of polio; or Ludwig van Beethoven, composing even after he had gone deaf.

The other convention Riordan draws on here is the idea that disability can be the gift of the gods. This belief goes a long way back into history. The Ancient Greeks called epilepsy "the sacred disease" because the sufferer was thought to be possessed by demons or gods; some truly impressive people throughout history were epileptic, including Alexander the Great, Julius Caesar, St. Paul, Joan of Arc, and Napoleon Bonaparte.

So the idea of disability as both the mark of a hero and an *advantage* to the hero is a solid tradition which Riordan uses in his own way to create the world of Percy Jackson.

Can You Read Ancient Greek? Dyslexia as the Gift of the Gods

Dyslexia is a language-based learning disability. It can occur at all levels of intelligence, and it is not a sight disorder, though it does affect the way people see words. It's a *decoding* problem. It most commonly causes trouble with reading; the word comes from the Greek words *dys*, meaning "impaired," and *lexis*, meaning "word." Dyslexia doesn't affect a person's ability to learn to talk, but it can produce trouble (and often does) with spelling, writing, and pronouncing words. It can hamper one's ability to read and process math problems too, although it doesn't adversely affect the ability to *do* math (that's called dyscalculia).

There are many different ways dyslexia can impair learning, and these usually overlap. Percy's dyslexia seems to be strictly visual, but of course we don't see him writing a lot of notes or trying to spell when he's in the middle of fighting off monsters. He doesn't seem to have any trouble filling out the delivery slip when he sends Medusa's head to Olympus in *The Lightning Thief*, at least. That his dyslexia is chiefly visual makes sense, though, because it's supposed to be connected to Percy's natural ability to read in another alphabet. For Percy and the other half-bloods, it's incredibly ironic that a reading disability with a Greek name is actually a sign of an innate ability to *read* Ancient Greek.

Because dyslexia makes learning to read so difficult, it can cause you social problems too, when other people don't fully understand or recognize your disorder. It can frustrate teachers and make them impatient; it can turn you into a target for other kids. If you've got other difficulties like ADHD, even though they may not be related to dyslexia, the separate problems can aggravate one another and you'll end up labeled as a Big Problem—like Percy—and maybe you'll get kicked out of six schools in as many years.

In the Percy Jackson books, the reader is given far more reminders of the difficulties dyslexia causes than about its supposed benefits. When Percy reads a sign or notice, there's often something wonky about it. "AUNTY EM'S GARDEN GNOME EMPORIUM" becomes the utterly unintelligible "ATNYU MES GDERAN GOMEN MEPROIUM" in *The Lightning Thief*; "CLOSED FOR PIRATE EVENT" really means "CLOSED FOR PRIVATE EVENT" in *The Titan's Curse*. But Percy can usually figure out pretty quickly from the context what written words mean, and sometimes he gets lucky, like when the "Kindness International" truck in *The Lightning Thief* has white letters reverse-printed on black, which makes it easier for him to read. Like many dyslexic kids, he's learned to compensate.

Of course, Percy isn't the only half-blood who is dyslexic: They all are. Annabeth Chase, daughter of Athena, has it; when she and Percy are on a quest together, they more or less have to guess at the signs along the way or else get someone like Grover Underwood, the satyr, to interpret. But that doesn't stop Annabeth from reading all the time. It's what she's doing when Percy first gets to know her (of course, she's reading in Greek, because it's easier). Nor does her dyslexia stop her from persistently pursuing her long-term plan to become an architect. And the message Riordan gives us is that it shouldn't stop anyone else either.

The Gods Are Impulsive: Attention-Deficit/Hyperactivity Disorder (ADHD)

Anyone, even mortals, can have Attention-Deficit/Hyperactivity Disorder (ADHD) along with dyslexia, but they are not related. ADHD is a neurological developmental disorder which affects 5 percent of the world's population. "Neurological" means related to the nervous system, and a "developmental disorder" indicates a lag—not necessarily permanent—in normal rate of growth. There are three main characteristics of ADHD: inattention, hyperactivity, and impulsivity. These characteristics combine to create each individual's own personal disorder: You can be mostly inattentive, mostly hyperactive and impulsive, or a combination of all three.

Percy, it seems, is meant to have the combined form of all three, but I think he's more convincing as the "mostly hyperactive and impulsive" type. He doesn't show many signs of being inattentive. His grasp of Greek myth is impressive, even if he sometimes complains that he can't remember it all. He remembers just about everything Annabeth ever says to him and keeps track of complicated plot twists and a huge number of friends and enemies with a whole lot more facility than I can as a reader. There is one place near the end of *The Titan's Curse* where Grover has to remind Percy of Apollo's instruction to find Nereus, the "old man of the sea," but as a reader I'd forgotten about it too, so plot-wise the timing was just about right for it to come up again.

The National Institute of Mental Health's Web site points out that "Not everyone who is overly hyperactive, inattentive, or impulsive has ADHD," and I do wonder about the Yancy Academy counselor who appears to have made the diagnosis. An ADHD diagnosis tracks consistent behavior over a six-month period and rates the problem level against a scale. The Yancy counselor must have been pretty hot off the mark to come up with an accurate diagnosis, given that Percy was only at the Yancy Academy from September to the following June. At the rate of six schools in six years, it doesn't really sound like Percy has had enough stability for anyone to have assessed his difficulties accurately.

But he is a good fighter (though modest about it). Impulsive behavior and hyperactivity in a half-blood are supposed to be connected to fighting ability, and a thing called "battle fury" or "battle ardor" is another commonly recognized motif in literature; it's even a historical phenomenon. ADHD seems like a clever way to explain the crazy impulsivity that can seize an enraged warrior. People who are fighting under the spell of "battle ardor" seem to go crazy and kill everything within reach without any thought for their own safety. Literary heroes who go into a "battle ardor" include Gawain, one of King Arthur's noblest knights (it gets him in trouble sometimes, because he is so uncontrollable when he's fighting); Cuchullain, the hero of Irish legend; and the Ancient Greek hero Achilles. Historically, Gaulish warriors were known and admired by the Romans for their battle frenzy. The English word "berserk" comes from "berserkers," the name of the Norse warriors who fought in a trance of rage.

At Camp Half-Blood, this fighting frenzy is most likely to turn up in the Ares Cabin. The sons and daughters of Ares are beyond impulsive (I suspect that the ADHD feature of a half-blood may vary in its intensity depending on which god your father or mother is). Not all warfare is dependent on pure fighting ability, and in fact there are two warrior gods in Greek mythology: Ares, the impulsive one, and Athena, patron of soldiers. But Athena doesn't fight impulsively. She's the goddess of *wisdom*. Thus, George Washington turns out to be a child of Athena: a general, a wise and careful planner, as well as a soldier. Ares wreaks mayhem; Athena inspires thought.

Historically, it is thought that battle rage was more likely to have been induced with mind-altering drugs than to be the result of a neurological disorder. In actual fact, anyone who is on medication— for ADHD or any other reason—would not be admitted to the U.S. military services. You can just imagine how useful a disorder that makes you inattentive and impulsive would be if you were holed up in a bunker in the Iraqi desert. But fortunately for Percy his battles are mostly with monsters, who tend to be extra stupid and have heads that turn you to stone or grow back in duplicate when you cut them off. A touch of impulsiveness in battle can't hurt against enemies like that.

Lame and Slow: Other Disabilities in the Percy Jackson Series

Dyslexia, a learning disability, and ADHD, a developmental disorder, are the two specific impairments that mark half-bloods, but other disabilities, particularly physical ones, can also hide remarkable characteristics in the world of the Greek gods. Chiron the centaur disguises his horse's body in a wheelchair. He appears to be a man who has lost the use of his legs, but in fact he is a powerful, beautiful being. Grover hides his satyr feet in oversized shoes which impede his ability to walk, and his hidden goat legs make him seem to have abnormal musculature development. Both Chiron and Grover endure the difficulties of these strange arrangements because by doing so they are *enabled*: They can inhabit two worlds, the world of gods and the world of men. The ability to pass between the two worlds makes the difficulty—the *disability*—worthwhile.

As with all Riordan's themes, this one of disability going hand-in-hand with giftedness has precedents in Greek myth itself. Hephaestus the blacksmith, Aphrodite's husband, is crippled and deformed, but he is a master craftsman who forged Apollo's chariot, Eros' bow and arrows, and many other heroes' weapons. Another disabled yet gifted Greek character, who did not turn up in the Percy Jackson series, is Tiresias, who is blinded by Athena because he has the bad luck of accidentally seeing her naked in her bath. When his mother pleads for him, Athena takes pity on Tiresias and compensates him for his blindness by giving him the gift of prophecy.

Tyson, Percy's Cyclops half-brother, is a character who appears to suffer from some kind of unidentified learning disability (compounded by his apparent homelessness)—he's extremely slow, and it shows in his speech, which isn't much more advanced than baby talk. His toddler's way of talking is strange coming out of his overgrown and lumbering body. Like the half-bloods' dyslexia, these defects are keys to his true nature. Tyson talks like a baby because he *is* a baby (although the full-grown Cyclops Polyphemus doesn't seem a whole lot more advanced than Tyson in intelligence, and Tyson has got it all over Polyphemus in emotional maturity).

Tyson is slow to learn the things we mortals value in school because they're fairly irrelevant to his inheritance or his existence.

What he *is* good at he excels at—communing with mythical sea beasts and making incredibly complex mechanical instruments, such as the watch that converts into a shield he makes for Percy. Tyson is the ultimate techie and a natural; his talent is innate. So his apparent defects, like those of the other half-bloods, both reveal his true nature and disguise it.

"Troubled Kid" with a Learning Disability = Probably a Demigod. Make Sense?

One of the keen readers in our house, who, like Percy in *The Lightning Thief,* is now in sixth grade, wolfed the first three books down in about ten days and is rereading them as I write—we have to fight over who gets the books because she wants to read them and I need to refer to them. But when I asked her what she thought of Percy's disabilities, she actually *denied* their existence.

"Percy's not dyslexic!"

She speaks with some experience of dyslexia, having a close friend who is severely affected by it. "Yes he is," I said. "It says so, here in the first chapter. And here later there's an example of him having trouble reading."

"Oh—" she said, looking at the proof. "Well, he doesn't seem dyslexic to me; he's very talkative." Her friend only talks to a small group of familiar people who can be trusted not to tease or ask embarrassing questions—or leave preschool picture books lying on her desk as a "joke."

Isabel Brittain has come up with a list of what she calls "The Six Pitfalls of Disability Fiction." Her research is based on several previous studies and is presented in a paper for the journal of the Society for Disability Studies based in Columbus, Ohio. (The word "pitfalls" is misleadingly negative, as here it simply refers to recurring themes in fiction featuring disabled characters; Brittain calls them pitfalls because they just don't offer the reader a particularly realistic option for living with or thinking about disability.) Very briefly, Brittain's "six pitfalls" are that the disabled character may be shown as 1) otherworldly, 2) extraordinary, and 3) only as a sidekick and not as a fully developed character (Tyson falls into this category); 4) the disability may not be accurately researched or described in detail; and 5) the impaired character may be alienated or isolated. The final "pitfall" is that 6) the author may not be able to see how the character can live successfully with his or her disability in the future.

Riordan's portrayal of Percy's own disabilities makes use of at least half of these, and all six turn up in his portrayal of disabilities in general, at least in the sense that characters like Grover will never be physically comfortable in the mortal world where they are required to spend so much of their lives. There is also a sense that few half-blood children will be able to function as happy, successful humans outside the boundaries of Camp Half-Blood.

I reckon our sixth grade reader didn't notice Percy's disabilities because Riordan doesn't always portray them consistently. In *The Lightning Thief* there are, if anything, *more* written signs, notices, and newspaper stories that Percy reads without any apparent effort than there are confusing ones. Percy is very quick to spot that Mr. D has misspelled his name on the form letter requesting he register to stay at Camp Half-Blood year-round.

Throughout these books Riordan does not so much *demonstrate* Percy's ADHD as he constantly *reminds* the reader with little narrative elbow nudges. Every time Percy does something without thinking it through, he attributes it to his ADHD through narration: "What I did next was so impulsive and dangerous I should have been named ADHD poster child of the year," or, "The ADHD part of me wondered, off task, whether the rest of [Hades'] clothes were made the same way" (*The Lightning Thief*). On most of these occasions, though, I didn't see why ADHD had to come into it. When Percy snatches the steering wheel of the bus from the driver in the Lincoln Tunnel, it's to avoid battling the three Furies, who are wielding fiery whips in the back. Given the alternative, running the bus out of control doesn't seem so crazy.

Without these occasional reminders, these verbal nudges, you might not notice Percy's lack of fixed attention. He seems extremely adaptable and capable—more so than most people, regardless of learning disabilities (though perhaps this is only true because we mostly see him thinking and acting in his predestined context as a hero). As far as getting kicked out of school is concerned, we don't have much of his past history, but the reality of the present is that it's never actually his fault. He is framed by monsters, teachers, classmates, and the press, time and again. Great bloody, godly battles during school museum trips and basketball games are not the way to lead a quiet life.

But whether or not the disabilities Riordan describes in the Percy Jackson series are convincing in their realism, his use of disability is an excellent device. Disability is both a mark of heroism and a way to disguise your heroism, but more importantly, it is a constant reminder that everyone is flawed in some way, even the bravest, strongest, and smartest people. In *The Titan's Curse*, the goddess Athena reminds Percy that every hero has a fatal flaw; Annabeth's is pride, and Percy's is personal loyalty.

Hang on—personal loyalty surely isn't a *flaw*! Fidelity is a virtue! But if it's used against our hero, in the wrong context, Percy refusing to sacrifice a loved one to save the world could mean the downfall of Olympus. Even a virtue can become a weapon for wrongdoing if it is manipulated by an evil force, just as a disability can serve as a mark of heroism and strength. And maybe, just maybe, that twist in point of view will make the reader think twice about those people who can't walk or read. Why not try to find out what heroic characteristics their disabilities disguise?

For further information on the disabilities discussed in this essay, check out these Web sites:

International Dyslexia Association
http://www.interdys.org

National Institute of Mental Health
http://www.nimh.nih.gov

For NIMH's information on ADHD, see
http://www.nimh.nih.gov/health/publications/adhd/complete-publi
cation.shtml

Epilepsy Foundation
http://www.epilepsyfoundation.org

● ● ● ●

Disability is a subject that is close to home for Elizabeth Wein. Her brother, who was severely brain-damaged in a car accident at the age of eleven, is permanently confined to a wheelchair. The hero of her young adult novels *The Lion Hunter* and *The Empty Kingdom* is missing an arm.

Elizabeth's most recent novel for young people is *Code Name Verity*, a thriller about an abiding friendship formed by two young women, one a transport pilot and the other a spy, during World War II. *Code Name Verity* was named a Boston Globe Horn Book Award Honor Book for 2012.

Elizabeth has a Ph.D. in folklore from the University of Pennsylvania. She and her husband share a passion for maps and fly small planes. They live in Scotland with their two children.

Elizabeth's Web site is www.elizabethwein.com.

Frozen Eyeballs

Oracles and Prophecies

Kathi Appelt

If you could consult the Oracle, would you? Knowing the future can be a very scary business, and divining your fate is not the same as controlling it. Just ask Oedipus. Kathi Appelt looks into her crystal ball to explain the prophecies of the Percy Jackson series and offer advice for those considering a visit to the Big House attic.

L et's talk about me. I'm five. My younger sister is four and possibly the most annoying creature ever born. She wants to do everything I do, including use the very same crayon that I am using at the same time that I am using it. Cardinal red. It's my favorite color, and I need it for the rainbow picture that I am making for my grandmother. All the other colors are filled in. I need the cardinal red crayon. All I want, all I ever wanted, is for this pesky little sister to go away and leave me alone, so I give her the "evil eye," which means that I'm crossing my eyes at her and sticking out my tongue. My mother is standing at the kitchen sink, her back to us, so how can she possibly know I am doing this mean thing to my little sister? But out of her mouth I hear this prophecy: "Your eyeballs are going to freeze like that."

Suddenly all I can think about are eyeballs, the one that must be hidden somewhere in the back of my mother's head and my own two that are about to turn into ice cubes. It's enough to make me quickly slip my tongue back into my mouth and uncross my eyeballs. Even though my tongue wasn't mentioned, can it be far behind?

Beyond that, which is more threatening? The prospect of my cold eyes forever seeing only the fuzzy ridge of my own nose, or my mother who seems to see all and know all? Here was a person in authority, who held some power over me and who also seemed to know what I was up to without even watching. My mother, ruler of the household, goddess of the realm. At that moment the future was certain. Frozen eyeballs were going to happen, unless. . . .

My omnipotent mother was just as convincing to five-year-old me as the Oracle at Delphi must have been to all those pilgrims who sought answers from her while she sat on her odd tripod perch, breathing in the wafting fumes from the fissure below her and delivering her pithy prophecies. Like the Oracle, there was no real explaining where or how my mother got her information. She just did.

In fact, every culture has had and continues to have its various prophets, seers, and soothsayers, from the ridiculous to the divine, and there are those who gaze into crystal balls and read tea leaves. There are those in the same league as John the Baptist, who foresaw the coming of Jesus in the New Testament. In fact, many of the most significant prophets were alike in that they foretold the coming of a divine figure.

Rick Riordan's Percy Jackson is hardly divine, but at the very core of his series is an overarching prophecy, one that we don't fully learn of until well into the third book, *The Titan's Curse*: "Years ago, Chiron had had a prophecy about the next child of the Big Three—Zeus, Poseidon, or Hades—who turned sixteen. Supposedly, that kid would make a decision that would save or destroy the gods forever." In *The Last Olympian* we finally get to hear the Great Prophecy in its entirety:

> *A Half-Blood of the eldest gods,*
> *Shall reach sixteen against all odds*
> *And see the world in endless sleep*
> *The hero's soul, cursed blade shall reap*
> *A single choice shall end his days*
> *Olympus to preserve or raze*

That, my friends, is one whopper of a prophecy! And while we certainly can't assume that Chiron is equal to John the Baptist, or that Percy, the half-human son of Poseidon, is divine, the larger prophecy does bespeak the coming of an important person, one who is born of both a human and one of the three major gods—Zeus, Poseidon, or Hades.

We eventually discover that, although Percy is the Half-Blood the prophecy speaks of, the hero is actually Luke. Percy doesn't know this until the moment before the prophecy comes true, however, and so it affects his actions in very important ways in the battles for Olympus and New York.

The Great Prophecy plays an integral role in the series, driving the gods' behavior as well as Percy's, but it's not the only prophecy that does so. Riordan uses prophecies to important effect throughout all five books, in both large ways and small.

— — —

Who among us isn't fascinated by the prospect of learning the future? Think about Genesis: Eve's transgressions were as much a result of temptation and curiosity as they were of inquiry. There is now and always has been an entire underground industry in fortunetellers, palmists, and psychics.

But there's a dark side to learning the future too. The future can be terrifying. And even when it isn't, having the knowledge of it is still a serious, often scary thing. Once you know something, you can't go back to not knowing it.

It's appropriate, I think, that a tree marks the border to Camp Half-Blood. Just as the tree in the Garden of Eden signifies knowledge, so too does the tree that stands at the entry to the camp. Once Percy discovers who he is and what is at stake for him, that knowledge seals the deal: He can't return to his prior innocence any more than Adam and Eve could return to theirs.

As well, it's no coincidence that the mist that surrounds the Oracle in the attic of Camp Half-Blood takes on the shape of a snake, "a huge green serpent . . . slithering back into the mouth of the mummy." The ancient Oracle at Delphi was known as Pythia, named for the great dragon that was slain by Apollo. The giver of prophecies—whether it's the mummy in the attic or the serpent in Eden—often dons the guise of something to be feared. Even in our popular games, the notion of prophesying takes on an ominous look. The triangular form of the popular Ouija board disc, after all, is the same shape as the head of a poisonous snake. (It's worth noting that it's also a "tripod," similar to the three-legged bench upon which the Oracle sat.)

The message is clear: Knowledge, especially the kind that comes from prophecy, is a very serious thing indeed.

— — —

The most obvious prophecies in the Percy Jackson series come from that musty old Oracle in the attic. She is one of the original Oracles who survived in freeze-dried condition, thanks to a curse from Hades that prevents the spirit of Delphi from passing to new maidens—at least until *The Last Olympian*, when Hades lifts the curse and Rachel takes over as the new Oracle. In Ancient Greece, the Oracle of Delphi was a kind of "channeler," typically a young priestess who received her information from the gods and then passed it on to a priest, who in turn shared it with whomever had come looking for an answer. According to Heraclitus (circa 500 B.C.E.), as related by Ron Leadbetter in the *Encyclopedia Mythica*, "the oracle neither concealed nor revealed the truth, but only hinted at it." In effect, the offering from the oracle was usually a puzzle, something to be unraveled and figured out by the recipient.

The original Oracle as portrayed in Riordan's stories is anything but a beautiful priestess perched on a tall stool. Instead, she appears as a mummified corpse and is described as looking like "death warmed over." She's not a reassuring motherly type, but her very age endows her with authority. And she lives right in the center of Camp Half-Blood.

Interestingly, according to legend, the site of the Oracle was known as the *omphalos*, which literally means "navel of the world." Camp Half-Blood, with its ability to protect its young, serves as a kind of central secure womb, at least for a little while. It's as safe as my mother's kitchen, but the connection to the outside world and what awaits the campers beyond its boundaries, the Oracle, resides in their midst. Right there in the attic. She's the belly button.

It's this figure that Riordan taps in order to offer up a prophecy for each of the four quests that Percy and his friends must embark upon. And in all four cases, Percy and his fellow sojourners use the different elements of her prophecies to guide their quests.

The first of the Oracle's prophecies is given to Percy himself. The quest is his to take:

> *You shall go west and face the god who has turned . . .*
> *You shall find what was stolen, and see it safely returned . . .*
> *You shall be betrayed by one who calls you friend . . .*
> *And you shall fail to save what matters most, in the end . . .*

Sure enough, the prophecy comes true, albeit in some surprising ways, particularly the part about being betrayed by "one who calls you friend." And this is an integral part of prophecies—they're not always what they seem on the surface. Back in the old days, the most famous of the ancient Oracles' prophecies was given to King Croesus of Lydia. When he asked her whether he should go to battle against the Persians, the Oracle replied that if he did, a great empire would be destroyed. So, Croesus invaded. The thing is, it wasn't the Persians who were brought down. Rather, it was his own empire that was lost.

Percy's prophecy is filled with riddles too. The first two lines are easy enough to figure out. But the last two are more obtuse. On the surface they seem obvious, but by the end of the tale, it's clear that they weren't exactly what they seemed. The last line especially appears to be the most ominous of all. What matters most to Percy—his mother—is also the one thing he can least afford to lose. By the end, we see that Percy does fail to save her; instead she saves herself by mysteriously dispatching her brutish husband Gabe. "She'd reported him missing to the police, but she had a funny feeling they would never find him."

As it turns out, it's not the fourth line that holds the most peril, it's the third. Until the very last chapter, Percy believes that it's Ares who is the traitor—the blustery god did pose as a friend, after all, and then turns his back. But in the very last chapter, the true traitor shows his face: Luke.

The very fact that Luke is a fellow camper and not one of the gods or even someone from Percy's human village makes him all the more menacing. And this holds true throughout the series, with Luke's power becoming increasingly stronger and more vengeful.

The quests in *The Sea of Monsters*, *The Titan's Curse*, and *The Battle of the Labyrinth* are also dictated by the Oracle's prophecies. But even though Percy is a hero in these three adventures, the Oracle's prophecies are not given directly to him.

The second prophecy in *The Sea of Monsters* is actually delivered to Clarisse, the daughter of Ares. Clarisse, like her father, is enigmatic, half-friend and half-nemesis. She's strong, brave, and competitive—the perfect qualities for a warrior, not necessarily perfect qualities for a friend. But unlike the prophecy given to Percy in book one, Riordan doesn't share this prophecy until close to the very end of book two. Only Clarisse knows what the Oracle has told her:

> *You shall sail the iron ship with warriors of bone,*
> *You shall find what you seek and make it your own,*
> *But despair for your life entombed within stone,*
> *And fail without friends, to fly home alone.*

By the time Percy discovers the prophecy, the first three lines have come to pass, so it's easy enough to figure out what they mean. It takes some brainwork to figure out what the last line means: Clarisse will have to take the Golden Fleece home by herself on a plane to Camp Half-Blood. The group does not have enough money to purchase more than one ticket.

As it did in *The Lightning Thief*, the Oracle's prophecy in *The Sea of Monsters* comes true. Just because this particular prophecy is not directly given to Percy, his combined experiences with the two prophecies allow him to trust in their efficacy. In this way, Riordan has infused the use of prophecy with reliability. While the meaning of the prophecy may not be clear at the outset, Percy can believe with some certainty that if he continues on his quest, the truth of the Oracle's messages will undoubtedly reveal itself.

By the time Percy gets to book three, the notion of prophecies and the power inherent in them are stronger than ever, which is both reassuring and terrifying. Here in our human world, for example, it's easy enough to shrug off our daily horoscope. But if that same horoscope continued to hold true day after day for an extended length of time, eventually we'd begin to trust that whatever it offered was going to occur, good or bad. It's no different with Percy. As each adventure unfolds, Percy can see that the words of the Oracle can be depended upon, even though he may not know what they mean at first. Ominous or not, confusing and strange, he can rely upon them to become true.

In *The Titan's Curse*, the Oracle again gives the prophecy to someone other than Percy. This time it's granted to Zoë Nightshade, Artemis' most faithful huntress.

> *Five shall go west to the goddess in chains,*
> *One shall be lost in the land without rain,*
> *The bane of Olympus shows the trail,*
> *Campers and Hunters combined prevail,*
> *The Titan's curse must one withstand,*
> *And one shall perish by a parent's hand.*

The prophecy in *The Battle of the Labyrinth* is given to Annabeth and is more enigmatic, a reflection of both Percy and Annabeth's increasing maturity and ability to analyze the Oracle's elusive meanings.

> *You shall delve in the darkness of the endless maze,*
> *The dead, the traitor, and the lost one raise,*
> *You shall rise or fall by the ghost king's hand,*
> *The child of Athena's final stand.*
> *Destroy with a hero's final breath . . .*

But just as Clarisse withholds her prophecy in the *Sea of Monsters* until the very end, Annabeth maintains claim to the final line of her prophecy until the close of *The Battle of the Labyrinth*. Her reasons are more personal than Clarisse's, however, and Percy, in his widening awareness of the power of prophecy, realizes that Annabeth's reasons for the secret are much deeper and more intimate than anything he has previously encountered. When Annabeth reveals that final line ". . . *And lose a love to worse than death*," its impact is powerful because it also reveals the depth of Annabeth's twin feelings of love for and sorrow over Luke. All at once, Percy realizes that Annabeth has gone to a place where he cannot go with her, a place filled with her own memories—memories that have nothing to do with Percy and their blossoming relationship. And at that moment Percy's own sense of loss is equally profound.

Just as the second prophecy is direr than the first, and the third is more menacing than the second, the fourth trumps everything to date, not because the physical challenges are greater, but because the emotional risks are so much higher. By the time the fourth prophecy rolls around, Percy takes it at face value. He knows with certainty that they will unfold, just as the Oracle predicted.

In all four of these tales, the Oracle is true. The prophecies that she espouses come to pass. And with each one, Percy comes to understand something more about prophecies themselves. In the first, he discovers their riddle-like nature; their face value is often misleading, hiding something underneath that same face. Because of this, Percy learns something about making assumptions. It isn't Ares who betrays him; it's Luke.

Nevertheless, by the time the second and third prophecies come to pass, the main thing that Percy has learned is that they are reliable. Which means he knows in *The Last Olympian* that the prophecy about a child of the Big Three will come true too, though he doesn't know exactly how, or to whom.

— — —

But the Oracle's prophecies are not the only ones guiding Percy Jackson. Recall that in *The Sea of Monsters*, *The Titan's Curse*, and *The Battle of the Labyrinth*, the prophecies pronounced by the mummy in the attic are not given to Percy; in some cases, he doesn't even learn the prophecy until that book's quest is over. Nevertheless, prophecy was at play. Only in these tales, the prophecies guiding Percy showed up in the form of dreams.

But are dreams the same as prophecies, one might ask?

I think that Riordan's Apollo would agree with me: "'If it weren't for dreams,' he said, 'I wouldn't know half the things I know about the future. They're better than Olympus tabloids.'"

In fact, *The Sea of Monsters* begins with Percy's nightmare, one that features his best friend, Grover, draped in a wedding dress and desperately trying to escape from . . . something.

Later, Riordan expands the dream so that it becomes a form of communication between Percy and Grover. He calls it "an empathy link." Does it seem far-fetched to presume that two friends like Percy and Grover could talk to each other through dreams? Perhaps. But one of the hallmarks of any good work of fantasy is the author's ability to ground that work in reality. For a fictional work to *work*, we must be able to empathize with the main character, regardless of how nonhuman that character may be. Any of us who have had a dream of warning can believe that the same could happen for Percy too. Who among us hasn't had that "naked on the school bus" dream? Or the one about showing up in our classroom for a test and not being able to remember a single answer?

We can take these as warnings: Get up in time to get dressed and study harder for the test. Percy's dreams of Grover are a warning too: Get there or risk losing your friend forever.

The prophecy given by the Oracle in book two is Clarisse's, and it is integral to her journey to recover the Golden Fleece. Percy is along to help, but his own quest is to rescue Grover. Percy's prophecy comes from his dream, not from the Oracle.

In *The Titan's Curse*, Percy's prophecy appears in the form of dream again. And again, the dream is about a close friend: Annabeth. But unlike the comfortable relationship that Percy shares with Grover, his feelings about Annabeth are more complex. In this case, he did not share the "empathy link" that allowed for communication.

No, this time it is left to Percy to figure out the meaning on his own, which he does.

And it's a good thing, too, because in *The Battle of the Labyrinth* Percy's dreams are not about his friends, but rather those he will soon encounter, namely Daedalus and his arch-enemy King Minos. Percy's dreams in this volume serve as both prophecy and history lesson, preparing Percy for the meeting we know is coming, but they also allow him to use his increasing maturity to see the complexities that underlie human (and godly) actions and decisions.

His dreams in book five further prepare Percy for the battles he must fight. He gets glimpses of the Titans planning their attacks on Olympus, and he also sees Rachel and clues to her impending role as the Oracle. Percy then uses the insights his dreams give into what other people are planning to guide his actions in the war and lead the half-bloods to victory.

I think it's important to note, though, that Percy's dreams are no less puzzling than the prophecies issued by the Oracle. He still has to learn to interpret them. They do, however, provide a more personal look at the way that Percy operates, especially in terms of his relationships with his fellow campers and friends. The dreams are his alone.

Boiled down, Riordan uses the Oracle for public prophecy and Percy's dreams for private prophecy. The former serves to illuminate the larger, global challenges for Percy and his friends. The latter allow us to get to know Percy at a more intimate level. A person who dreams of his friends, who recognizes through those dreams that his companions need him, is a person we can pull for.

— — —

But where does Percy's loyalty come from? To answer that, we have to go back to our early glimpses of Percy. And we find out through them that Percy has, in a way, always been a child of prophecy.

When we first meet him, we discover that by the age of twelve, he's already been put on probation for misbehavior resulting from his inability to sit still, a product of his ADHD, and he's about to be faced with the challenge of a field trip. Nothing has ever gone right on the field trips that Percy has taken before. Why should it be any different this time? The headmaster has threatened him "with death by in-school suspension if anything bad, embarrassing, or even mildly entertaining happened on this trip." It doesn't take an oracle to see the writing on the wall. Percy is bound for trouble. No ifs, ands, or buts. Because he himself believes that he can't avoid trouble, or that trouble can't avoid him, he is the perpetual victim of what is known as a "self-fulfilling prophecy." He sees himself as the source of trouble and so becomes the source of trouble. Trouble seems to single him out.

His inability to concentrate and control his reactions have made it pretty much impossible for him to function in a regular school, and so he's enrolled in Yancy Academy, "the school for loser freaks who couldn't make it elsewhere." And now he's about to be kicked out of there as well. His success—or lack of it—in school is a foregone conclusion. A prophecy.

Not only that, but Percy is also the child of an undereducated (albeit smart) mom, who is married to a brutish oaf of a man, Percy's stepfather. Percy's real dad is completely missing in action. Even without Percy's issues with ADHD, his situation on the home front doesn't give him much hope. All things considered, it would be easy enough to plant a big fat prophecy on Percy's head, one that does not include things like college, law school, or a great job with benefits.

As it turns out, prophecies based on circumstances such as Percy's are fairly easy to make, and all of them include the word *struggle*. From the very first page, even though there are no Olympians present, we can peg Percy. We know his type. We've met him in our classrooms, our neighborhoods, our soccer teams. Even without special powers, we can predict what is in store for someone like him:

a lot of hard work. So it makes sense that even before Percy Jackson discovers that he isn't completely human, he's seen the future.

So what Rick Riordan has ingeniously done with Percy in his *human* world is to prepare him for the obstacles he'll have to face as a half-blood. The challenges Riordan placed upon Percy in his younger life—his learning disabilities and his family situation—served their purpose of "toughening up Percy" for the obstacles, namely the monsters, he will be forced to face in each and every quest.

The very first prophecy the Oracle delivers to Percy is presented by his human familiars. As Percy recounts it:

> Gabe turned toward me and spoke in the rasping voice of the Oracle: *You shall go west, and face the god who has turned.*
>
> His buddy on the right looked up and said in the same voice: *You shall find what was stolen, and see it safely returned.*
>
> The guy on the left threw in two poker chips, then said: *You shall be betrayed by one who calls you friend.*
>
> Finally, Eddie, our building super, delivered the worst line of all: *And you shall fail to save what matters most, in the end.*

The attentive reader will realize the Oracle is no dummy. Percy will face many monsters in his quests, but at this particular moment, the worst among them are the sneering men around the poker table, lead by his stepfather, Gabe Ugliano.

Annabeth confirms this when she reminds Percy, "The real world is where the monsters are. That's where you learn whether you're any good or not."

— — —

Percy's genetics are at play here as well. Embedded in everyone's genes lay a million small and large prophecies. Our penchant for music or science or art, the hand we write with, the way we laugh or cough, the turn of our feet when we walk—so much is decided before we're even born. Suffice it to say that our parentage is the first factor in determining who we are, how we are, and the ways our lives turn out. (That said, I never inherited my mother's third eye.)

The ADHD that caused him so many difficulties in the world of humans, it turns out, is a necessary trait for heroes. As Annabeth explains, "And the ADHD—you're impulsive, can't sit still in the classroom. That's your battlefield reflexes. In a real fight, they'd keep you alive. As for the attention problems, that's because you see too much, Percy, not too little. Your senses are better than a regular mortal's."

Thanks to his father's DNA, Percy gains power from submersion in bodies of water. He can breathe underwater and communicate with the creatures of the sea. The water is his friend. From the moment he emerged from his mother's watery womb, every cell in his body had a prophecy: born to swim! And throughout the stories, Percy uses these abilities time after time to rescue himself and his friends.

— — —

And speaking of friendship, this leads us to what may be the largest prophecy of all when it comes to Percy Jackson: his fatal flaw.

One of the trademarks of the stories given to us by the Greeks is the notion that every hero has a tragic shortcoming. Perhaps the most famous can be found in Homer's *The Iliad*. Achilles, the hero of Troy, was the strongest, bravest warrior of all; his body could withstand any assault. He believed that he was immutable, unassailable, immortal. His only weak point on his entire body was his heel, and who knew anything about that? Sure enough, someone shot an arrow right into his heel, and that was the end of Achilles—and

Troy too. From that day forward, our "Achilles' heel" has been syn-onymous with our weak point, and nothing supposedly makes us weaker than a fatal flaw.

Like Achilles, Percy needs invulnerability for the battle for Olym-pus in *The Last Olympian*, and so he swims in the Styx. The only catch is that, to survive while bathing, he has to imagine one thing that will tie him to the living—an anchor point that will connect him to his humanity. Percy thinks of Annabeth and chooses the spot opposite his navel as his weak point.

But it's another kind of "fatal flaw" I'm thinking of, which Percy also learns about earlier in the series, from Annabeth, when she tells him about her own: *hubris*. "Hubris means deadly pride, Percy," she tells him. "Thinking you can do things better than anyone else . . . even the gods."

But why is a fatal flaw so instrumental in a good story? The Greeks inherently knew that the most important rule that a writer can never break is to "worry the reader." Once we become aware of the hero's weakest point, then we are constantly worried about whether or not the hero's enemies will discover that weakness and use it against him or her. Once we know what the hero's soft spot is, we can foresee—we can prophesize—that the hero will have to reckon with it. The flaw itself is where the potential for failure lies. You could say that a hero without a flaw is *less than human*. And therein lies the rub. Percy is *more* than human. He's a half-god.

Unlike the Oracle's pronouncements and Percy's dreams, which to a great extent come from external sources, his fatal flaw is inter-nal, something that comes from within. Annabeth's mother, Athena, pegs it when she and Percy have their talk on Mount Olympus: "Your fatal flaw is personal loyalty, Percy. You do not know when it is time to cut your losses. To save a friend, you would sacrifice the world. In a hero of the prophecy, that is very, very dangerous."

As Percy grows in both years and experience, he also makes more and more of his own choices. And at the end of the day, isn't choice a distinctly human quality? Despite the circumstances of our births, our families, our economics, and our traits, humans continue to overcome even the direst of situations. Percy is part god, but he is also part human, and his loyalty to his friends is, at its heart, human.

Percy's personal loyalty turns out to be his greatest asset, though Riordan appropriately keeps us worried throughout the series about whether it will turn out to be his greatest flaw instead.

It's also true that one's greatest weakness can also be one's greatest strength. I'm not sure who said that, but in the meantime we can take heart in the fact that though we are all, like Percy, to a certain extent children of prophecies—whether those prophecies have to do with our genes, our circumstances, or whatever gods and goddesses (a.k.a. parents, grandparents, teachers, and—okay—higher powers too) look over us—we can make our own choices. We can face down those monsters in our paths. We can take whatever the fates have handed us and use it for the greater good. No matter what our bloodlines, we can still be heroes.

We can thaw out our eyeballs and focus on something besides our noses.

• • • •

Kathi Appelt is the *New York Times* bestselling author of more than 40 books for children and young adults. Her novel *The Underneath* was a finalist for the National Book Award and a Newbery Honor book and won the PEN USA award. Her newest novel, *The True Blue Scouts of Sugar Man Swamp*, will be available in July 2013. Her newest picture book, *Mogie: The Heart of the House*, illustrated by Marc Rosenthal, will be released in 2014. You can learn more at her Web site: www.kathiappelt.com.

The Language of the Heart

Sophie Masson

> What makes a monster scary? The worst are the ones we believe in—the ones we know are real. Oh, you can say they are only stories. But deep in our hearts, we recognize them. They stir primal fears. They make us remember our earliest nightmares. Sophie Masson takes us on a tour of the subconscious, which holds more monsters than Tartarus ever could.

When I was about nine, I had a horrible recurring dream. It was pretty simple. All I could see was a face, which at first was small and in the distance, but then got bigger and bigger till it seemed to be right on top of me. I couldn't see a body, just a face. It was a monstrous face: very, very pale, almost gray-skinned, with big staring eyes so pale they seemed almost white and a thin pale mouth that opened on to long yellow teeth tipped with red. Straggly hair that seemed to move and lift in an invisible wind blew out around the face as if there was an electric current running through it, or as if each hair was alive and wriggling horribly. I always woke up just as the mouth opened wide on a terrible scream, and I'd be screaming myself, yelling my head off.

My mother would come running, but I was so scared of that dream I could not bring myself to tell her about it. I also thought that maybe if I said nothing, then I would forget it and it would go away. So I dreamed it three times before my mother finally persuaded me to tell her about it. As I described it to her, stammering over the words, I was suddenly filled with a frightening thought. What if telling her, describing the face in words, made it leave my dreams—but come into my real life? Or what if now I could never forget it, because I had fixed it in words, made it almost solid? I thought that my mother would tell me not to be scared, that it was just a nightmare, that it wasn't real. That she wouldn't understand what it was like to stand there paralyzed in your dream as the monster came closer and closer and you couldn't move or scream or do anything at all. Except wake up. And then lie there worrying about whether, if you closed your eyes, it would come back.

But instead she said to me, "Did that monster remind you of anything?"

"Anything real?" I whispered.

"Real, or in a story."

I thought about it. I loved stories. I loved reading them and listening to them and trying to write my own. I'd learned to read very early and spent as much time with books and stories as I could. My favorites were fairy tales, legends, and myths. The monstrous face could be like the wicked witch out of *Hansel and Gretel*. It could belong to some monster King Arthur killed. But as I thought about it, I knew what the monster actually reminded me of. Earlier that year I'd been given a marvelous book called *Tales of the Greek Heroes*, written by Roger Lancelyn Green. It was about Hercules and Theseus and Jason and Perseus and others, about the adventures they had and the monsters they had to fight. I loved that book and read it several times. I especially loved the story of Perseus, with its high glamour, its rich fairy tale atmosphere: the prophecy about Perseus' birth, his mother, Danae, locked up in a stone tower by her father, Zeus coming to Danae in a shower of gold, the mother and child being cast away to die in the sea, the rescue by a fisherman, Perseus growing to manhood, the magic gifts the gods and nymphs had given him, the way he rescued Andromeda from the dragon, and. . . .

Now I said to my mother, "I think it was like Medusa." Medusa, the most terrible of the monstrous Gorgon sisters, with her snake hair and her cold, cold glance that would turn you to stone on the spot if you looked into her face. "But she was real, in my dream."

"Of course," said my mother. "She was real to Perseus too. What did he do to defeat her?"

"He used the shield Athena gave him like a mirror, so he wouldn't look into her eyes and be turned to stone. Then he cut off her head," I said promptly.

"Then," said my mother, smiling, "you know what to do. Don't be afraid. Just think about lifting up your shield and swinging your sword, and it won't be able to hurt you anymore."

Am I supposed to dream that? I thought, puzzled. *Am I meant to try to make myself dream about defeating Medusa? I don't think I can do that. I've tried to stop myself dreaming about that Medusa face, and I can't. I've tried to make myself have nice dreams every night, and I can't.* But if I said I couldn't do it, perhaps my mother would take away my beloved *Tales of the Greek Heroes* because it was too frightening for me, giving me nightmares. I didn't want that to happen. So I said, "Okay," as if I knew what to do.

That night I lay in bed worrying about it. I tried to will the picture into my head, of me holding up a shield as a mirror toward that horrible face so that I would dream about it when I fell asleep. But it felt silly. I wasn't Perseus. I didn't have a shield. Or a cap of invisibility or magic shoes, much as I wanted them. What would you use, if you weren't an Ancient Greek hero and a horrible face haunted your dreaming self and turned you to stone, unable to move or run away? Then I thought, *Of course! You'd just use an ordinary mirror.* Not the big one in the bathroom that you couldn't get off the wall, but a little one, like the one my mother had on her dressing table. I imagined myself picking up that mirror and holding it up in front of me. It didn't seem like much of a weapon against a monster, but it would have to do. And what would happen next? Perseus had chopped off the Gorgon's head with the strongest weapon in the world, the adamantine sickle the god Hermes had given him. I didn't have anything remotely like that. My little brother had a toy sword, but a very small one, made of plastic. Not the kind of thing you'd want to use against an ancient monster. Not at all the sort you . . .

Worrying about it, I fell asleep. I didn't even know I had, until the next morning when I woke up. The face hadn't appeared in my dreams. It wasn't because I'd forgotten what I dreamt. I never forgot it if the face appeared. But it hadn't come. I hadn't had to fight it, with or without the hand mirror and the toy sword. It just hadn't come.

It didn't come the next night, or the next, or the next. In fact, it never came back. Not once. I never forgot that dream, but I never had it again. I had other bad dreams from time to time and lots of good ones. (I still have lots and lots of very vivid dreams, some of which have gone into my books and inspired some of my stories.) I kept reading *Tales of the Greek Heroes* and every time I had a little shiver over the Medusa story. It was a kind of mixed shiver: fear mixed with pleasure. Pleasure because I thought I'd done what Perseus had—I'd defeated the monster. I did not have to literally fight it, with actual weapons. But I know that it isn't coincidence it went away when my mother's questions helped me to *recognize* the monster and think what I could do to fight it. And because of that, the dream-monster lost the power to frighten me. It vanished, never to return.

But the memory of that dream still lived at the back of my mind. Many years later, when I'd become a writer myself, I watched a really creepy old movie called *The Medusa Touch* (starring Richard Burton) about a guy who had Gorgon eyes—he could stop people's hearts and make planes fall out of the sky like stones. And I remembered my Medusa dream. Though she'd never come back in a dream, I could still see that face so clearly. I'd grown up by then, and life had taught me that there were all kinds of monsters in the world, not just dream ones or ones in stories. I knew that some of them were not terrifying at first sight like Medusa but might wear normal or even friendly faces. I had come to understand that monsters lived in the human heart and sometimes caused people to do the most dread-ful and horrific things, things that would turn you to stone if you thought about them for too long. Monsters might also be pitiable, like Medusa, turned to a ravening, hate-filled, vengeful monster by the gods because she dared to love who she must not love. The word we often use in our society for a monstrous personality is "psycho-path," a word that comes from two Greek words: *psyche*, meaning the soul, and *pathos*, meaning suffering, or sickness. So "psychopath" literally means "soul-sick," as good a description of a monster-like Medusa as any other.

I had come to realize that the amazing world of fairy tales and legends and myths, where gods, heroes, monsters, fairies, and witches share an enchanted and scary space, isn't just about adven-ture and magic. It isn't even just about monsters and defeating them. It has a lot to tell us about the world of flesh and blood and suffering and glory in which we live, and about our inner selves as human beings. These stories speak in the language of the human heart: a language of courage and terror, joy and pain. A language that is still intensely relevant. The old stories tell us about ourselves—what we are capable of, what we might do. We might not know exactly what it is like to be an ancient hero defeating a superhuman monster, but we all know what it's like to be afraid of evil and danger. And we hope that, faced with a challenge, we too will take our courage in both hands and go out to do what must be done. We might not exactly be princesses shut up in towers by tyrannical fathers, like Perseus' mother, Danae, was. But we all know young people who are in similar sorts of situations in the everyday world. The old stories open us up to possibilities all around us.

Myself, I write fantasy, that inheritor of myth and fairy tale, because I feel it also speaks with the language of the heart. It possesses the realism of the soul, a heightened sort of realism where a hero can defeat a fearsome monster with his or her wits and courage, not just a mirror and a sword, and can learn all kinds of things about himself or herself while doing so.

— — —

I'd never forgotten *Tales of the Greek Heroes*. I'd often wondered why no one, including myself, ever used the Greek myths as background for fantasy novels. We used Celtic myths—a lot—Norse myths, Arthurian myths, and others, occasionally, including Russian, Chinese, and Japanese. But not Greek myths. And yet Greek myth is at the foundation of so many of our stories in Western Civilization.

I thought about it for a time. If I was going to write something based on Greek myth, I thought, I'd pick the story of Perseus. It had the right elements to make it really interesting. Perseus wasn't a guy of extraordinary strength, like Hercules. He didn't go seeking riches, like Jason, and betray the woman who had helped him. Besides, he was the one who had defeated Medusa, so I always felt close to him, because of that dream. And as well as Hermes' sickle and Athena's shield, he had those cool magic gifts from the nymphs: the Shoes of Swiftness and the Cap of Darkness, which made him invisible. You could write a really great updated version of his adventures, I thought. I'd get around to it maybe, one day, I mused vaguely. Very vaguely. There was always another book to write, another story that clamored to be written down first.

So imagine the mixture of delight and dismay when I first picked up Rick Riordan's *The Lightning Thief*! But sweet delight very quickly won over sour old dismay. After a very short cross writer's moment in which I thought, *Blast, this guy's pipped me to the post about an updated Perseus*, I got thoroughly immersed in the story and the way in which the writer had been able to stay true to a good deal of the savage power and magic of the Greek original whilst also being able to totally bring the story into the twenty-first century. Riordan makes us really believe in Percy and his fellow half-bloods, troubled offspring of gods and humans, a world where Olympus is on the 600th floor of the Empire State Building; war god Ares is a red-eyed biker; the Delphic Oracle is a mummified Woodstock hippie; the three Fates knit the socks of Death; a Hitlerian Hades is defended by a (literal) skeleton army; and the Mother of Monsters, Echidna, chucks a hissy fit (most amusing to us Australian readers) about the "ridiculous animal" that bears her name in the Antipodes. A world in which a burger-cooking, seemingly sweet, veiled old lady with a warehouse full of fearful-faced stone statues is the dread Medusa. Dread, and deadly dangerous, but also pitiable. . . .

What wonderful invention! What fun! What a glorious mixture of humor and adventure and gruesomeness and tragedy we rollick through in these pages as Percy and Annabeth and all their friends battle it out with scores of monstrous enemies in order to try to forestall a war between gods that would shake the world to its core! Reading it, I felt plunged back into the world of my younger self, into a landscape where everything was possible, where gods and monsters lived in all kinds of guises and might not only pop up in your dreams but in your life too. But I also read it very much as an adult, as writer as well as reader, and was enormously impressed. For the series is more than just a very skillful, clever, imaginative use of the Greek myths in a wonderful fantasy adventure for kids. It delves into characters' motivations, into their backstories, their troubles and traumas—especially Percy's, as he tries to be brave and make sense of a world that has suddenly become bewildering and dangerous. It also successfully transposes the setting for the gods, heroes, and monsters. As the wheelchair-bound centaur tutor Chiron tells Percy, in chapter five of *The Lightning Thief*:

> The gods move with the heart of the West . . . What you call Western civilization. Do you think it's just an abstract concept? No, it's a living force. A living consciousness that has burned bright for thousands of years. The gods are part of it. You might even say they are the source of it, or at least they are tied so tightly to it that they couldn't possibly fade, not unless all of Western civilization were obliterated.

He tells Percy that this living force started in Greece and went on to Rome, Germany, Spain, France, England—wherever the flame of Western Civilization was strongest, there were the gods. And now they are in Percy's own country, the United States: "Like it or not— and believe me, people weren't very fond of Rome, either—America is now the heart of the flame. It is the great power of the West. And so Olympus is here. And we are here."

A year or two before I read *The Lightning Thief*, I read Neil Gaiman's extraordinary (adult) novel, *American Gods*, in which Gaiman imagines a United States in which all the gods brought over with the diverse multitudes of immigrants are struggling to keep their niches and make a home in a place that has half-forgotten them. They scratch out livings in corners and run various scams and get involved in all sorts of things, especially the trickster gods like the Norse god Loki and the West African god Anansi. It's an amazing and vivid and detailed picture of a weird and yet totally believable world, and in many ways reading Percy Jackson reminded me of reading it. The Percy Jackson series is aimed at kids rather than adults, but it is just as strong and interesting and unusual and does not underestimate its readership. And it is just as focused on the concept that it is America that is the new home of the gods, America where important, world-changing battles are fought.

For the non-American reader, that can be a bit of a challenge—and yet Riordan carries it off with such *élan* and pizzazz that you can't be offended. You really enter into the whole idea. You feel as though he has completely, and successfully, re-imagined modern America as the new home of myth, where just about anything can happen. In *A Midsummer Night's Dream*, by William Shakespeare, one of the characters (incidentally named after one of the Greek heroes, Theseus) talks of "airy nothings"—the enchanted world of myths and legends and fairy tales—being "given a local habitation and a name." And that's what Riordan has done, with his daring re-imagining of the myth in an American setting: He has given them a new "local habitation and a name." And it works. In fact, it works very well.

But of course, if Percy's country is the new home of the gods, then it follows it's also the new haunt of the monsters. And like the gods, they've come back in forms different from how they presented themselves in the original myths. They, too, have moved with the times. They come at Percy from all angles, and he has to learn to fight them, as well as try to accept he's actually a demigod. And through his fights with the monsters, as well as his confrontation with Hades, he also learns another important thing: that death may not be the ultimate enemy. No, the thing that crouches in the pit, waiting to rise again—the ironically timeless evil that is the Titan Kronos, devouring old Father Time himself—is the ultimate enemy. And he's the scariest and most powerful monster of them all, for he devours everything.

I think about the child that I was, waking from that Medusa nightmare, and I know she would have *loved* this book. She would have carried it around with her, like she carried around the *Tales of the Greek Heroes*. She would have wished herself into Percy's world (probably in Annabeth's shoes, she sounds cool!) and tried out all the wonderful magic gifts and gadgets in her imagination. She would have wondered about whether she was brave enough to fight the monsters. Maybe she would even have dreamed of Medusa as a scary old lady in a warehouse full of statues.

For with this series Rick Riordan has accomplished something extraordinary: He has become a keeper of the flame, writing in the language of the heart. He is fighting Father Time and the wiping-out of memory and tradition by keeping alive the deepest old stories and traditions of the West, in a form that has renewed their glorious and grand and exciting and scary appeal for a whole new generation.

• • • •

Born in Indonesia of French parents and brought up in Australia and France, Sophie Masson is the author of more than 50 novels for children, young adults, and adults, published in Australia and many other countries. Her historical novel *The Hunt for Ned Kelly* (Scholastic Australia) won the Patricia Wrightson Prize for Children's Literature in the 2011 New South Wales' Premier Literary Awards. Her most recent novels are the YA fairy-tale novel, *Moonlight and Ashes* (Random House Australia, 2012), the fantasy adventure for younger readers, *The Boggle Hunters* (Scholastic Australia, 2012), and the historical novel for older readers, *Ned Kelly's Secret* (Scholastic 2012). She has also written under the name of Isabelle Merlin. Her novel *The Madman of Venice* was published in the United States in 2010 by Random House. She writes regularly on literary matters at the Writer Unboxed blog, www.writerunboxed.com. Her Web site is at www .sophiemasson.org.

A Glossary of Ancient Greek Myth

Nigel Rodgers

A

Achilles

Son of Peleus and the nymph Thetis. When Achilles was born, Thetis held him by one foot and dipped him into the River Styx in an attempt to make him immortal. She almost succeeded; only the spot on his heel by which she held him while he was immersed remained a point of vulnerability—the origin of the term Achilles' heel, meaning a weakness. Aside from the spot on his heel, Achilles was completely invincible. When he was older, his father sent him to be raised by Chiron the Centaur on Mount Pelion. He is most famous for being a great warrior and for his participation in the Trojan War. He fought on the side of the Greeks under their leader, Agamemnon, after his best friend, Patroclus, was killed. He slew Prince Hector in battle before he himself was killed by an arrow Paris, the Trojan prince, shot at his heel. (*See Amazons, Centaurs, Diomedes, Hephaestus, Nereids, Peleus, Trojan War*)

Aegis

A sacred adornment of great importance, normally worn as a medallion or necklace around the chest of a god (or a man worshipped as a god, such as Alexander the Great), or carried on its own in solemn procession. Zeus, king of the gods, first gave an aegis to his daughter Athena, patron goddess of Athens, which made her invulnerable even to his thunderbolts. Fringed with snakes' heads and decorated with images of the Gorgon—the dread creature that turned viewers to stone—the aegis brought victory to whichever side the god wearing it supported.

(See Athena, Perseus)

Aegean Sea

The main sea around Greece, which took its name from Aegeus, king of Athens. When Aegeus' son Theseus, as a young man, sailed off to Crete as part of Athens' tribute to the Minotaur, he promised his father that he would change the color of his ship's sails from the normal black if he had returned safely. Although he did escape alive from Crete, Theseus failed to do so, and Aegeus threw himself, in grief, into the sea—which was thenceforth known by his name.

Aeneas

Son of the goddess Aphrodite and the Trojan prince Anchises, and hero of The Aeneid. Aeneas escaped from Troy as it fell, carrying his aged father. His subsequent wanderings around the Mediterranean led him to Carthage, where he had a passionate affair with Dido, the city's founder and queen, and when his god-given duty called him reluctantly away, Dido in despair committed suicide. Aeneas then visited the Underworld to meet the ghost of his father, who had since died, and hear of his part in Rome's future greatness before sailing on to Latium (now Lazio, central Italy). There Aeneas married Lavinia and founded Lavinium, a city on the coast that was the precursor to Rome. The Romans venerated Aeneas. Julius Caesar claimed to be descended from him, as did Augustus, during whose reign Virgil wrote The Aeneid.

(See Aphrodite, Trojan War)

Aeolus

King of the winds. This disheveled, white-haired and -bearded god lived in isolation on the island of Aeolia, where he kept the winds penned in a cave. He could release the wind at will to cause all kinds of storms, a power he sometimes lent to travelers. Odysseus was one such traveler; in *The Odyssey* Aeolus gave him a bag of wind to help him on his journey home.

Amazons

Female warriors. While real women in Greece were secluded indoors, unable to vote let alone fight, one mythical race rejected male dominance: the Amazons. Their name may come from *Amazona,* meaning "without breasts," for they reputedly cut off their right breasts in order to shoot better, but in Greek art they are always shown with both breasts. The Amazons lived in Pontus (the north coast of modern Turkey) and other remote, legend-misted regions around the Black Sea. Here they formed societies where the women ruled and men either did the domestic work or were excluded altogether. Above all, the Amazons fought, invading many territories and even founding cities such as Ephesus (on the Aegean coast of modern Turkey). Theseus of Athens, who had joined Hercules on one of his adventures, abducted Antiope, an Amazon princess, and took her home to Athens. In revenge the Amazons invaded Greece and were only defeated right outside Athens. During the Trojan War, the Amazon queen, Penthesilea, went to Troy's aid, fighting valiantly until killed by Achilles. Most unusually, Achilles wept at her death. Later, Alexander the Great reputedly loved an Amazon queen whom he encountered in central Asia.
(*See Theseus*)

Andromeda

Mythical princess, the daughter of Cepheus, king of Ethiopia, and Cassiopeia. Andromeda rashly boasted that she was more beautiful than the Nereids, and the angry sea nymphs complained to

Poseidon, the sea god, who sent a flood and monster to ravage the land. To appease the angry god, Andromeda was chained to a rock as a sacrifice to the monster. But Perseus, the hero who had just killed the hideous Medusa, saw Andromeda and fell in love with her. He killed the monster and married Andromeda, and their son (also named Perseus) became the ancestor of the Persians. Along with Cepheus and Cassiopeia, Andromeda and Perseus were later raised to the heavens as constellations.
(*See Perseus*)

Antaeus

Son of Poseidon and Gaia. Antaeus was a giant of great strength so long as he maintained contact with the ground. Once lifted into the air, all his strength vanished. He would challenge passersby to wrestle him; he would kill them and take their skulls to use as building material for a temple to his father. Hercules discovered Antaeus' secret and defeated him in a wrestling match by lifting him into the air.

Aphrodite

Goddess of love and the most beautiful of the Olympian deities. Aphrodite was worshipped in many forms across the Mediterranean; doves were sacred to her and she was often shown attended by Eros, mischievous god of desire. However, Aphrodite had disconcertingly foul origins. The god Kronos, urged on by his mother Gaia, castrated his father Ouranos and threw the severed genitals into the sea. Out of the resulting foam rose Aphrodite, the "foam-born." Blown ashore by Zephyrus, the west wind, she landed at Cyprus, where she was dressed and bejewelled by the Horae, goddesses embodying the four seasons. Now dazzlingly lovely, she caused amorous chaos on Olympus, for every god adored her. Zeus married her off to Hephaestus, the blacksmith god, but it did not prove a marriage made in heaven. Aphrodite soon grew bored with her lame (and ugly) husband and had an affair with Ares, the war god. When Hephaestus realized this, he threw a steel net over the sleeping couple that chained them to their bed. The other gods looked on, laughing. Aphrodite had affairs with other gods such as Hermes and men such as the Trojan prince Anchises (the father of her son Aeneas). Aphrodite's beauty bewitched another Trojan prince, Paris, and when he was called on to judge who was the most beautiful, Athena, Hera, or Aphrodite, Paris chose the love goddess. In return he was gifted with great sex appeal, which won him the heart of Helen, the loveliest woman alive. Unfortunately, Helen was married already—to Menelaus, king of Sparta. By eloping with her, Paris started the Trojan War.

(See Aeneas, Ares, Athena, Eris, Hephaestus, Hera, Jason, Nereids, Ouranos)

Apollo

God of music, poetry, medicine, light, and science, and for many the archetypal Greek deity. Apollo was born with his twin sister Artemis on the island of Delos. His father was Zeus, king of the gods, and his mother was Leto, a Titaness. The baby god was fed nectar and ambrosia rather than milk, giving him the strength he used to kill the serpent Pytho, which had molested his mother. He named the site of his victory Delphi, and it became the seat of his Oracle, the greatest in Greece. Each winter Apollo went far north to the land of the mysterious Hyperboreans in a chariot drawn by white swans and returned with the spring. He was master of the lyre, Greece's main musical instrument, and of the bow. On Mount Parnassus near Delphi he held court, playing his lyre and attended by the Nine Muses. Apollo could be dangerous if crossed. The satyr Marsyas rashly challenged him to a musical contest, and when Apollo won, he had Marsyas flayed alive. He could dispense sickness as well as medicine, sending plagues if angered. But generally Apollo was a beneficent god, honored by humans and the other Olympians. Depicted always as a serenely handsome, beardless young man, Apollo had many, often unhappy, love affairs, most notably with Daphne, a nymph. Apollo pursued her passionately but in vain, for she prayed to her father, the river god Peneus, and he turned her into a laurel tree just as Apollo was about to grasp her. One of his other love affairs was with the princess Coronis. When Apollo discovered she had left him, he shot her with one of his arrows, and repented of his rage too late to save her. Their son Asclepius was saved by the centaur Chiron, however, and grew up to be a divine healer. Apollo also fell in love with Hyacinthus, a Spartan prince, whom he taught to throw the discus. When Hyacinthus was killed by a flying discus, the first hyacinth flower sprang from the ground stained by his blood. Apollo was at times identified with Helios, the sun god, but they were really distinct deities.

(See Artemis, Delphi, Hecate, Helios, Hercules, Hermes, Laurel, Mount Olympus, Nymphs, Oracles, Orpheus, Python, Zeus)

Arachne

Daughter of a Lydian dyer, who rashly challenged the goddess Athena to a weaving contest. The tapestry Arachne wove depicted the scene of Athena's contest with Poseidon with such brilliant realism that the goddess, jealously enraged, destroyed Arachne's works. Athena then turned the weaver herself into a spider, doomed to repeat forever her compulsive weaving. From Arachne's name come the terms *arachnid* and *arachnophobia* (fear of spiders).

Ares

God of war. Irascible and cruel, Ares was disliked both by other gods and by human beings. Although the son of Zeus and Hera, and so part of Olympus' "royal family," Ares was not loved by his parents. Only Aphrodite, bored by her blacksmith husband Hephaestus, loved him, and even then only briefly. More usually, he spent his time haunting the battlefield with his supporters, the lesser gods Deimos (fear) and Phobos (panic), killing at will. But Ares was not invincible, for he lacked intelligence as well as charm. Athena often managed to outwit him and even Hercules, who was a mere demigod, at times defeated him. Ares was worshipped by men only in Thebes, a city noted for its militarism and dullness.

(See Aphrodite, Diomedes, Eris, Hephaestus, Hera)

Ariadne

Daughter of King Minos and Queen Pasiphae of Crete. Ariadne fell in love with Theseus of Athens when he came to Crete as one of the sacrificial victims for the Minotaur, and so she gave Theseus a thread to help him find his way back out of the Labyrinth, the maze in which the Minotaur was held. After Theseus had killed the monster, the couple escaped from Crete together. However, Theseus—for reasons still debated—abandoned Ariadne on the island of Naxos. There she was rescued by the god Dionysus, who married her. Ariadne, in origin, was probably a Minoan goddess connected with the Great Mother.

(See Dionysus, Minotaur, Theseus)

Artemis

Daughter of Zeus and Leto and twin sister of Apollo. In one avatar she was a chaste huntress, slim, athletic, and short-skirted (Greek women usually wore long robes). Protector of young wild animals, she roamed the woods with a bow and was attended by nymph-huntresses sworn to celibacy like her. (These twenty shadowy nymphs, immortal but with no real power, were nameless apart from Callisto. Callisto, daughter of Lycaon, was seduced by Zeus while he was disguised as the goddess herself. When Artemis discovered this, she shot the unfortunate Callisto.) When the hunter Actaeon came upon Artemis bathing naked, she angrily transformed him into a stag and he was devoured by his own hounds. Often shown with the crescent moon, Artemis was sometimes associated with Selene, the Titan moon goddess, and even with Hecate, the fearsome queen of darkness. As Selene, she fell in love with the beautiful youth Endymion, who was put by Zeus into an immortal sleep to preserve his beauty. Artemis was also worshipped as the Great Goddess, an older

multi-breasted fertility goddess venerated in a huge temple at Ephesus in Asia Minor. (This is the temple of Diana that St. Paul later
attacked; Diana is the Latin form of Artemis.)
(See Apollo, Hecate, Nymphs, Zeus)

Athena

Goddess of wisdom. Athena was born fully formed from the forehead of Zeus. Unlike most other gods, Athena showed almost no
interest in sex and was often called *Parthenos* (virgin). Still, she was
affronted when Paris, the Trojan prince, chose Aphrodite over her
in the Judgment of Paris. In the Trojan War that followed, Athena
favored the Greeks, especially the wily hero Odysseus, whom she
helped on his long wanderings as he made his way home. Athena
was the patron goddess of Athens, especially of its craftsmen, and
her temple the Parthenon, the most perfect temple in the Greek
world, still rises above the city. She had won Athens' devotion with
the olive tree, which the Athenians preferred to Poseidon's gift of a
freshwater spring. Another of her titles was *Promachos*, defender or
champion, for she was a fighter goddess, shown always with spear,
helmet, and shield. She sported the hideous snake-haired aegis of
Medusa, who was killed by Athena's protégé Perseus, and was frequently pictured with a snake coiling beside her and an owl, a symbol of wisdom, on her shoulder.
*(See Aegis, Aphrodite, Arachne, Ares, Daedalus, Diomedes, Eris, Furies,
Hercules, Medusa, Nemean Lion, Pegasus, Perdix, Perseus, Poseidon, Zeus)*

Atlas

Titan punished by Zeus for joining the "revolt of the Titans." Atlas
was forced to stand forever at the world's western edge and support
the weight of the heavens on his shoulders. Only once did he have
a break: Hercules, on his mission to fetch the golden apples of the
Hesperides, agreed to take on his great burden if Atlas fetched the
apples. This done, Hercules promptly gave the crushing weight of

the heavens back. Atlas was the father of Calypso and of the Pleiades, who became a constellation. He gave his name to the Atlas Mountains in Morocco, the westernmost area the Greeks knew. *(See Calypso, Hesperides, Titans)*

B

Briares

Son of Uranus and Gaea, called Briares by the gods and Aegaeon by men. Briares, one of the three Hekatonkheires, had fifty heads and 100 arms like his brothers. According to Homer, he successfully aided Zeus, with his brothers, against the Titans. Another version has him as one of the attackers on Olympus, who when defeated was buried under Mount Etna. Yet another version depicts Briares as Poseidon's enemy and a sea giant who invented warships.

C

Cadmus and Europa

Son and daughter of Agenor, king of Tyre in Phoenicia (modern-day Lebanon). Cadmus, along with his brothers, was sent to Crete to rescue his sister Europa when she was abducted by Zeus (who had taken the form of a beautiful bull to seduce her). There Europa bore the god three children, Minos, Rhadamanthys, and Sarpedon, before marrying Asterion, king of Crete. Cadmus never found his sister because he landed in central Greece. There, following orders from the Oracle at Delphi, he founded the city of Thebes after killing a dragon. From the dragon's teeth sprang up a race of formidable fighting men, with which Cadmus peopled his new city.

Calypso

Nymph daughter of Atlas and the Titaness Tethus, who lived on the magical island of Ogygia. Calypso rescued Odysseus from a shipwreck and they lived in bliss together for seven years. But Calypso would not let her still-homesick lover leave, vainly promising him immortality if he stayed. Finally, after Zeus ordered her to release Odysseus, she bade him a reluctant farewell, equipping him for his voyages. They had two sons: Nausithous and Nausinous.

(See Atlas, Odysseus, Ogygia)

Centaurs

Dangerous wild creatures who were half-human (from the waist up) and half-horse (from the waist down). Invited by King Pirithous of the Lapiths to his wedding feast, the centaurs became drunk and attacked the bride. The Lapiths won the battle that followed, but from then on there was war between centaurs and men. Hercules killed the centaur Nessus for attacking his wife. One or two centaurs were different, however. Chiron was famous for his wisdom and taught the young Achilles and Jason.

(See Apollo, Chiron, Hercules, Jason)

Cerberus

Ferocious many-headed dog that guarded the entrance to the Underworld. Cerberus had a baying brass voice and a shaggy mane that sprouted snakes. Despite such horrors, he was lulled asleep by Orpheus' songs, enabling the poet to regain his wife Eurydice from the Underworld, and later he was overwhelmed and chained up by Hercules.

(See Hades, Hercules, Hydra, Orpheus, Orthus)

Charon

Spectral boatman who ferried the spirits of the dead across the River Styx to the Underworld. He demanded payment of one obol (a small coin) from the dead for this service, so corpses were always buried with a coin.

(See Hades, Hermes, Orpheus, River Styx)

Charybdis and Scylla

Whirlpools (Charybdis) and rocks (Scylla) encountered by Odysseus on his travels around the Mediterranean, which he only escaped by clinging to a tree as his ship went down. Both Charybdis and Scylla had once been beautiful nymphs but were transformed, Charybdis by Zeus and Scylla by Circe.

Chimera

Bizarre monster killed by the hero Bellerophon. According to Homer the chimera had a lion's head and feet, a goat's body, and a serpent's tail. According to other accounts it breathed fire, had six heads, and was related to the similar monsters Eris and Typhon. The name has come to mean something obviously impossible and fantastic.

Chiron

The wise, aged centaur who tutored heroes such as Jason as children. Chiron was regarded as a great educator and was also reputed to be learned in medicine, astrology, and astronomy.
(*See Achilles, Apollo, Centaurs, Jason*)

Circe

Daughter of the sun god Helios, aunt of Medea, and a powerful sorceress. Circe lived on the fabulous island of Aeaea (meaning "wailing") at the edge of the world. When Odysseus' men landed on Aeaea, she transformed them into swine. Odysseus alone escaped, thanks to the magical herb "moly" given to him by the god Hermes, and forced Circe to change his followers back into men. They stayed on her island for a year before Circe sent them off with advice on how to escape the Sirens, whose seductive singing lured sailors to their doom, and how to enter the Underworld. Later, when Jason and the Argonauts reached her island, she purified them of the guilt of murdering Medea's brother.
(*See Charybdis and Scylla, Medea, Odysseus, Sirens*)

Clazmonian Sow

Son of Typhon and Echidna, this huge, winged pig terrorized the village of Clazomenai. There is no mention of its death in any accounts. There are also mentions of a Crommyonion Sow in mythology. She was named Phaea, and was killed by Theseus.

Cocalus

King of Sicily, who saved Daedalus' life by hiding him from Minos. When Minos arrived in Sicily looking for Daedalus, Cocalus convinced Minos to take a bath before retrieving Daedalus. While he was bathing, Cocalus' daughters killed him.
(See Daedalus, Minos)

Colchis

Home of the Golden Ram, located in the southeast corner of the Black Sea. Jason and his followers, the Argonauts, sailed to Colchis to capture the ram's fabulous fleece. Colchis was also the birthplace of Medea, daughter of King Aetes, who fell in love with Jason and fled with him after he found the fleece.
(See Golden Fleece, Jason, Medea)

Cyclopes

One-eyed giants who, according to Homer, lived on a distant primitive island where they kept sheep. Looking for food, Odysseus and his crew landed on the Cyclopes' island and entered a deep cave. They were trapped in it by Polyphemus, the Cyclops to whom the cave belonged, who had returned and rolled a boulder across the entrance. Polyphemus, on discovering his intruders, ate two of the Greeks raw before Odysseus managed to blind the giant while he slept. (By calling himself "nobody" when Polyphemus asked who he was, Odysseus tricked Polyphemus into shouting, "Nobody is hurting me!" when he yelled for help after being blinded. The other Cyclopes thought that if nobody was hurting their comrade there was nothing to worry about and left him alone in his cave with the Greeks.) The Greeks then escaped by clinging to the underside of Polyphemus' sheep when the giant let his animals out in the morning, for Polyphemus checked his flock by touching them on their backs. Once back on board ship, Odysseus taunted Polyphemus, thinking he was safe. He was not, for Polyphemus was the son of Poseidon, and Odysseus then had to face the sea god's wrath on his storm-tossed journeys. Another legend portrays the Cyclopes as giant craftsmen, blacksmiths working with Hephaestus.

(See Helm of Darkness, Hekatonkheires, Kampê, Mount Etna, Odysseus, Polyphemus, Poseidon)

D

Daedalus

Athenian master craftsman and great artist, attributed with building the Labyrinth used to hold the Minotaur. Daedalus had two sons, Icarus and Iapyx, and a nephew, Perdix, his sister's child. Daedalus was so accomplished that he could not bear for his greatness to be surpassed. When his nephew started to show signs of ingenuity, Daedalus pushed him off a high tower in order to get rid of his competition. However, Athena witnessed Daedalus' wrongdoing and saved Perdix by changing the boy into a partridge. For his crime, Daedalus was banished from Athens. Daedalus was recruited to build a labyrinth for King Minos, who used it to imprison the Minotaur. Daedalus was later detained in the Labyrinth with Icarus, in one story so that he could not tell anyone else the secrets of the Labyrinth, and in another story as punishment for giving Ariadne, Minos' daughter, the thread that allowed the hero Theseus to escape the Labyrinth after killing the Minotaur. Daedalus escaped from imprisonment with Icarus by creating a pair of wings for each of them and flying out of Crete. Daedalus hid from Minos in King Cocalus' court, where Minos was tricked and killed by Cocalus' daughters during his search for the escaped craftsman.

(See Icarus, Minos, Cocalus, Labyrinth, Minotaur, Pasiphae, Perdix)

Delphi

Site of the holiest Greek Oracle, located 2,000 feet up on the southern slope of Mount Parnassus in central Greece. In it was the *omphalos* (navel), a numinous stone considered to mark the center of the world. Delphi was sacred to the god Apollo, who had slain (or tamed) the serpent Pytho, and established his own Oracle, the Pythoness. This act symbolized the triumph of Greek reason and order over primeval earth deities. Vapors rising from a cleft in the earth intoxicated the Oracle, a priestess seated on a tripod above the chasm. She answered questions put to her in famously cryptic verses that could be interpreted ambiguously. For example, Croesus, king of Lydia, asked if he should attack Persia, his powerful eastern neighbor. "If you cross the River Halys [the frontier], you will destroy a great kingdom," declared the Oracle. Encouraged, Croesus went to war and indeed destroyed a kingdom—his own. Delphi's prophetic reputation, however, remained unharmed. (Other major Greek oracles were Apollo's at Delos and Zeus' at Dodona and Olympia.)

(See Apollo, Cadmus and Europa, Oracles, Python)

Delphin

A dolphin in the service of Poseidon. He convinced the nymph Amphitrite to marry Poseidon, and to reward him for this deed, Poseidon placed him in the stars as the constellation Delphinus.

Demeter

Goddess of all vegetation and therefore life on Earth. Demeter had a daughter by her brother and called her Persephone, or simply *Kore*, "girl." When Persephone disappeared, Demeter wandered the Earth looking for her, disguised as an old woman with a torch. At Eleusis, near Athens, Demeter learned that Persephone had been abducted by Hades and taken to the Underworld. In gratitude she taught Eleusinians the secrets of agriculture, but in anger she blighted the earth so that nothing grew, causing universal famine. Finally Zeus ordered Hades to let Persephone go. At Eleusis the Mysteries of the Two Goddesses (as Demeter and Persephone were known) were held each year in the fall, after the harvest was gathered. These mysteries remain mysterious, but as far as historians can tell, they involved initiates fasting, spending the night in darkness, and then being granted a dazzling revelation of a golden ear of wheat.

(See Hades, Kronos, Persephone, Tantalus)

Diomedes

Two Greek mythic characters go by the name of Diomedes. The first Diomedes was a son of Ares and Cyrene. Similar to his dad in that he enjoyed a good war, he was a giant man who kept man-eating mares for pets. Hercules visited Diomedes once, intending to use the mares to drive a chariot back to King Eurytheus as part of a challenge. When Diomedes violently objected, Hercules fed him to his own horses before driving them away.

The second Diomedes was a son of Tydeus and Deipyle. He fought in the Trojan War alongside the warriors Achilles, Ajax, and Odysseus, and was regarded as one of the best fighters of the Achaeans. He is also one of the soldiers who rode in the belly of the Trojan Horse to begin the sack of Troy. He wore a cuirass (a piece of armor that covers the body from neck to waist) made by Hephaestus, and was the only person ever to attack and wound an Olympian immortal (and it wasn't just any immortal—he managed to stab *Ares* with a spear). Diomedes was a favorite of Athena, and after he died, she made him immortal.

(See Hercules)

Dionysus

God of wine, ecstasy, and intoxication. Dionysus was the "most terrible and sweet" of deities and his wild worship transgressed all the normal bounds of social life. The son of Zeus and Semele, a Theban princess, Dionysus was called "twice-born" because he was snatched from the womb of his dying mother (who Hera killed out of jealousy) and sewn up in Zeus' thigh. Delivered safely, he was brought up by nymphs and satyrs. He then set out on a triumphal journey to India in a chariot drawn by panthers or tigers, accompanied by Maenads (ecstatic female worshippers) and satyrs, teaching the world the joys of wine. He often appeared somewhat effeminate, with long hair, but he was a dangerous god to cross. On Dionysus' return to Greece, Pentheus, uptight king of Thebes, arrested him. This was a big mistake. Ivy, sacred to the god, burst through the prison walls and Dionysus was freed. Meanwhile Agave, Pentheus' mother, had joined the drunken worshippers in the mountains outside the city. Pentheus, lured by Dionysus to spy on the women in drag, was seized by Agave and other women and torn to pieces. Similar fates befell other rulers who failed to accept the god. Dionysus was the god of Greek theater, both tragic and comic, and many festivals were held in his honor. He was married to Ariadne, who he rescued when the Cretan princess was abandoned on Naxos by Theseus.

(See Ariadne, Hephaestus, Maenads, Nymphs, Satyrs, Zeus)

Drachmae

Standard currency of Athens and other Greek cities, often minted coins of great beauty.

Dryads

Nymphs who lived in groves and forests. There were many types of dryads, each associated with a different sort of tree. They included

Daphnaie (laurel trees), Hamadryads (oak trees), Meliads (ash and fruit trees), and Oreads (pines). Although dryads could leave their trees, a dryad's existence was bound up with her tree; if the tree died, then the dryad died with it. When a tree was cut down, its dryad could be heard screaming and might exact revenge if not appeased by proper prayers and sacrifice.
(*See Nymphs*)

E

Echidna
Mythical half-woman, half-snake creature who gave birth to Typhon, one of the numerous monsters killed by Hercules. According to some sources, the Scythians (of southern Russia) were her descendants.
(*See Clazmonian Sow, Hydra*)

Elpis
The spirit of hope. The daughter of Nyx by some accounts, Elpis was sometimes depicted as a young woman, usually carrying flowers or a cornucopia. She remained the only item left in Pandora's Box after Pandora opened it, leaving humanity with hope despite the many other ills that were unleashed.
(*See Epimetheus, Pandora*)

Elysian Fields/Elysium
The paradise that awaited a highly select and very fortunate few. Elysium was located at the ends of the Earth. Gentle breezes blew over it all the time and there fortunate heroes enjoyed a life generally like that of the gods. Menelaus, Helen's husband, went there, but most dead people, even if heroes, did not—they ended up in the gloomy Underworld.
(*See Hades, River Lethe*)

Empousai

Monsters that took the form of beautiful women with one leg of brass and the other of a donkey. The empousai were sent out by Hecate to frighten travelers, but if a traveler insulted them, they would shriek and run away. They share a name with Empusa, a Greek demigoddess who feasted on men's blood.

Epimetheus

Titan whose name means "afterthought," in contrast to his brother Prometheus, whose name means "forethought." In one myth, he and Prometheus were charged with distributing traits to mankind and animals. When Epimetheus used up the positive traits on animals before bequeathing anything to man, Prometheus stole fire from the gods and gave it to humanity to make up for his brother's lack of gift. Zeus was angry about the theft, and as part of a larger plan to quash man's pride, he had the first woman created—Pandora—as a wife for Epimetheus. In one lesser-known version of the myth of Pandora's Box, Pandora offered the box to Epimetheus to open, and not being one to think things through, Epimetheus opened the box, unleashing all of the ills of humankind upon the world. (You can thank him for sickness, disease, and homework.)
(See Pandora, Prometheus, Titans)

Eris

Goddess of strife or discord. Eris was the daughter of Nyx (night) and the mother of Toil, Pain, Strife, and Lies. She was also the sister of Ares, the war god. By stirring up jealousy between the three great Olympian goddesses, Aphrodite, Athena, and Hera, she was partly responsible for the Trojan War.
(See Chimera)

Erymanthian Boar

Giant savage pig that lived on the slopes of Mount Erymanthus in the Peloponnese. The boar ravaged the lands until it was captured

by Hercules, who tied it up and took it back to Tiryns, his home. There, its size so terrified Eurystheus, the king who had sent Hercules to capture it, that he jumped into a bronze jar to hide.
(See Hercules)

Eurytion
Son of Ares and guardian of Geryon's cattle. Hercules slayed Eurytion in order to take Geryon's cattle.
(See Geryon)

F

Fates
Daughters of Nyx (night) who embodied the inevitable fate for every human being. Also known as the Moirai, they were three in number: Clotho, who spun life's thread; Lachesis, who represented the element of chance in everyone's life; and Atropos, inescapable fate. Even the gods—even Zeus himself—were not entirely free of their powers, having to accept what was fated.

Fields of Asphodel
A sort of grassland in the Underworld where the spirits of most of the dead, even illustrious heroes, went.

Furies
Daughters of Nyx (night) and among the most feared supernatural beings. There were three Furies, or Erinnyes: Alecto, Tisiphone, and Megaera. They were dark, elemental forces, older than any Olympian god, and avenged crimes such as patricide, matricide, and perjury, hunting the guilty across the face of the Earth. Portrayed as repulsively ugly, with wings and snakes instead of hair, they were at times euphemistically called the Kindly Ones, or Eumenides, to disguise their horrific nature. In Aeschylus' play *Eumenides* they were tamed

by the goddess Athena and made benevolent guardians of justice in Athens.

G

Gaia

Goddess of the earth. She married her son Ouranos, and with him bore twelve sons: the Titans.

(See Antaeus, Aphrodite, Hesperides, Kronos, Oceanus, Ophiotaurus, Ouranos, Titans, Typhon)

Ganymede

Son of King Tros of Phrygia (now western Turkey). Zeus, king of the gods, was so charmed by this beautiful boy that he swept down in the form of an eagle—his special bird—and carried Ganymede off to Mount Olympus. There he became cupbearer (wine waiter) to the gods during their eternal banquets. In return King Tros was given some marvelous horses.

(See Mount Olympus)

Geryon

Medusa's grandson, a much-feared giant who lived on the island Erytheia. Geryon had three bodies, including three heads with human faces and six arms, and took the form of a warrior. He owned a magnificent herd of red cattle that Hercules was sent to acquire as his tenth labor. When Geryon tried to battle Hercules (after the hero first slayed Geryon's two-headed dog, Orthus, and Eurytion, the cattle's guard, in order to take the cattle), he was killed by Hercules' poison arrow.

(See Eurytion, Hercules, Orthus)

Golden Fleece

Fleece from a magical flying ram on which Phrixus and Helle, children of King Athamas of Boeotia, had fled from their wicked stepmother. Helle fell off the ram's back but Phrixus reached the distant land of Colchis in the Black Sea, where he sacrificed the ram to Zeus. Its fleece was hung in a river where it soon filled with gold dust. It became world-famous but was guarded by a terrible dragon. When Jason and the Argonauts arrived on their quest to find the fleece, they were helped by Medea, the king's daughter, to overcome the dragon. They then returned to Greece with the fabulous fleece.

(See Hylas, Jason, Medea, Peleus, Orpheus)

Gray Sisters

Three hideous hags, gray-haired from birth, who were related to the Gorgon sisters. Also called the Graiai ("crones/old women") in Greek, the Gray Sisters' names reflected their horrific appearance: Deino, or Dread; Enyo, or Horror; and Pemphredo, or Terror. They had writhing, snake-like hair, gnashing fangs, and a deadly glare. But as they only had one eye and one tooth between them, which they had to take turns to use, they were vulnerable. Perseus caught their eye as it was being passed around and so forced the Graiai to reveal the next stage in his quest.

(See Perseus)

Greek Fire

Weapon developed in c. 700 A.D. by the Byzantine Greeks to help protect Constantinople (now Istanbul) against Arab attack. Like an early flame-thrower, it jetted a stream of flame onto ships. Its inextinguishable fire was made of a mix of petroleum, sulphur, and nitre.

H

Hades

Hades was the name given both to the god of the Underworld and to his realm, where he ruled over the spirits of the dead. Hades was the son of Rhea and Kronos and fought alongside his brothers, Zeus and Poseidon, against the Titans but had none of their majestic splendor. Hades evoked only fear and his name was mentioned with reluctance by the living. To find a wife, he had to kidnap Persephone, Demeter's beautiful daughter, whom he kept imprisoned underground for half of every year. Hades was seldom seen outside his kingdom, partly because he had a cap made of wolf skin that made him invisible. Down in the bowels of the earth, he piled up riches—one of his names was *Pluton*, meaning "wealth"—which he gained from buried treasure and from the earth's minerals. The realm of Hades, the Underworld, where the ghosts of the dead flitted around restlessly like bats, was where most dead Greeks went. It was a dismal place, bound by the River Styx, across which the boatmen Charon ferried the dead, and guarded by Cerberus, the hideous many-headed watchdog. In Hades, King Minos of Crete and his brother Rhadamanthys, lords of legendary wisdom, judged the dead. While a lucky few found bliss in the Elysian Fields, a grim fate was reserved for the very wicked: They were imprisoned in Tartarus, the lowest part of Hades.

(*See Demeter, Helm of Darkness, Hercules, Hermes, Kronos, Minos, Mount Olympus, Orpheus, Persephone, Poseidon, River Lethe, River Styx, Theseus, Titans, Zeus*)

Harpies

Three terrifying half-human creatures who had scaly wings, sharp curved claws, and long flowing hair. Flying faster than any bird, these daughters of the monster Typhon would descend with shrill

cries like vultures at feasts to snatch away the food and break up the party. They attacked Jason and the Argonauts on their quest.
(*See Jason*)

Hecate

Goddess of the moon and the night. Hecate could be either terrifying or benevolent, and her "triple aspects"—shown in her statues with three heads—represented the three phases of the moon: waxing, full, and waning. As the daughter of Asteria, a star goddess who was the sister of Leto, Hecate was a first cousin of Apollo and Artemis and honored as such, but she was never one of the official Olympian deities. Instead, she was often worshipped outside the city at crossroads and in graveyards, with sacrifices of goats and fish. (The usual offerings for a god or goddess were bulls, sheep, or chickens. Both goats and fish were considered a bit offbeat.) Hecate could be portrayed as a blood-drinking sorceress with serpent-hair and baying hellhounds, as she was linked with suicides and other violent deaths. Olympias, mother of Alexander the Great, sacrificed to Hecate, and she long remained an infernal goddess; she is invoked by the three witches in Shakespeare's play *Macbeth* (1605).
(*See Artemis, Empousai*)

Helen

Greatest beauty in Greek legend. The daughter of Zeus, who disguised as a swan had seduced her mother Leda, Helen was born from an egg. As Greece's most beautiful woman, she was wooed by many heroes before she chose Menelaus, the powerful and muscular king of Sparta. But although Menelaus was a great warrior, Helen fell in love and ran off with the handsome Prince Paris of Troy when he visited Sparta. Helen's flight—or abduction, depending on the storyteller—sparked the ten-year Trojan War, as the Greeks united under Agamemnon, King of Mycenae and brother of Menelaus, to avenge the insult. When Troy was finally captured and Paris killed, Helen returned peacefully to Sparta with Menelaus to live out her days.

(See Aphrodite, Elysian Fields/Elysium, Trojan War, Zeus)

Helios

God of the sun, later identified with Apollo, the god of light and reason. Helios was especially worshipped on the island of Rhodes, where a huge statue, the "Colossus of Rhodes" (one of the Seven Wonders of the World), was erected in his honor at the harbor entrance. Reputedly it was so tall that ships could sail between its legs. Each day Helios rose from the east and, in a chariot drawn by eight winged horses, traversed the skies before setting in the western ocean. He then returned east every night in a barque, a type of sailing vessel. One day Helios' son Phaethon insisted on driving the heavenly chariot himself. But he proved unable to control the fiery steeds, who flew so close to the sun that the chariot was scorched. Finally Zeus had to kill Phaethon with a thunderbolt. After that, Helios took the reins again.

(See Apollo, Circe, Hyperion, Medea, Selene)

Hekatonkheires

Giants with fifty heads and 100 arms each. The Hekatonkheires aided Zeus against the Titans' attack. In Latin poetry, the Hekatonkheires were known as the Centimani, which translates to "Hundred-Handed Ones." As storm gods, they represent the major forces of nature, such as earthquakes and sea waves.

(See Briares, Kampê, Telekhines)

Helm of Darkness

Part of Perseus' magical equipment when he set off on his quest to kill the Medusa. Originally created by a Cyclops for Hades, Lord of the Underworld, the helmet made the wearer invisible, as if it were night—hence its name, the Helm of Darkness.

Hephaestus

God of fire and metal-working. Hephaestus was sweaty, ugly, and lame, quite unlike the other glamorous Olympian gods. He became lame when, as a child, he intervened in an argument between his parents, Zeus and Hera, and Hera threw him from Mount Olympus. Falling down into the sea, he was rescued by Thetis, a sea nymph. In revenge he created a magical gold throne for Hera. She sat on it and became trapped, unable to move. After Dionysus persuaded Hephaestus finally to free his mother, the soot-stained god demanded as his reward marriage to Aphrodite, the love goddess. But Aphrodite soon fell in love with Ares, the war god, making Hephaestus ragingly jealous. He forged a net of gossamer-light steel and draped it over the sleeping lovers. They awoke trapped in their bed by the steel net, as the other Olympians gathered to laugh. Usually, however, Hephaestus was busy at his furnace, which was situated beneath Mount Etna in Sicily, an active volcano (Hephaestus' Latin name was Vulcan), and he was much admired for his skills. He built wonderful palaces for the gods on Mount Olympus and made the armor for the Greek warrior Achilles, since Achilles' mother, Thetis, had helped the god when he was in the sea, taking care of him until he had recovered enough to return to land.

(See Aphrodite, Ares, Cyclopes, Diomedes, Hera, Mount Etna, Mount Olympus, Talos)

Hera

Goddess of childbirth and marriage, mother of Ares and Hephaestus and both the sister and wife of Zeus, king of the gods. Hera, as queen of Olympus, was majestic rather than beautiful. This encouraged the notoriously promiscuous Zeus to pursue other females, mortal and divine, which fueled Hera's sometimes deadly jealousy and their terrible rows. At one point Zeus in exasperation hung his wife upside down from Mount Olympus, but usually Hera could more than hold her own against any of the Olympian deities. She intervened to great effect against the Trojans in the Trojan War (because Prince Paris of Troy had preferred Aphrodite to her in the Judgment of Paris). The triple crown that Hera often wears reveals her links with the pre-Greek Great Goddess of Asia—each part of the crown represents one aspect of a woman's life: maiden, mother, and crone. Hera was also often accompanied by a peacock, another of the Great Goddess' attributes. *(See Aphrodite, Ares, Dionysus, Eris, Hephaestus, Hercules, Hesperides, Iris, Jason, Kronos, Zeus)*

Hercules

Archetypal Greek hero. Hercules had a divine father, Zeus, king of the gods, and a mortal mother, Princess Alcmene. Though his exploits inspired later heroes such as Alexander the Great, they made for a grueling life, despite help from the goddess Athena. Hercules was harassed from birth by Hera, ever-jealous of the children of Zeus' lovers. She sent two snakes to kill him in his crib but the muscular infant easily strangled both. Later Hera drove him so mad that he killed his wife Meagre and his family. To atone for this terrible crime, Apollo ordered Hercules to perform Twelve Labors to benefit humanity. These tasks, beyond the powers of any normal human, traditionally were:

1. To kill the man-eating Nemean Lion, whose hide Hercules then wore, making him almost invincible.
2. To kill the Hydra of Lerna, a many-headed dragon.
3. To capture the Golden Hind (deer) of Cerynaea.
4. To capture the Erymanthian Boar.
5. To clean the filthy Augean stables in one day.
6. To destroy the iron-clawed Stymphalian Birds.
7. To capture the Cretan Bull.
8. To steal the wild horses of Diomedes.
9. To steal the girdle of Hippolyta, the Amazon queen.
10. To obtain the Cattle of Geryon.

11. To steal the Golden Apples of the Hesperides in the farthest west.
12. To descend to the Underworld, capture Hades' guard dog Cerberus, and bring him back.

In all these he was triumphant. Hercules' end, however, was horrific. He was persuaded to wear a tunic soaked in the blood of Nessus, a centaur he had killed for trying to force himself on Hercules' second wife, Denaira, and the poison it contained tormented him. In agony, he set fire to the shirt, killing himself. But his soul rose up to heaven as a constellation, and he was worshipped as divine after his death.

(See Amazons, Antaeus, Ares, Atlas, Centaur, Cerberus, Charybdis and Scylla, Diomedes, Echidna, Erymanthian Boar, Eurytion, Geryon, Hesperides, Hydra, Hylas, Jason, Nemean Lion, Orthus, Pankration, Peleus, Prometheus, Stymphalian Birds, Theseus)

Hermes

God of travelers, merchants, and thieves. A son of Zeus, Hermes was unusual in relying more on his quick wits, good luck, and intelligence than on superhuman strength. He was only a few hours old when he stole some cattle belonging to his half-brother Apollo by using winged sandals, one of his many cunning devices. He deflected Apollo's anger by giving him another of his cunning devices: the lyre. (Hermes invented many things, among them the alphabet, numbers, and weights and measures.) Hermes often wore a broad-rimmed winged hat and carried a magic wand, the Caduceus, with two snakes entwined around it that sent people to sleep. His smooth talk and notorious good luck made him the patron god of both merchants and thieves. In his capacity as the messenger god—for he was always swift-footed—he was kept busy carrying messages from Olympus down to Earth. He often traveled farther down still, for he also led the souls of the dead to Charon, the boatman on the River

Styx in Hades. Hermes was also the protector-god of travelers, and herms (stone statues) were set up by them in his honor on doors and at crossroads.

(See Aphrodite, Circe, Medusa, Pan, Pandora, Persephone, Perseus, Typhon)

Hesperides

Daughters of Hesperis, goddess of the morning star, and the Titan Atlas. The Hesperides, who numbered three to seven depending on the version of the tale, were famed for their wonderful singing and guarded a tree of golden apples given by Gaia (Earth) to Hera. The magic apple tree grew on islands in the farthest west, beyond the reach of any normal human, but the hero Hercules succeeded in obtaining several apples with Atlas' help, after killing Ladon, the dragon who acted as watchdog.

(See Atlas, Hercules)

Hestia

Goddess of the hearth, and the eldest daughter of Kronos and Rhea. A gentle, benevolent goddess, she never married or had any children of her own. Zeus assigned her the duty of feeding and maintaining the Olympian hearth fires. The hearth was an important part of Greek households, essential for warmth, food, and making sacrifices to the gods. Because of the Greeks' high regard for it, Hestia received the first offering at every sacrifice. Depictions of this goddess vary in mythology. She is sometimes portrayed as a woman wearing a simple cloak.

(See Kronos)

Hippalektryons

Beast with the foreparts of a horse and the tail, wings, and back legs of a rooster. Hippalektryons may be an earlier version of the winged horse Pegasus.

Hippocampi

Mythical seahorses that pulled the chariot of Poseidon, god of the sea, or cavorted through the waves alongside him, in company with tritons (mermen) and mermaids.

Hydra

Monster from the same alarming family as the Gorgons and Cerberus. Its father was the monster Typhon and its mother Echidna, and it had at least eight heads (some writers gave it 1,000), toxic blood, and breath so venomous that it poisoned all who breathed it. Hercules' second labor was killing it—a major task even for him. He had to drive it out of its lair by shooting burning arrows at it and cutting off its myriad heads. These kept sprouting back from the creature's many necks until he burnt them off. He buried the last head under a boulder.
(See Hercules, Typhon)

Hylas

An exceptionally attractive boy brought up by the hero Hercules. Hylas accompanied Hercules and Jason on the voyage of the *Argo* in the quest of the Golden Fleece. When they stopped at Cius on the Black Sea, the naiads, nymphs of the spring where Hylas was looking for fresh water, found him so delightful that they seized him and would not let him go. Hercules and his companions spent hours looking for him in vain.

Hyperion

Eldest Titan, whose name means "the one above." He married Theia, who bore Helios, Semele, and Eos (the sun, the moon, and the dawn, respectively).
(See Titans)

I

Icarus

Daedalus' son. Icarus escaped with his father from imprisonment in Crete by using the wings Daedalus had created, but despite his father's warning, he flew too close to the sun. The heat caused the wax holding the wings together to melt, and Icarus fell to his death. The waters into which Icarus fell is called the Icarian Sea.
(See Daedalus)

Ichor

Blood of the gods. The gods were perfect superhuman beings, and they were also immortal. In battle they could be wounded but never killed, partly because they did not have human blood. In their veins flowed not blood but ichor, which was poisonous to mortals.

Iliad, The

First of Homer's two great epic poems. *The Illiad* related scenes from the ten-year long Trojan War (Ilium was another name for Troy). Most Greeks thought it the greatest poem ever written and knew it by heart.
(See Trojan War, Quintus)

Iris

Goddess of the rainbow and mother of Eros, god of desire. Iris acted as a messenger of the gods, often being used by Zeus, and sometimes by Hera, to carry messages. She was called "wind-footed" and "stormy-footed" because her rainbow either warned of storms to come or showed that storms had passed.
(See Zephyr)

Ithaca

Island kingdom of Odysseus, to which he constantly tried to return after the Trojan War. In Ithaca his ever-faithful wife Penelope waited for him, putting off the suitors who, believing Odysseus dead, wanted to marry her and so gain the kingdom. Ithaca is generally identified with the island that still bears that name in the Ionian Sea off the west coast of Greece. The description given by Homer in *The Odyssey*, however, does not match the island closely, so many people think the ancient kingdom was somewhere else.

(See Odyssey, Odysseus)

J

Janus
God of doors and gates and beginnings and endings. From Saturn, Janus received the gift of seeing both the past and future. He is most often depicted with two heads facing opposite directions, and he is accordingly representative of the progression of time and transitions, as well as peace and war.

Jason
Among the greatest of Greek heroes, and the son of King Aeson of Iolcus. As King Aeson had been deposed by his brother Pelias, Jason was brought up in exile by the wise centaur Chiron. When Jason returned to Iolcus, he was soon recognized by his uncle, who sent him on a perilous quest: to win the Golden Fleece from Colchis in the eastern Black Sea. Jason chose heroes such as Hercules and Theseus of Athens to crew his ship the *Argo* (thus their name, the Argonauts). Their quest was aided by two goddesses—Hera, who helped them fight off aerial attacks by the Harpies, and Aphrodite, who made Medea, daughter of the king of Colchis, fall in love with Jason. The Colchian king gave Jason a task to prove himself worthy of Medea: He had to plow a field with wild bulls and sow it with dragon's teeth. When angry warriors sprang up from the dragon's teeth, Jason persuaded them to fight one another, not him. With Medea's help, Jason seized the Golden Fleece, and they both

sailed off in the *Argo*. Jason became king of Corinth, a wealthy city, but soon left Medea for another woman. In fury, Medea torched the palace and killed most of the royal family before fleeing to Athens. Jason escaped unharmed, and was eventually killed when a beam of the by-then rotten *Argo* fell on his head.

(See Centaurs, Circe, Chiron, Colchis, Golden Fleece, Harpies, Hylas, Medea, Orpheus, Sirens)

K

Kampê

A female monster with a female head and torso and a scorpion's tail, sometimes described as having wings. She guarded the Hekatonkheires and Cyclopes when Kronos trapped them in Tartarus, and was killed by Zeus when he rescued them for help in the battle against the Titans.

Kronos

Youngest of the Titans, son of Uranus and Gaia, who castrated and overthrew his father. Kronos married his sister Rhea, who gave birth to many of the Olympian gods (Demeter, Hades, Hestia, Hera, Poseidon, and Zeus). Fearing that his children would overthrow him as he had overthrown his own father, Kronos swallowed them all as babies except the youngest, Zeus, for whom Rhea substituted a stone. Later Zeus led a revolt against his father, making Kronos vomit back up all the gods he had swallowed. Kronos was then imprisoned in Tartarus, the depths of the Underworld. Paradoxically, Kronos' reign was later also remembered as a Golden Age, a utopian era in which there was universal peace and humanity did not have to work, as the earth produced food for free.

(See Aphrodite, Hades, Hestia, Kampê, Ouranos, Titans, Zeus)

L

Labyrinth

Maze built on the island of Crete to hide the Minotaur, the half-bull, half-human offspring of Queen Pasiphae and a bull. King Minos ordered the Athenian master craftsman Daedalus to create an impenetrable maze with countless twists and turns to conceal this monster of royal birth, and the Minotaur grew up in the Labyrinth's center, living off of the sacrificial victims that were sent to feed him. Thrust into the Labyrinth, these victims became hopelessly lost in its corridors until the beast loomed up out of the darkness to devour them. The word "labyrinth" possibly derives from the same root as *labrys*, the ancient name for a double-headed ax, a common Cretan religious symbol.

(*See Ariadne, Minos, Minotaur, Pasiphae, Theseus*)

Laistrygonians

Cannibalistic giants who lived in the land of Lamus, somewhere in the western Mediterranean. Odysseus and his sailors, going ashore for water and food during their long wandering, encountered the Laistrygonians. Two of them were eaten by the Laistrygonians before the rest of the crew managed to escape.

Laurel

Plant with leaves sacred to Apollo, the god of poetry, sport, and music. Crowns of laurel leaves were usually given to victors in poetry and athletic contests (and were the only prizes given to winners at the ancient Olympic Games). Today national poets are often called *poets laureate* after this tradition.

(*See Apollo, Dryads*)

Lotus

Plant with leaves that, when eaten, make you forget all desires. Odysseus on his long voyages around the Mediterranean came to the mysterious Land of the Lotus Eaters (which may have been in modern Tunisia, north Africa), whose inhabitants lived idle, contented lives thanks to their diet of lotus leaves. Some of Odysseus' sailors who tried eating the lotus plant lost all their longing to return home and had to be dragged back to the ships by their comrades.

M

Maenads

Manic, intoxicated female followers of the wine god Dionysus. Maenads took part in drunken *orgia* (orgies) on the mountainside outside Greek cities, dancing alongside the god of ecstasy to the sound of drums and flutes. It was death to any man to stand against them, as Pentheus, king of Thebes, and the grieving poet Orpheus discovered: Both men were torn apart by these raving female worshippers.

(See Dionysus, Orpheus)

Master Bolt

Final, most awesome weapon of Zeus, which he only unleashed after consulting with the other gods.

Medea

Granddaughter of Helios, the sun god, and daughter of the king of Colchis, home of the Golden Fleece. As the niece of Circe, the witch who turned Odysseus' men into swine, Medea had magic in her blood and knew the lore of sacred herbs and potions. She helped Jason win the Golden Fleece before sailing off with him to become queen of Corinth. When Jason left her for another woman, however, she revealed her full fury. She murdered Jason's new bride and also

her own children by him, then flew off to Athens in a winged chariot drawn by dragons. In Athens she seduced the elderly King Aegeus and tried to poison Aegeus' young son Theseus when he turned up in disguise. Foiled just in time when Theseus revealed his true identity, Medea again took off in her chariot, returning to Colchis.
(*See Circe, Colchis, Golden Fleece, Jason, Talos, Theseus*)

Medusa

One of the three Gorgons. Medusa and her sisters, Stethno and Euryale, had wings, bronze claws, and glaring eyes, and their horrific appearance alone was enough to turn all who looked on them into stone. She was killed by the hero Perseus, who, with the help of the goddess Athena and the god Hermes, surprised her while she slept and cut off her head. From Medusa's severed neck sprang the winged horse Pegasus, on which Perseus fled from the other enraged Gorgons.
(*See Andromeda, Athena, Geryon, Helm of Darkness, Pegasus, Perseus*)

Minos

Legendary king of Crete who lived three generations before the traditional date of the Trojan War. The son of Zeus and Europa, a princess whom Zeus had carried off from her home, Minos was renowned for his kingly wisdom. He drew up laws with his brother Rhadamanthys and, in the Underworld, was said to judge the dead. But he wasn't always wise. One day Minos prayed to Poseidon, god of the sea, to send him a fine bull to sacrifice. Minos was so impressed by Poseidon's bull that he decided to keep it—an unfortunate decision, for his wife, Pasiphae, became besotted with it. From her passion was born the half-human Minotaur, which was kept in the Labyrinth under Minos' palace in Knossos. Minos also built the first navy that ruled the waves, making him *thalassocrat*, sea ruler. When the Athenians killed his son Androgeus, he made them send an annual tribute of seven youths and seven maidens to be sacrificed to the Minotaur, which continued until Theseus killed the monster. The name Minoan is used by modern archaeologists for the whole Ancient Cretan civilization of the Bronze Age.

(See Ariadne, Cadmus and Europa, Cocalus, Hades, Labyrinth, Minotaur, Pasiphae, Theseus, Zeus)

Minotaur

Son of Queen Pasiphae of Crete and a bull sent to Pasiphae's husband, King Minos, by Poseidon, god of the sea. It had a bull's head and legs but the body of a man. King Minos of Crete, appalled by his queen's monstrous offspring, had the Labyrinth built to contain it. The Minotaur lived in its center and was fed on a diet of human sacrifices from Athens. The Minotaur, though possessed of immense strength, finally met his match in Theseus, the Athenian hero who killed him with the aid of Princess Ariadne, the Minotaur's half-sister.

(See Aegean Sea, Ariadne, Labyrinth, Minos, Pasiphae, Pankration, Theseus)

Morpheus

God of dreams. The son of Somnus, he is often depicted as a chubby, winged child holding poppies.

Mount Etna

Volcano in eastern Sicily. Mount Etna was the highest volcano known to the Greeks. Reaching almost 11,000 feet, it is snow-capped much of the year. It is also frequently volcanically active, although its damage does not usually spread far. In its fiery depths Hephaestus, the blacksmith god, was said to have his main furnace, where he hammered away at his magical forge with the assistance of one-eyed giant Cyclopes. The philosopher and magus Empedocles met his death by throwing himself into Etna's molten mouth.

(See Briares, Hephaestus, Typhon)

Mount Olympus

Highest mountain in Greece. Rising to 9,677 feet, Mount Olympus' peaks are often shrouded in clouds or covered in snow. This led the early Greeks to consider the mountain the home of their main deities, the twelve "Olympian" gods. (Only Hades, Lord of the Underworld, shunned it, preferring his own gloomy realm.) Life in the palaces built by Hephaestus on Olympus was splendid. At their great banquets the gods drank ambrosia, their divine liquor, served by Ganymede, their beautiful cupbearer, while Apollo played the lyre and the Muses sang. Mortals and demigods were permitted to visit occasionally, but Olympus was no heaven in a Christian sense; the spirits of dead humans descended to Hades' Underworld.
(See Ganymede, Hephaestus, Hera, Mount Othrys, Zeus)

Mount Othrys

Mountain in north-central Greece. Mount Othrys was seized by the Titans in the war that they fought against Zeus and his brother gods, the Titanomachia. But Zeus had already occupied the far grander peak of Mount Olympus; Mount Othrys is only 5,610 feet high.

N

Naiads

Nymphs who lived in fresh water, especially in streams and brooks. Like other nymphs, they were generally benevolent and were often worshipped by human beings. Though not always immortal, they had very long lives and remained always young and beautiful.
(See Hylas, Nymphs)

Nemean Lion

Enormous lion that terrorized the area around Nemea. The Nemean Lion's hide was so thick that normal weapons—arrows, swords, clubs—were useless against it. Killing it was the first of the Twelve

Labors performed by Hercules, and he finally succeeded by closing in and sticking his arm down the creature's throat to choke it to death. He then tried to skin it, but was unable to do so until the goddess Athena showed him how: by using the lion's own savage claws. Wearing the lion's hide made Hercules almost invincible.
(See Hercules)

Nemesis

Goddess of vengeance (to the people she punished) and arbiter of justice. The daughter of Themis, at times she is depicted with a helm and wheel and has also been portrayed driving a chariot pulled by griffins. Her name comes from the Greek word *némein*, meaning "to give what is due" and is now also synonymous with the word *enemy*.

Nereids

Fifty sea nymphs, or mermaids, daughters of the sea nymph Doris and Nereus, the old man of the sea. The Nereids lived in the depths of the ocean and loved to play amid the waves. Three Nereids were brought up by Aphrodite, the goddess of love: Acis, Arethusa, and Thetis, all of whom were golden-haired and beautiful. Thetis was especially attractive. She caught the eyes of mortals and gods and was desired by both Zeus and his brother Poseidon. To avoid family quarrels, Zeus arranged for the (human) king of Thessaly, Peleus, to marry her. Thetis disliked Peleus, however, and tried to escape him. From their unhappy union was born the hero Achilles, the greatest warrior of the Trojan War.
(See Andromeda, Nereus, Nymphs, Poseidon)

Nereus

Minor sea god renowned for his wisdom and prophetic powers and known as the "old man of the sea." Nereus lived in the ocean's depths, but surfaced at times to help shipwrecked sailors. His daughters with the sea nymph Doris were known as the Nereids.
(See Nereids)

Nymphs

Minor female divinities personifying aspects of wild nature. They came in many different guises: Dryads and hamadryads were tree nymphs; lemoniads were meadow nymphs; oreads were mountain nymphs; naiads were fresh water nymphs; the Nereids and oceanids were sea nymphs. All were beautiful and forever young, and so loved by both men and gods. (The Greek word *nymphe* also meant "unmarried young woman.") Nymphs themselves also sometimes fell in love with mortals, occasionally abducting especially handsome boys. Nymphs often accompanied gods such as Dionysus, Pan, Artemis, and Apollo, while satyrs pursued them ardently if not always with success. Nymphs were often worshipped by mortals, and they could grant humans minor favors such as helping the sick and guiding lost hunters.
(See Andromeda, Artemis, Charybdis and Scylla, Dionysus, Dryads, Hylas, Naiads, Nereids, Oceanus, Pan, Satyrs, Zeus)

O

Oceanus

Titan, and the all-encompassing *Ocean*. This was a great freshwater river rather than a sea that, according to early Greek geography, encircled the whole inhabited Earth beyond the east and west and fed all the Earth's rivers through subterranean sources. As a god, Oceanus was considered to be the son of Ouranos (the sky) and Gaia (the earth), the two primeval deities. He was the father of the oceanids (sea nymphs), and was considered a great, mainly benevolent cosmic force, essential for maintaining the Earth's natural life by renewing the rivers and streams.

Odysseus

King of Ithaca, a tiny island. Odysseus is the focus of Homer's second grand poem, *The Odyssey*, which relates Odysseus' adventures on his long way home from the Trojan War (the real distance from

Troy to Ithaca is small but the legendary distance is vast). The poem opens with Odysseus still held captive by Calypso, a bewitching nymph, after ten years. Released on Zeus' orders, he set out with his companions on an epic journey. On the way he encountered Cyclopes, one-eyed, man-eating monsters; sailed past Sirens, whose songs lured sailors to their death; outwitted the witch Circe, who turned men into pigs; and visited the Underworld. A colorful, wily hero, he survived more by his wits than his strength. Finally shipwrecked, with all his crew drowned, Odysseus reached the land of the Phaecians. There the beautiful princess Nausicaa found and befriended him, and introduced him to the king. The Phaecians listened to his tales, gave him gifts, and sent him back to Ithaca. But his adventures did not end when his ship touched his native shores, for in his twenty-year absence his faithful wife Penelope had been pestered by suitors. Thinking Odysseus dead, they wanted to marry her and gain the kingdom. In disguise, Odysseus returned to his palace to take revenge—by killing all the suitors with a great bow that he alone had the strength to draw. Then at last he and Penelope were reunited in the great marriage bed he had made long ago.

(*See Aeolus, Athena, Calypso, Circe, Cyclopes, Diomedes, Ithaca, Laistrygonians, Lotus, Medea, Odyssey, Polyphemus, Poseidon, Sirens*)

Odyssey, The

Second of Homer's great epic poems. *The Odyssey* relates the adventures of Odysseus on his long way home from the Trojan War to Ithaca.

(*See Aeolus, Ithaca, Odysseus, Polyphemus*)

Oedipus

Son of Laius, king of Thebes. To avert a prophecy that his son would kill him, Laius ordered a shepherd to expose baby Oedipus on a mountainside. But the shepherd saved Oedipus, who was brought up by the king of Corinth as his own. Oedipus, warned by an oracle

that he would kill his father and marry his mother, fled Corinth to avoid this. But at a crossroads near Thebes he met and killed Laius, who he failed to recognize, and won a debate with the Sphinx, an enigmatic lion-like creature. Reaching Thebes, Oedipus was hailed as king and married the widowed queen Jocasta. Years later, as plague ravaged Thebes, Oedipus heard from the Delphic Oracle that the killer of Laius was the plague's cause. Finally he realized that *he* had killed his own father. Hearing the news of her husband's murder and her own incest, Jocasta committed suicide. Oedipus blinded himself and went into exile.
(*See Sphinx*)

Ogygia

Calypso's island home, where Odysseus washed ashore after his men perished. There is much speculation regarding Ogygia's location. Some associate Ogygia with present-day Gozo, in the Mediterranean Sea. Others associate Ogygia with the lost Atlantis.
(*See Calypso*)

Ophiotaurus

Hybrid monster whose front resembled a bull's and whose rear resembled a serpent's. This creature, which was among Gaia's weirdest offspring, became an ally of Zeus and was killed with an adamantine axe by Briares, one of the Titan's allies, during their war against the gods of Olympus. The Ophiotaurus' entrails, when set alight, produced a fire so great that it could have destroyed any of the gods, even Zeus. After the Ophiotaurus' death, it was placed by a grateful Zeus in the heavens as the combined constellations Taurus (bull) and Cetus (whale).

Oracles

Places where the Greeks asked advice from the gods. There were several important oracles: Dodona in northwest Greece, reputedly the oldest oracle, where Zeus spoke from a grove of sacred oak trees; the island Delos, where Apollo was honored; Siwah, in the western desert of Egypt, where Amon, the Egyptian equivalent of Zeus, was worshipped, and which Alexander the Great visited in 331 B.C.; and above all the Pythian Oracle of Apollo at Delphi, the most sacred site in the Greek world. (*See Delphi, Python*)

Orpheus

Son of the god Apollo and the Muse Calliope. Orpheus was the archetypal poet, whose music had magical powers. He accompanied Jason and the Argonauts on their quest for the Golden Fleece, and proved useful when his music was able to refloat their ship when it stranded, and when he was able to counter the song of the Sirens with his own, thus saving the ship's crew from certain death. He loved his wife, Eurydice, so deeply that when she died from a snake-bite, he descended to the Underworld. His singing charmed the ferryman Charon, the infernal watchdog Cerberus, and even Hades himself. The god agreed to let Eurydice return with Orpheus provided he did not look back at her until they had left the Underworld. But he could not resist glancing round at her on the long path toward daylight, and so lost her forever. Grieving, he retired to the wilderness, where his music charmed the animals. Still mourning Eurydice, he spurned all women, until the Maenads, enraged by his celibacy, tore him to pieces. However, his head, still singing, floated over the waters to the island of Lesbos. Many mystical poems about immortality, written after his death, were later attributed to him. (*See Cerberus, Maenads, Sirens*)

Orthus

Two-headed dog owned by Geryon. Orthus was the brother of Cerberus, the two-headed dog that guarded the gates of Hades. He guarded Geryon's magnificent red cattle. He was slain by Hercules. (*See Eurytion, Geryon*)

Ouranos

Divine personification of the starry sky, also known as Uranus. The son of Gaia, the earth goddess, he was also her husband. They had twelve sons, the Titans, one of whom, Kronos, castrated his father and threw his genitals into the sea. From the resulting foam was born Aphrodite, the Olympian love goddess.

(See Aphrodite, Gaia, Oceanus, Titans)

P

Pan

Rustic god, son of the Olympian messenger god Hermes and a nymph. He was the patron god of shepherds, woods, and wild animals, and also of goats and sheep. Born with goat-like cloven feet, horns, and legs, Pan haunted the woods and pastures of Arcadia (a wild part of southern Greece), playing his pan pipes, or *syrinx*, that he had cut from reeds. He loved and pursued several nymphs, including Echo. The Athenian runner Phidippedes, on his way back from begging Sparta for help against the invading Persians, encountered Pan, who promised Athens victory. When the Athenians won—the god induced "panic," which the Greeks considered to be a special power of Pan's, in the Persian ranks at the battle of Marathon—the city built a temple to him. Pan's name—*pan* means "all" in Greek—later led to some Greeks' belief that he must be the god of all things, and they worshipped him as the one true god of all the universe.

(See Nymphs, Satyrs)

Pandora

The first woman to walk the earth, created on Zeus' orders as a punishment for mankind after Prometheus gave them fire stolen from the gods. By some accounts, the god Hermes gave her a golden box (which is also sometimes depicted as a jar or *pithos*) upon her creation and told her not to open it, instilling in her the trait of curiosity and ensuring that she would later open it. When she married Epimetheus, either he or Pandora (depending on whom you ask) eventually succumbed to temptation and opened the box, releasing the ills it contained upon the world. Only Elpis, the spirit of Hope, remains in the bottom of the box, giving humanity a reason to continue living.

(See Elpis, Epimetheus)

Pankration

An Ancient Greek fighting style resembling a blend of boxing and wrestling. It is said that Hercules and Theseus created this form of martial arts, which Theseus used to defeat the Minotaur in the Labyrinth. Pankration was also an event in the Olympic games, and part of combat training for Greek soldiers.

Pasiphae

Wife of Minos, king of Crete. Minos prayed for a specially fine bull to sacrifice to the sea god Poseidon, but then decided to keep it for himself. Angered, Poseidon made Pasiphae fall in love with the bull. To consummate her passion, she got Daedalus, the Athenian master craftsman, to build a cow in which she lay to seduce the bull. From this monstrous mismatch was born a monster, the half-bull, half-man Minotaur, who was hidden away in the Labyrinth.

(See Ariadne, Labyrinth, Minos, Minotaur)

Pegasus

Immortal winged horse that sprung from the severed head of Medusa. Tamed by the hero Bellerophon with the aid of a gold bridle given him by the goddess Athena, Pegasus carried Bellerophon on his mission to kill the chimera. Pegasus could create springs by stamping his foot—doing so caused water to spring forth from the earth.

(See Hippalektryons, Medusa, Perseus)

Peleus

Son of Aeacus and Endëis. Peleus was a friend of Hercules, and served with him on his quest for the Golden Fleece. After the death of his first wife, Antigone, whom he accidentally killed, he married the nymph Thetis. Achilles was their son.
(See Nereids)

Perdix

Daedalus' nephew and apprentice, credited with creating the first saw. Athena turned Perdix into a partridge in order to save him when Daedalus pushed him from a tall tower out of jealousy of the boy's ingenuity.
(See Daedalus)

Persephone

Daughter of Demeter, the goddess of wheat, and Zeus. Persephone's original name was Kore, meaning simply "girl." Persephone lived happily on Earth until one day while she was picking flowers, Hades, the god of the Underworld, burst out of the ground and carried Persephone off in his chariot to his miserable realm, where she became his reluctant queen. Demeter frantically searched the Earth for her missing daughter, blighting the crops in her despair until Zeus sent Hermes to persuade Hades to release Persephone. This Hades did, but not before he had tricked Persephone into eating some special pomegranate seeds so that she still had to spend the winter months of each year with him. As queen of the Underworld, Persephone wielded great power, but she was also worshipped when she was above the earth alongside Demeter at the city of Eleusis near Athens, where the citizens had told Demeter about Hades' abduction of Persephone and so had been rewarded with the divine secrets of fertility.
(See Demeter, Hades, Tantalus, Theseus)

Perseus

Son of Danae, the daughter of King Acrisius of Argos, and Zeus, king of the gods, who seduced Danae by appearing to her in a blaze of gold. Perseus grew up with his mother on the island of Seriphus, whose king Polydectes fell in love with Danae. Danae disliked Polydectes, however, so Perseus agreed to go on a quest to kill Medusa, a hideous snake-haired creature whose stare turned men to stone, if Polydectes would leave his mother alone. With the help of the goddess Athena, who gave him a polished shield, and the god Hermes, who provided winged sandals and a magic cap that made Perseus invisible, Perseus surprised Medusa while she slept. He cut off her head, using the shield as a mirror to avoid her petrifying glare, and escaped on the winged horse Pegasus, which had sprung from Medusa's severed neck. Flying back with the Medusa's head, after capturing the eye of the Gray Sisters and forcing them to reveal the next stage in his quest, he saw the lovely princess Andromeda chained to a rock and guarded by a sea monster. Perseus turned the sea monster to stone by displaying the Medusa's head, freed Andromeda, and later married her. Back in Seriphus, he used the Medusa's head to turn Polydectes to stone, and then handed the head over to Athena. The goddess made it part of her aegis, worn around her neck, and Perseus ended his life as king of Tiryns in the Peloponnese, a major kingdom in Greek myth.

(*See Andromeda, Athena, Gray Sisters, Helm of Darkness, Medusa*)

Polyphemus

Cyclops featured in *The Odyssey*. Polyphemus loved Galatea, a sea nymph, who preferred Acis, the son of Pan and a river nymph. Polyphemus crushed Acis with a rock but it didn't help him win Galatea's affections. Nor did he fare better in his encounter with Odysseus and his men. The cunning Greek hero managed to blind him while he slept in his cave and then escaped by clinging to the underside of the Cyclops' sheep. Once back on his ship, Odysseus taunted the blind giant—rashly, for Polyphemus threw huge boulders at him and called on his father the sea god to take revenge. Poseidon duly made the rest of Odysseus' voyage even harder.

(See Cyclopes)

Poseidon

God of earthquakes, horses, and the sea. Zeus' elder brother and second in majesty only to him. Poseidon was a formidable, half-savage deity. He became lord of the sea, while Zeus ruled the skies and their other brother, Hades, ruled the Underworld. Wielding a divine trident, Poseidon rode the waves in a chariot drawn by sea horses. He married Amphitrite, one of the Nereids, but had affairs with many other beings, human, divine, and bestial. Among his stranger children were the Cyclopes, one-eyed, man-eating giants. Although Poseidon supported the Greeks in the Trojan War, he was an enemy of Odysseus and made his wanderings yet more difficult by sending storms. Sailors and fishermen prayed to Poseidon for fair weather, and a famous temple on the promontory of Sunium was dedicated to him. Poseidon failed to win the affection of the Athenians, however. In a competition with Athena, he offered the city a freshwater spring, while she offered an olive tree. The Athenians chose the latter; olive trees were a vital part of Athenian agriculture.

(See Andromeda, Antaeus, Arachne, Athena, Briares, Cyclopes, Delphin, Hades, Hippocampi, Kronos, Minos, Minotaur, Nereids, Pasiphae, Polyphemus, Theseus, Titans, Zeus)

Procrustes

Gigantic brigand who lived on the Isthmus of Corinth and preyed on travelers. Procrustes forced his victims to lie on special beds he had made, and if his victims proved too short for these "beds of Procrustes," he would stretch them until they fit; if they were too long, he hacked off their limbs. His evil-doings were ended by the young

prince Theseus, who overcame him and forced Procrustes onto one of his own beds.
(See Theseus)

Prometheus

Titan. Prometheus differed from his often mindless brothers in his cunning "forethought" (as his name implies). Neutral in the war between the Titans and Zeus, Prometheus was admitted to Olympus—but secretly he hated Zeus. He took his revenge on the gods with a cunning trick. The Greeks sacrificed animals to the gods, butchering and cooking them on fires outside temples, but some parts were left for the worshippers to eat. Prometheus, by hiding the best meat of a sacrificial ox he had cut up under its guts—which struck both gods and men as repellent—and putting the bones under a layer of appealing fat and skin, persuaded Zeus to agree to choose the latter. From then on in sacrifices the gods received only the fat and bones—which were burnt—and humanity got the best meat. Enraged, Zeus withdrew the gift of fire from mankind. But Prometheus, lighting a torch from the sun's fiery chariot, gave fire back. For this "theft," Zeus chained Prometheus to a rock in the Caucasus Mountains, where a vulture devoured his liver. Every night Prometheus' liver magically grew back, only to be eaten again the next day. He was finally freed from 30,000 years' torment by Hercules.
(See Epimetheus, Titans)

Python

Ancient female earth serpent (or dragon) killed by the young Apollo when he made Delphi his main shrine. The Python's name and aura lived on, however, in the Pythoness, the priestess who gave cryptic answers to the questions that people brought to Delphi, the greatest of Greek oracles. Traditionally the Pythoness sat in the innermost sanctuary on a tripod above an immeasurably deep chasm. The

fumes rising from the chasm threw her into a trance, in which the god spoke through her in verses so ambiguous they could never be proved wrong, no matter how events turned out.
(*See Delphi*)

Q

Quintus

Quintus was a common Greek name. One notable Quintus, Quintus Smyrnaeus, was a Greek epic poet who continued Homer's stories, although his poetry was said to be of inferior quality to Homer's. He's best known for his work *Posthomerica*, which covers the time period between the end of *The Iliad* and the end of the Trojan War.

R

River Lethe

One of the rivers of Hades, the Underworld. The River Lethe flowed around the Elysian Fields, the brightest parts of the Underworld, and then around Tartarus, the Underworld's most gruesome quarter. Any spirits who drank from its "lethal" waters forgot everything about their former life on Earth.

River Styx

Another of the rivers of Hades, the Underworld. The black waters of the River Styx surrounded the Underworld with nine loops, one of which was the River Acheron. To cross it the shades of those who had recently died had to pay the infernal boatman Charon an obol, a small coin traditionally buried with the dead.
(*See Achilles, Charon, Hades, Hermes*)

S

Satyrs

Exuberant, mischievous, exclusively male creatures who had a goat's horns, pointed ears, tail, and cloven hooves but were otherwise human. They were among the followers of Dionysus, the wine god, and were often drunk and always chasing women—both mortals and nymphs. Pan had many of the characteristics of a satyr. Often seen carousing with satyrs was Silenus, a fat but jolly old man who was so drunk he kept falling off his donkey.

(See Dionysus, Nymphs)

Selene

Goddess of the moon and daughter of Helios, the sun god. Selene rode a lunar chariot that was drawn through the sky by silver horses. She fell in love with the incredibly handsome youth Endymion, a mortal son of Zeus. When Selene begged Zeus to keep Endymion immortally young, Zeus granted her wish, but caused Endymion to sleep non-stop. Despite this slumber, Endymion remained Selene's sole lover.

(See Artemis)

Sirens

First recorded *femmes fatales*, literally fatal to sailors who heard their alluring songs. With birdlike bodies and fish tails, but the faces and busts of beautiful women, the three Sirens inhabited an island near Scylla and Charybdis, where the shores were extremely dangerous. Warned by the witch Circe, Odysseus stuffed his sailors' ears with wax and ordered them to tie him to the mast as they approached the area. This ensured that, though he could hear the Sirens' sweet voices, he would not be lured to his doom. Despite Odysseus begging his men to let him free, the crew obeyed his orders and Odysseus escaped. Later, when Jason and the Argonauts passed by the

Sirens, the poet Orpheus launched into a counter-song so powerful that the Sirens themselves were turned to rocks.

(*See Circe, Odysseus, Orpheus*)

Sphinx

Hybrid monster with a woman's breasts and face, a lion's body and claws, and a serpent's tail and wings, which originated in Egypt but was adopted by the Greeks. The Sphinx lived outside Thebes in central Greece, terrorizing travelers with baffling enigmatic riddles. Finally Oedipus, on his way from Corinth, answered the Sphinx's riddles correctly. (The most famous riddle asked: *What goes on four legs in the morning, two legs at noon, and three legs in the evening?* The answer is a human being, who crawls as a baby, walks as an adult, and uses a stick in old age.) As a result, the Sphinx either committed suicide or died at Oedipus' hands, depending on the version of the tale.

(*See Oedipus*)

Stymphalian Birds

Man-eating birds with iron claws and beaks that infested Stymphalus, a city in the Peloponnese. Hercules killed them as his sixth Labor.

(*See Hercules*)

T

Talos

Giant animated bronze figure made by blacksmith god Hephaestus to guard the princess Europa and the shores of Crete. The Talos could throw stones an immense distance. Its vital fluid was kept in a magic membrane within its foot; Medea cast the Talos into a deep sleep with her spells and then killed it by cutting this membrane.

Tantalus

Fabulously wealthy king of Sipylus (in modern-day Turkey). One of the first mortals honored by being allowed to dine with the gods, Tantalus offended Zeus by stealing the ambrosia served at the divine feasts and giving it to mortals, as well as by reporting the gods' gossip. He also chopped up his son Pelops and served his meat in a stew, although only Demeter, distracted by the loss of her daughter Persephone, ate any. To punish these crimes, Zeus chained Tantalus in a pool with a fruit tree just above his head. Whenever Tantalus tried to eat any of its fruit, the tree was raised out of his reach. Whenever he bent to drink any water, it shrank away from him. Thus was Tantalus eternally "tantalized."

Tartarus

Deepest region or pit of the Underworld. Enclosed within bronze gates and triple walls, Tartarus was a penal colony for the dead, where the especially wicked, such as the Titans who had revolted against Zeus, were incarcerated forever.
(See Hades, Kampê, Kronos, River Lethe, Titans, Typhon)

Telekhines

Sea spirits often described as having dogs' heads and flippers instead of hands. The Telekhines were skilled metal workers and created Poseidon's trident. They are sometimes considered to be related to the Hekatonkheires because of their ability to control the weather. When they began to use their powers for evil, Zeus sent them to their destruction in the depths below the sea.

Theseus

Archetypal Athenian hero and the city's great legendary king. Theseus reputedly had two fathers: the sea god Poseidon, and Aegeus, king of Athens. Aegeus had slept one night with Aethra, unmarried daughter of king Pittacus of Troezen, and left his sword and sandals under a huge rock on his departure the next morning. When he was sixteen, Theseus lifted this boulder and discovered the identity of his (mortal) father. Armed with the royal sword, he set out for Athens. On the way he killed Procrustes, the robber plaguing the Isthmus. When he reached Athens, Medea, his father's new wife, tried to poison Theseus but failed and fled. Aegeus recognized Theseus as his heir, but he had problems: King Minos of Crete, in revenge for the murder of his son, had imposed a yearly tribute on Athens of seven youths and seven maidens, who were sacrificed to the Minotaur in the Labyrinth. Volunteering to go himself, Theseus led the Athenians to Crete. There the princess Ariadne fell in love with him, and gave him a ball of thread to guide him back out through the Labyrinth once he had killed the Minotaur. After, he married Ariadne and fled from Crete with her, only to abandon her on the island of Naxos. As his ship neared Athens, he forgot to change its black sail to white as he had promised his father, and in despair, thinking his son dead, Aegeus killed himself. So Theseus became king. He united Attica (Athens' territory) but he himself still roved far and wide, going east to the Black Sea. There he abducted the Amazon queen, Antiope (or Hippolyta), which caused the Amazons to later invade Attica. He also went adventuring with his friend Pirithous, a Thessalian prince. Trying to abduct Persephone from the Underworld, he was trapped by Hades and only freed by Hercules (Pirithous was left to rot in Hades). Theseus' second marriage, to Princess Phaedra of Crete, Ariadne's sister, proved disastrous, for she fell in love with Hippolytus, Theseus' son by Antiope. When Hippolytus, who had sworn a vow of celibacy, refused her advances, Phaedra told Theseus that Hippolytus had tried to rape her. Enraged, Theseus called on Poseidon to kill Hippolytus, only discovering his son's innocence too late. Theseus finally died in Scyros island, whose jealous king killed him. But at the battle of Marathon in 490 B.C., Theseus' ghost re-appeared to fight alongside Athenian soldiers against the Persian invaders.

(*See Aegean Sea, Amazons, Ariadne, Clazmonian Sow, Dionysus, Jason, Medea, Minos, Minotaur, Pankration, Procrustes*)

Titans

Among the first primeval gods; the children of Gaia (earth) and Ouranos (sky). Traditionally they were very large and strong but not very bright, with the exception of Prometheus. Among notable Titans were Atlas, Epimetheus, Hyperion (light), and Kronos. Kronos was the father of several Olympian gods. Because he feared they would supplant him as he had his own father, he swallowed each of his children as his wife Rhea gave birth to them. Rhea substituted a stone for Zeus, however, and with Rhea's help Zeus later forced Kronos to vomit back up the others. When the Titans revolted against the Olympians' new order, Zeus, helped by his brothers Poseidon and Hades, crushed them, imprisoning most of the Titans in Tartarus.

(*See Atlas, Briares, Gaia, Hades, Hekatonkheires, Hyperion, Kronos, Mount Othrys, Ophiotaurus, Ouranos, Prometheus, Tartarus, Zeus*)

Trojan War

Greatest war in Greek myth and the subject of Homer's grand epic, *The Iliad* (although the Greeks themselves thought of it as history, not myth at all). The Trojan War began when Paris, handsome son of King Priam of Troy, left Sparta with Helen, beautiful queen of Sparta. Menelaus, Sparta's king and Helen's husband, was the brother of Agamemnon, the most powerful Greek ruler, and Agamemnon summoned all Greece to help him revenge the insult to his family's honor. The Trojans responded by calling on their allies across Asia. When the Greeks landed on the beach near Troy, they had no way of capturing the high-walled city. So the war became a series of individual combats between heroes that could become full-scale battles. At times the Greeks were victorious, nearing the gates of Troy; at times the Trojans, led by Priam's eldest son, Prince Hector, drove the Greeks almost back to their ships. (Paris did little fighting.) The Greek cause was harmed by quarrels between Agamemnon and young Prince Achilles, their finest warrior, when Achilles refused to fight. Only after Patroclus, Achilles' best friend, was killed did Achilles return to the war, slaying Hector before being killed himself. Troy was finally captured using the now-famous Trojan Horse ruse. The Greeks pretended to sail away, leaving a huge wooden horse as an offering to the gods. Delighted, the Trojans took the horse inside their city. But the horse was hollow and filled with warriors. That night the Greeks inside emerged from its wooden belly to open the gates and let other Greeks in. Troy was sacked and its people killed or enslaved—except for Helen, who was restored to Menelaus, and Aeneas, hero of *The Aeneid*, who escaped with his father.

(*See Achilles, Amazons, Aphrodite, Athena, Diomedes, Eris, Helen, Hera, Iliad, Ithaca, Minos, Nereids, Odysseus, Odyssey, Poseidon, Quintus, Zeus*)

Typhon

Monstrous son of Gaia (earth) and the god Tartarus. Typhon was as large as a mountain, with a hundred dragon heads, a snake's body, and blazing eyes. He fathered other monsters, such as the Hydra and chimera, and for a time so frightened many Greek gods that they fled to Egypt, disguising themselves as animals (this is how the Greeks explained Egypt's animal-headed gods such as Anubis). Zeus and Hermes finally trapped Typhon under Mount Etna in Sicily, from the volcanic depths of which he still spouted fire and sent forth sudden storms: *typhoons*, which were named for him.

(*See Chimera, Clazmonian Sow, Echidna, Harpies, Hydra*)

U

Underworld

Gloomy realm beneath the earth to which the spirits of almost all the dead went, ruled by the god Hades, whose name the Greeks preferred not to utter. (Hades also became another name for the Underworld.)

(See Aeneas, Cerberus, Charon, Circe, Demeter, Elysian Fields/Elysium, Fields of Asphodel, Hades, Helm of Darkness, Hercules, Kronos, Mount Olympus, Odysseus, Orpheus, Persephone, Poseidon, River Lethe, River Styx, Tartarus, Theseus, Zeus)

Z

Zephyr

God of the west wind, the gentlest of the four winds, associated with the soft, sweet-smelling showers of spring. (The others were Boreas, the north wind; Notus, the south wind; and Eurus, the east wind.) Zephyr's wife was the flower goddess Chloris, and their son was Carpus, which meant harvest or fruits. But Zephyr also married Chloris' sister Iris, goddess of the rainbow.

(See Aphrodite)

Zeus

King of the gods and lord of the sky. Zeus was the supreme patriarchal god, who ruled both Mount Olympus, home of the twelve Olympian gods, and the world of men below. Zeus was the son of the Titans Rhea and Kronos. Kronos had swallowed his other sons for fear they would overthrow him, but Rhea saved Zeus by offering her husband a stone instead and hiding the baby on Mount Ida in Crete, where he was brought up by nymphs. Zeus later deposed Kronos and made him vomit the other gods back up. Among them were Poseidon and Hades, with whom Zeus divided the world: Zeus took the skies, Poseidon the oceans, and Hades the Underworld. The other Titans revolted against this new order but were suppressed in battle. From then on Zeus governed the cosmos. His thunderbolt was his most dramatic weapon, with which he blasted any who opposed him, but all men, including kings, and all the other gods had to obey him. Zeus was a king, however, not a tyrant. He himself obeyed the cosmic laws of Fate. Zeus was the supreme guardian of justice, human and divine, punishing wrong-doers, and was the protector of strangers and of beggars. He married Hera, his sister, whose heart he had won by taking the form of a cuckoo, and she became queen of Olympus. The divine couple did not get along, however. Hera objected violently to Zeus' colorful love life, for he was a notorious seducer of women, both mortal and divine, often taking the shape of animals to do so. Among his conquests were Leto, a Titaness and the mother of Apollo and Artemis, who became Olympian gods; Themis, another Titaness, who gave birth to the Horae, the goddesses of the hours; Europa, the daughter of the Phoenician (Lebanese) king Agenor, whom Zeus carried off while in the guise of a bull to Crete, where she gave birth to Minos and Rhadamanthys; and Leda, whom he seduced disguised as a swan, and who gave birth to the incomparably beautiful Helen, later the cause of the Trojan War. Having Zeus as a lover could be dangerous for mortals. The Theban princess Semele, whom Zeus always visited in the dark, insisted on seeing him in his full glory. When he finally revealed his divinity, she was burnt up. However, Zeus did save her unborn child, who became Dionysus, the wine god. Athena, the patron goddess of Athens, was Zeus' most original offspring, for she sprang, fully formed and already armed, from his forehead. Zeus was identified with the Roman Jupiter and has obvious affinities with the Sanskrit (early Hindu) sky god Dyaus Pater. Zeus was worshipped across Greece, and the grandest temples and most opulent statues—such as the huge gold and ivory statue made by the sculptor Pheidias at Olympia, site of the Olympic Games—were created in his honor. The oldest oracle in Greece was that of Zeus at Dodona, where the god's pronouncements were written on oak leaves.

(See Aegis, Aphrodite, Apollo, Ares, Artemis, Athena, Atlas, Briares, Cadmus and Europa, Calypso, Charybdis and Scylla, Delphi, Demeter, Dionysus, Epimetheus, Fates, Ganymede, Golden Fleece, Hades, Helen, Helios, Hekatonkheires, Hephaestus, Hera, Hercules, Hermes, Hestia, Iris, Kampē, Kronos, Master bolt, Minos, Mount Othrys, Nereids, Odysseus, Ophiotaurus, Oracles, Pandora, Persephone, Perseus, Poseidon, Prometheus, Selene, Tantalus, Tartarus, Titans, Typhon)

● ● ● ●

Nigel Rodgers, who has a degree in history and history of art from the University of Cambridge in England, has written widely on history, art, mythology, and philosophy. Among his most recent books are *The Ancient Greek World* (Lorenz, 2008), *Roman Empire* (Lorenz, 2006), and *Philosophers Behaving Badly* (Peter Owen, 2005). His Web site is http://nigelrodgers.co.uk.

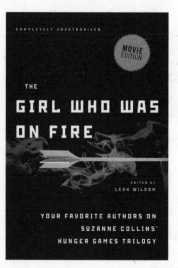